The

Maddoc opened his e̶... ...t strong, coming so close to the ke̶e̶p̶... ...if it were her, if she were releasing so much power, it could well mean that the Emergence had finally taken place.

When he'd first initiated his plan to resurrect Asvoria and make her magic his own so many months ago, he'd underestimated just how powerful the sorceress' spirit would be, not to mention how resourceful her host, Nearra, would prove. But he'd made alterations in his plan, researching new spells and waiting for the day the little fools would walk right into his trap.

It appeared that day might finally have arrived.

THE NEW ADVENTURES

SPELLBINDER QUARTET

Volume 1
TEMPLE OF THE DRAGONSLAYER
TIM WAGGONER

Volume 2
THE DYING KINGDOM
STEPHEN D. SULLIVAN

Volume 3
THE DRAGON WELL
DAN WILLIS

Volume 4
RETURN OF THE SORCERESS
TIM WAGGONER

THE NEW ADVENTURES
VOLUME
4

RETURN
OF THE
SORCERESS

TIM WAGGONER

COVER & INTERIOR ART
Vinod Rams

MIRROR STONE

Cover art by Vinod Rams
Cartography by Dennis Kauth
First Printing: November 2004
Library of Congress Catalog Card Number: 2004106860

9 8 7 6 5 4 3 2 1

US ISBN: 0-7869-3385-2
UK ISBN: 0-7869-3386-0
620-17959-001-EN

U.S., CANADA,   EUROPEAN HEADQUARTERS
ASIA, PACIFIC, & LATIN AMERICA   Wizards of the Coast, Belgium
Wizards of the Coast, Inc.   T Hofveld 6d
P.O. Box 707   1702 Groot-Bijgaarden
Renton, WA 98057-0707   Belgium
+1-800-324-6496   +322 457 3350

Visit our web site at **www.mirrorstonebooks.com**

FOR ERIC,
WHO'S NOT JUST MY BROTHER BUT ALSO MY BEST FRIEND.
(THERE, I DEDICATED A BOOK TO YOU.
NOW WILL YOU STOP BUGGING ME?)

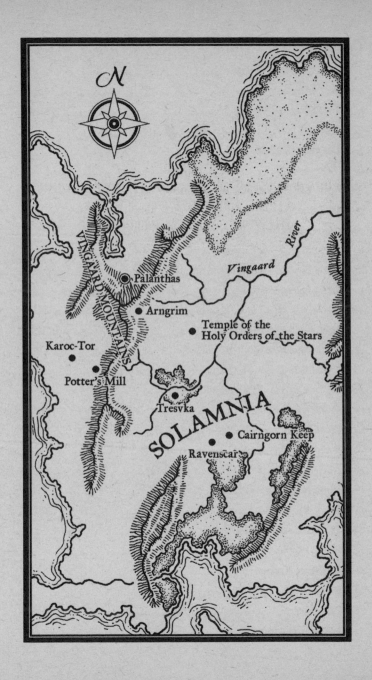

Contents

UNWELCOME VISITORS

W hat business do you have in Ravenscar?"
Two broad-shouldered men armed
with swords stood in the middle of the muddy road, blocking the
way. The first man's tone was neutral, but the hard look in his
eyes sent a shiver down Nearra's spine. This was someone who
would kill without thought or remorse.

"Why should we tell you?" Davyn said.

The second man scowled and dropped his hand to his sword,
though he made no move to draw the weapon.

Nearra tensed. She wished she was holding her dagger. But
she knew if her hand so much as twitched in the direction of her
blade, the two thugs—who, it seemed, were Ravenscar's unofficial
welcoming committee—would be on them in an instant.

It was early spring in Solamnia. The trees were beginning to
bud, and while the air was still cool enough for the five companions to wear their fur cloaks, there was a fresh, green smell
in the breeze that promised warmer weather to come. The road
that led into Ravenscar was muddy from recent rains, and dotted
with mounds of horse manure, fruit rinds, and gnawed meat
bones. The town, if it could be called that, was little more than

a collection of ramshackle buildings made from weathered and rotting wood. It seemed to Nearra as if one good strong wind could turn the entire town into kindling.

Catriona, Elidor, and Sindri remained silent and Davyn spoke again.

"Our business is our own. Since when did the folk of Ravenscar start asking questions of visitors?"

"Since we felt like it," the first man growled. He was tall and clad in leather armor and wore a snake-skin sword-belt.

"But if you don't want to answer in words, you can always answer in coin," the second thug added. He was dressed like the first, except his belt was plain leather, and he wore a cloak made from the hide of a mountain cat. The second bully began to draw his sword, and his companion did likewise.

Catriona reached for the steel dragon claws tucked beneath her belt, while Sindri raised his hand, the one with the silver ring, in preparation of casting a spell. But before a fight could break out, Elidor drew a fat coin purse from his tunic.

"In that case, here's our answer." The elf shook the purse, jingling the coins inside. "I suspect it's your favorite language."

The first thug—Nearra thought of him as Snake Skin—stopped drawing his sword, but he didn't slide the blade back into its sheath. "That it is," he allowed. "But how many words of it do you intend to speak?"

"As many as necessary," Elidor replied.

The two men stared at the purse for a moment, sizing it up, and then looked at each other. The barbarians sheathed their swords, and Nearra let out a breath she hadn't known she was holding.

Elidor tossed the money pouch and Snake Skin snatched it out of the air. He opened it and both men examined the contents. Satisfied, Snake Skin closed the purse and stepped aside.

"Enjoy your stay in Ravenscar," Snake Skin said.

"For as long as it lasts." Cat Hide smirked. "Or maybe I should say for as long as *you* last!"

Both men laughed, but Nearra and her companions did their best to ignore them as they walked past. When they were out of earshot, Elidor said, "It truly pains me to have to part with so much steel."

"It's a good thing you did," Davyn said. "If we hadn't paid them, a fight might have broken out, and the last thing we want to do is draw attention to ourselves. Remember, we've come here to contact an old friend of mine who can help us sneak into Cairngorn Keep."

"I still don't see how a centaur is going to get us into Maddoc's home," Elidor said.

"Ayanti is Bolthor's gamekeeper," Davyn explained. "She often goes to the wizard's keep to deliver supplies and pick up Maddoc's latest, uh, creation for Bolthor's amusement. But she won't be able to help us if we're imprisoned—or dead. So let's be careful, all right?"

Despite everything Nearra had been through since awakening with no memories on a forest trail so many months ago, she didn't think she'd ever become completely used to being in dangerous situations. And from what Davyn had told them, Ravenscar was a dangerous place indeed.

The friends continued walking through the town, doing their best to ignore the stares of the residents they passed.

"Look at *him*!" Sindri said, pointing at a man standing in front of one of the buildings. He held a long metal staff with axe heads at both ends, and his face was covered with a skull tattoo.

"What an interesting tattoo. Do you think it means anything? And I wonder if he'd consider trading his staff for mine. I think I'll go over and ask."

But before Sindri could take a step toward the man with the death's head tattoo, Davyn put a hand on the kender's shoulder and stopped him.

"What did we all agree on before entering town?" Davyn asked.

"Not to talk with anyone and to avoid eye contact whenever possible," Sindri said in a sullen tone.

"And therefore you . . .," Davyn prompted.

"Will stay with the rest of you and keep my mouth closed." Sindri sounded miserable. Kender lived to satisfy their boundless curiosity, and not being able to do so was killing him.

"And make sure you don't use any magic," Davyn continued. "We're only a couple miles from Cairngorn Keep, and the wizard will detect any magic in the area."

Sindri nodded.

Davyn kept his hand on Sindri's shoulder a few moments longer, as if to make certain the kender was going to do as he said. When he was satisfied, Davyn removed his hand and Sindri remained where he stood, his lips pursed in an unhappy pout.

"Come on," Davyn urged. "It's best to keep moving in Ravenscar. Stand still long and you're liable to become a target."

"All right, boss," Catriona said with a grin.

Davyn scowled. "I thought we settled that. Don't call me *boss*."

Catriona's grin widened. "Of course, b—" But Davyn shot her a venomous look, and still grinning, she fell silent.

Nearra didn't have to ask what Davyn meant by becoming targets. There were other people walking down the street, standing in doorways of shacks and lean-to's, lurking in the spaces between buildings that weren't quite large enough to be called alleys. Most were human, though over by a cutler's cart a trio of dwarves garbed in red cloaks stood drinking from wineskins

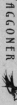

while they listened to a bearded half-elf strum a lute. But while there was wide variety in the way the denizens of Ravenscar looked and dressed, they all shared a single trait: their eyes were cold, calculating, and full of potential menace.

But regardless of the danger, Nearra was determined to do whatever she must to finally regain her memories and win her freedom from the spirit that Maddoc had instilled in her. That was the reason the companions had come to Ravenscar in the first place. They had grown tired of always being on the defensive against the evil wizard. This time they were bringing the fight to Maddoc.

"It's not really a town though, is it?" Elidor said. "I see no people working, no families, no children, and these shacks are so poorly built they don't deserve to be called buildings."

"You're right," Davyn said. "In many ways, Ravenscar is more like a camp for bandits and mercenaries. It came into existence centuries ago, when Asvoria lived in the keep that the *wizard* now occupies."

There was bitterness in Davyn's voice and Nearra noted that he didn't say *Maddoc* or *my father*. He'd barely spoken of the evil wizard at all since learning what Maddoc had done to his true father. And now Davyn had to live with what he'd been forced to do to free his real father from the wizard's curse.

Davyn went on. "It was a place for those who served the sorceress to drink, gamble, and fight while they awaited their mistress' orders. After Asvoria fell from power, outlaws continued using Ravenscar as their headquarters. Once the wizard took up residence in Cairngorn Keep, he established a similar business relationship with the criminals from the town. While he maintains a small staff of servants in the keep, when he needs certain supplies to be acquired or a *special* task to be done, he turns to the folk of Ravenscar."

From the rough and dangerous appearance of the people they'd seen so far, Nearra had no trouble picturing Maddoc recruiting them for whatever dirty work he needed done.

They passed a pair of old weathered buildings that leaned upon one another as if for mutual support. Catriona asked, "What are all these buildings for? There are no signs to help visitors tell one from the other."

"There are no signs because the buildings are apt to change owners suddenly, not to mention violently," Davyn said. "So what might once have been a tavern will be a fur trader's on your next visit. People probably got tired of constantly making signs, so they just gave up."

"How does anyone know where anything is then?" Nearra asked.

"You ask around," Davyn said.

"But how can we do that?" Sindri said. "You told us not to speak with anyone!"

Davyn smiled. "We don't need to ask. We're going to visit the one establishment in Ravenscar that never changes. The Pit."

Sindri's eyes widened and he turned to Nearra. "I just thought of something. If Asvoria used to live around here, does that mean you remember this place?"

"It doesn't work that way," Nearra said. "Asvoria's spirit may dwell within my body, but we are two separate beings. I no more know her thoughts than she does mine."

This wasn't entirely true. There'd been numerous times when she'd sensed Asvoria's thoughts, often hearing them as a voice speaking in her mind. And from time to time, she'd been able to tap Asvoria's power. Or perhaps the sorceress' spirit had simply worked her magic through her body. Whichever the case, Nearra didn't want to let the others know how blurred the boundary between her spirit and Asvoria's had become—especially after she'd been drenched by the mystic blood of the dragon well. One reason she wished to keep the full extent of the truth from her friends was because she didn't want them to worry about her. But she was also afraid that if they knew how strong Asvoria had become they would not trust her. Look how long it had taken them to trust Davyn after he'd revealed the truth about his relationship to Maddoc and his role in the wizard's grand scheme to resurrect and control Asvoria. Catriona still didn't trust him completely. How would they treat her if they knew the truth?

They continued walking toward the center of Ravenscar, doing their best to ignore the town's inhabitants and be ignored by them. Before long they heard cheers and laughter, but these sounds had a decidedly dark and nasty edge. They turned a corner and saw a crowd gathered in a circle.

"There it is," Davyn said. "Looks like there's a match going on." He looked at the others. "What goes on in the Pit isn't very pleasant, but do your best not to let your true feelings show. If there's even a hint that we don't approve of what's going on, it could give us away."

The five companions approached the crowd and got as close to the edge of the Pit as they could. They received a few looks from spectators—mostly due to Sindri's presence. There had been no sign of other kender in Ravenscar, and Nearra thought Sindri might be the only one. And given the kender habit of "accidentally" procuring objects that weren't theirs—a habit which Sindri believed in his case was due to an ability to magically conjure items—it was no surprise that people would eye him warily. But no one said anything, and as long as Sindri kept his hands to himself there shouldn't be any trouble.

At least, that's what Nearra hoped.

The Pit was exactly as its name implied: a round pit thirty feet across and twenty feet deep. The walls and floor of the Pit were lined with stone blocks, and a rusted metal grate in the center served as a drain for rainwater and, Nearra guessed with a clench of her stomach, other liquids. Sharp iron spikes a foot long ringed the edge of the Pit. Many of the spikes were covered with reddish-brown stains that Nearra hoped were rust but knew were not.

Despite herself, Nearra found her gaze drawn to the battle taking place within the Pit. Two dire wolves attacked a lone ice bear, their fangs sinking into the helpless creature's neck. Nearra turned her head away, disgusted.

While most of the audience stood around the Pit, one man sat in a fine oak chair mounted on a raised platform to give him a better view. From what Davyn had said Nearra knew this was Bolthor, the unofficial ruler of Ravenscar, while the bandits, barbarians, and other unsavory types who made up the crowd cheered, the outlaw chieftain remained silent, his face impassive. His eyes glittered with intensity as he watched the action below.

Looking at his thick brow, cruel eyes, and tangled black hair and beard, Nearra could believe he was half-human, half-ogre. Standing on either side of him were two elves—one male, one female. Their bodies were covered with tribal tattoos and they wore tunics made of deerskin over leather armor.

"Who are the elves?" she asked Davyn in a whisper.

"Kuruk and Shiriki," he said. "Fierce Kagonesti warriors who serve as Bolthor's bodyguards. They're also cousins."

Nearra glanced at Elidor. He was half Kagonesti, on his father's side, though he dressed more like his mother's people, the Silvanesti. Elidor was looking at the elf guards and scowling.

Nearra leaned close to him and whispered. "Davyn told us to mask our feelings, remember?"

Elidor hrumpfed, but he stopped scowling and turned his attention to the Pit.

Small tin whistles hung on chains around the necks of the elf guards. They lifted the whistles to their mouths and blew. Shrill high-pitched tones cut through the air and Nearra gritted her teeth and clapped her hands to her ears, as did most of the crowd. Bolthor, however, seemed unaffected by the sound. The bear and the wolves responded at once to the signal, moving to opposite sides of the Pit and lying down, though in the bear's case, it was closer to collapsing.

On the other side of the Pit from where Nearra and her companions stood, the crowd parted for a quartet of men who carried a long wooden ramp. With ease they lowered the ramp into the Pit and stepped back.

Davyn leaned close to Nearra. "Here comes Ayanti," he whispered.

Nearra heard the sound of clopping hooves and then Ayanti came into view. Nearra gasped when she saw the centaur. There was something almost regal in the graceful way she moved. Nearra had imagined that she would be awkward, her body an unnatural blend of human and equine, but nothing could've been further from the truth.

Ayanti stepped to the edge of the Pit and clapped her hands. "Gerda, Mottul, come!" she commanded.

With happy yips and wagging tails, the two wolves bounded up the ramp, which was designed to fit over the metal spikes jutting from the Pit's edge. Once the wolves were out, Ayanti leaned over, her human half bending where it joined her horse half. Her chestnut-brown hair matched the color of her equine coat and it spilled into her face as she scratched the wolves behind the ears. Then she straightened and said, "You're done for now. Go rest, you two." She nodded to one of the men who'd brought the ramp, and he whistled for the wolves. They ran to him, eager as puppies, and he led them away.

The centaur then turned her attention to the wounded bear. The animal lay on its side, breathing hard, its fur matted with blood. Ayanti scowled and gave Bolthor an angry glance, as if she blamed him personally for inflicting the bear's injuries.

"Finish him off!" someone in the crowd shouted. The rest of the crowd cheered.

Nearra turned to Davyn. "Will she?"

But before he could answer, Ayanti drew a dagger from her belt sheath and pointed it at the crowd. "If you don't shut up, I'll come up there and slit a few throats until you do!"

The crowd suddenly grew quiet, and Bolthor laughed. Ayanti sheathed her dagger and clopped over to the ice bear. She bent of her forelegs and knelt next to the animal. She spoke soothingly to him as she examined his wounds. Then, with much coaxing, she led the bear up the ramp. One of her assistants was waiting with a muzzle, but Ayanti waved him away. She walked off, the wounded ice bear limping behind her.

"Are you certain she'll help us?" Catriona whispered to Davyn.

"Ayanti and I grew up together," Davyn said. "My—the *wizard* didn't approve of a human and a centaur having a personal relationship. But we became friends anyway. She'll help us."

After a time, Ayanti returned, pulling a wagon with an iron cage in the back. Inside the cage was a strange beast that resembled a boar, though it was closer to the size of a bull. Instead of fur, it was covered in greenish-black scales, and it had long lizard-like tail. The beast snorted and rammed its curved tusks against the iron bars of its cage, impatient to be free.

Nearra was horrified. "Is that abomination Maddoc's doing?"

Davyn nodded. "That's how he pays Bolthor. Bolthor gets the wizard whatever supplies and servants he wants, and in return, the wizard uses his magic to create monsters to fight in the Pit. This one looks to be a cross between a boar and a lizard."

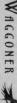

The beast slavered and whipped its tail about, eager to get to killing.

"It's disgusting!" Catriona said.

"I wonder what sort of spell Maddoc used to create the animal," Sindri said. "Do you think he might tell me?"

Ayanti pulled the wagon up to the ramp at the edge of the Pit and started to unlock the cage door. Though the centaur had showed affection for the wolves and the bear, it was clear from her expression that she held little love for the lizard-boar. Nearra couldn't blame her.

As soon as the door was open, the lizard-boar jumped onto the ramp and ran down into the Pit without any urging from Ayanti.

"What now?" Nearra asked.

Before anyone could say anything else, a shout came from edge of the crowd.

"Cheaters! Thieves!"

The crowd grew quiet, and turned to look at the cause of the commotion. The two bullies who had "greeted" the companions at the edge of town were pushing their way through, weapons drawn and faces twisted into masks of fury.

The crowd lost no time parting to make way for the angry thugs.

"I think perhaps it's time we were going," Elidor said nervously. But before any of them could move, Snake Skin saw them and jabbed his sword in their direction.

"You gave us iron coins coated with steel!"

His partner grinned and brandished his weapon. "So now it's time to give you a taste of *our* steel!"

The two thugs rushed toward Nearra and her friends, swords raised high and murder in their eyes.

2

All Bets are Off

As the thugs approached, Nearra and the other companions turned to look at Elidor.

The elf thief smiled apologetically. "I told you it pained me to have to part with that much steel. So I, uh, gave them coins that were, shall we say, less than pure?"

Catriona scowled. "Well, that was brilliant."

Elidor shrugged. "I didn't think they'd check, at least not so soon."

Nearra wondered where Elidor had gotten hold of counterfeit steel. She decided it didn't matter. He was a thief, and he could've gotten it almost anywhere.

Bolthor stood and roared at the approaching thugs. "You two fools had better have a good reason for interrupting the games!"

The bullies stopped running and turned to Bolthor's dais. His elf bodyguards had drawn their swords but they made no move to attack.

I guess no one trusts anyone in Ravenscar, Nearra thought. She nudged her companions, encouraging them to begin moving through the crowd.

"A group of travelers entered town a short time ago," Snake Skin said. "We asked them to provide us a few coins as, uh, a tax—"

Cat Hide interrupted. "When we checked the coins, we discovered they were nothing but steel-coated iron!"

The outlaw chieftain cut the bully off with an impatient gesture. "Where are these travelers now?" he asked.

Snake Skin and Cat Hide pointed at the companions. "There!" they shouted in unison.

"Run! Davyn shouted.

Catriona grabbed Nearra by the arm and started pulling her away from the crowd. Davyn drew his hunting knife since there wasn't enough room to use his bow. Elidor's throwing knives appeared in his hands with a speed that seemed almost mystical. Only Sindri didn't prepare to escape.

"But I want to stay and watch the monster boar!" he protested.

Davyn grabbed the kender's purple cape and pulled him away from the Pit. "We'll be fed to that monster for a snack if we don't get out of here!" Davyn snapped.

"Do you really think so?" Sindri said sounding intrigued.

Before Davyn could reply, the crowd turned on the companions. Dozens of hands clutched for them, desperate to please Bolthor and claim whatever reward he might offer. Or perhaps the people were interested in watching what Snake Skin and Cat Hide would do to the companions.

Elidor and Sindri evaded the crowd's grasping hands with the grace and agility of their respective races. Davyn whipped his hunting knife back and forth, keeping the blood-thirsty men and women at bay. The grim expression on Catriona's face—coupled with the single dragon claw in her hand—was enough to deter most from even attempting to grab her.

Nearra was armed with her staff, but she needed two hands to wield it effectively, and Catriona had hold of one of her arms. But just as she was about to ask her friend to let go so she could fight, someone latched onto Nearra's free arm and yanked.

"C'mere, blondie! I bet Bolthor would like to have a word or two with you for disrupting his games!" It was a white-bearded dwarf.

Nearra tried to pull away from him, but the dwarf's grip was too strong. "Catriona!" she shouted.

But the red-haired warrior was unable to come to her aid. One of the Kagonesti bodyguards—Kuruk—had managed to make his way through the crowd and was coming toward Catriona, sword in hand.

"Let go of my arm!" Nearra shouted to Catriona. "I need both hands to fight!"

The warrior glanced at Nearra, then at the elf coming toward her, torn with indecision. It was Kuruk who finally made the choice for her. He ran forward and swung his sword in a sideways swipe designed to take off Catriona's head. The warrior released her grip on Nearra, drew her second dragon claw, and moved to block the bodyguard's strike.

Nearra's hand was free to wield her staff, but this also meant that there was no longer an opposing force pulling against the dwarf. Nearra was yanked backwards, and she dropped her staff as she stumbled into the dwarf. He let out a surprised yelp and they tumbled together toward the edge of the Pit. It was a twenty-foot drop to the stone floor, and there was nothing she could do to stop her fall.

Nearra suddenly jerked to a halt and hung in midair. At first she was confused, but then she looked up and saw Sindri standing at the edge of the Pit, frowning as he concentrated, and she realized what had happened. The kender had used his magic powers to stop her fall.

Sindri hadn't done the same for the dwarf. He hit the bottom of the Pit with the harsh snap of breaking bones. The dwarf shrieked in agony, but his cries of pain turned to screams of terror as the lizard-boar gave an excited snort and starting shuffling toward him. The little man didn't scream for long. Nearra resisted the temptation to look down. She knew she didn't want to see what the beast was doing to the dwarf.

She cupped her hands to her mouth. "Sindri!" she called. "Can you levitate me all the way out of here?"

The kender's face appeared over the edge of the Pit. His brow was furrowed in concentration and sweat trickled down his face.

"I'm trying, but it's difficult . . . so much going on . . . hard to concentrate . . ."

Nearra suddenly dropped a couple feet, and she let out a cry of surprise. And then she heard the lizard-boar's snort as the monstrous beast leaped for her.

Sindri fought to concentate as the lizard-boar jumped for Nearra and missed.

"Sindri!" Nearra shouted.

"I'm working on it!" the kender replied through gritted teeth.

Nearra began to rise faster, but her flight wasn't smooth. Sindri felt as if he were lifting his friend with a weak, trembling hand that might lose its grip on her any moment.

The lizard-boar leaped again, and this time one of its tusks managed to graze Nearra's foot. She screamed. The beast fell back into the Pit without getting hold of her. If the creature managed to get its teeth on her foot Nearra would be dragged down into the Pit and then . . . Sindri didn't want to think about what would happen then.

Stay calm and stay focused, he told himself.

"Got you, kender!"

TIM WAGGONER

Sindri was yanked backward. He turned his head to see that Cat Hide had hold of his cape. The kender grabbed two of the iron spikes that jutted from the Pit's edge to give him more leverage against Cat Hide, but the thug was much larger and stronger than the kender. With a last hard yank, Cat Hide broke Sindri's grip and pulled him away from the edge. The last shreds of Sindri's concentration vanished, and he felt the magic power that was holding his friend aloft fade. Nearra screamed as she fell toward the lizard-boar.

Sindri tried to shout "No!" but he couldn't get the word out. The collar of his cape was tight against his skin and cutting off his air. Cat Hide laughed as Sindri's vision began to go gray around the edges.

Instinctively, Sindri reached into one of the many pockets sewn into the inner lining of his cape, and his fingers closed around a slender metal object.

Sindri leaped backward and turned as he pulled the silver candlestick from its hiding place within his cape. Cat Hide's eyes widened in surprise as Sindri swung the makeshift club toward his head and thunked into the thug's left temple. With a groan, Cat Hide collapsed to the ground. Sindri landed on top of him.

But the kender took no time to exult in his victory. Nearra needed him! He tried to pull away from Cat Hide, but the man still held his cape tight. Sindri quickly undid the cape's clasp, shrugged it off, then ran back to the edge of the Pit and looked down.

Nearra, appearing dazed and confused, but otherwise uninjured, stood with her back against the wall of the Pit, watching the lizard-boar finish off what was left of the white-bearded dwarf. The hideous creature then turned its attention to her, and as the monster advanced, it opened tusked jaws to reveal two rows of sharp blood-stained teeth.

Sindri began to concentrate, ready to attempt to levitate Nearra to safety. But before he could begin to work his magic, Nearra started speaking in a language the kender didn't recognize. A series of words came out of Nearra's mouth in soft, liquid syllables of power. She pointed her index finger at the lizard-boar, and a ball of fire materialized at the tip. With a whoosh the fireball shot toward the beast and engulfed it in flame.

The lizard-boar shrieked in agony and fell to the floor of the Pit. It rolled back and forth in a frantic attempt to put out the flames that covered it, but this was no ordinary fire. These flames would continue to burn until they had no more to feed on. Soon the air was filled with greasy black smoke and the sickening stench of burning flesh. Even Sindri—who was something of an aficionado of strange odors—couldn't stand the stink.

Looks like Bolthor is going to dine on roast lizard-pork tonight, Sindri thought. Soon, the lizard-boar ceased its thrashing and grew still. The flames began to diminish, for there was little left to burn beside bone. Even though the creature was an unnatural abomination and had tried to kill Nearra, Sindri couldn't help feeling sorry for it. What a horrible way to die.

Sindri tore his gaze away from the grisly sight and looked at Nearra. He expected to see that she was equally disgusted by the beast's death, but was surprised to see that she was smiling.

"Are you all right?" Sindri called.

"Just fine," Nearra said. "Best I've been in ages, as a matter of fact."

"That was amazing!" Sindri said. "The fireball, I mean! How did you do it?"

Nearra shrugged. "I'm really not sure, to be honest. But we can figure that out later, *after* you levitate me out of here."

There was a haughtiness in Nearra's words that was unlike her. It was almost as if she were giving Sindri a command. Still, the kender decided she was right; time enough to worry about what had happened to her, if anything, after she was safe. Sindri concentrated and Nearra began to rise slowly. He couldn't help noticing that she was still smiling.

Two miles to the east, the black-robed wizard called Maddoc looked up from the spellbook he had been studying and frowned.

There was magic in the air. Someone was working an enchantment nearby. A mile away, two at the most. In the direction of . . . he closed his eyes and murmured a spell. In the darkness of his mind a pinprick of light appeared. The light lay in the direction of Ravenscar.

He opened his eyes. A burst of mystic energy that strong, coming so close to the keep . . . could it be Nearra? And if it were her, if she were releasing so much power, it could well mean that the Emergence had finally taken place.

Maddoc felt a wave of exhaustion crash into him. His head swam and his vision blurred. For a moment he feared he might lose consciousness. But the sensation passed, though he remained weakened.

Ever since the death of Shaera, his beloved falcon familiar, Maddoc had been in ill health. The bond between a wizard and his familiar was a strong one, and it ran deep in both of their beings. When the bond was broken by the death of one, it was as if the other died as well, or nearly so. With a supreme effort, Maddoc stood and walked away from the reading table. The magic in Ravenscar needed to be investigated at once.

When he'd first initiated his plan to resurrect Asvoria and make her magic his own so many months ago, he'd underestimated just how powerful the sorceress' spirit would be, not to mention how resourceful her host would prove. But the death of Shaera had driven home the truth to him, and since then he'd made alterations in his plan, researching new spells and waiting for the day the little fools would walk right into his trap. It appeared that day might finally have arrived.

Since Maddoc no longer had a familiar to send to investigate on his behalf, he would have to make do with one of his more macabre servants.

Excited, Maddoc shuffled out of the library, into the cold stone hall of his keep, and headed toward one of the chambers where he conducted his magical experiments, a chamber known as the Ossuary.

The Ossuary contained a number of wooden tables covered with all manner of bones—some animal, some human, some unidentifiable as either—along with spools of wire, leather straps, and metal pins. This was the chamber where Maddoc conducted his experiments in necromancy. And the results of his most successful experiment stood in the middle of the chamber, hidden by a large woolen blanket.

Maddoc pulled the cover off his greatest creation, and looked into its empty eye sockets. "To Ravenscar!" he commanded. "Go now, and go swiftly! Bring me the girl called Nearra!"

Though the undead thing possessed no vocal chords, it nevertheless let out a loud screech and then crawled across the floor toward an open window, bone-talons clacking hollowly on stone. It climbed onto the sill and leaped out into space. Artificial wings stitched together from leather spread wide and began to flap, bearing the skeletal creature toward Ravenscar.

As Maddoc watched his undead creation soar off, he smiled a dark smile. Soon, the power that he had worked so long and hard to possess would be his at last.

CHAPTER 3

FROM BAD TO WORSE

Davyn heard the lizard-boar scream in agony, but he was too busy trying to keep Snake Skin from cutting him to pieces to investigate.

Snake Skin swung his sword at Davyn's midsection in a clumsy but powerful blow. Davyn was able to block the strike with his hunting knife, but the barbarian was so strong that Davyn feared his blade might break. As it was, the vibrations from the impact made his hand go instantly numb. As if sensing Davyn's injury, Snake Skin grinned and raised his weapon high, clearly intending to bring the blade down upon Davyn's head for a killing blow.

Stupid, Davyn thought. The idiot should take a thrust at my heart. He moved to block the blow, but his knife arm felt heavy as lead, and he knew he wouldn't be able to parry Snake Skin's strike this time.

So instead of waiting for Snake Skin's blow, Davyn leaped forward and rammed his head into the barbarian's gut. Snake Skin let out a whoof of air and staggered back. Davyn didn't give him time to recover. He gripped his bow in his good hand and hit Snake Skin as hard as he could on the side of his head.

21

But instead of falling to the ground unconscious, as Davyn had hoped, Snake Skin's face flushed a fiery red and fury filled his eyes. The guard gave an angry roar and came at the young ranger, wildly swinging his sword.

Davyn turned and ran toward the edge of the Pit. Thick black smoke rose from the sunken arena, making it difficult to see. But when Davyn judged he'd gone far enough, he stopped and fell on his hands and knees. Snake Skin couldn't stop in time. His foot hit Davyn's side, and the thug tripped and fell forward right onto the spikes jutting from the Pit's edge.

Davyn stood. He checked his bow and was relieved to see that it wasn't broken. His side ached from where Snake Skin had struck him, but the leather armor he wore beneath his tunic had kept any ribs from breaking. He felt no triumph at defeating Snake Skin; he'd simply done what was necessary to survive.

Davyn took a quick glance to see how his other friends were faring. Catriona was battling Kuruk while Elidor fought Shiriki. The Kagonesti elves fought like a pair of dervishes, moving with speed and grace. Elidor, half Kagonesti himself, was having little difficulty matching Shiriki blow for blow, her sword and his two daggers ringing like musical instruments as they collided time and again. Catriona, however, was having a harder time of it. Though still technically a squire, she had trained to be a Solamnic Knight, and since the five companions had come together in Treskva, she'd gained even more training and experience. But in the end, she was only human, and though she had acquitted herself well so far, she couldn't hope to stand against Kuruk for much longer.

Davyn's hand was still too numb to effectively wield his hunting knife, so he dropped his blade and took hold of his bow. His numb fingers would still be a liability, but he thought he could—

"Davyn! Look out!"

Davyn turned just in time to see Bolthor coming at him, no doubt furious at having his beloved games interrupted. The outlaw chieftain gripped a curved scimitar that had been honed to a deadly sharp edge.

"Davyn, eh?" Bolthor said as he approached. "I thought I recognized you! You're Maddoc's whelp, aren't you?"

Forcing his numb fingers to move as swiftly as he could, Davyn strung his bow, drew an arrow from the quiver on his back, nocked it and took aim at Bolthor's heart. But he didn't fire.

"That's right," Davyn said in his best haughty voice. "And my father is going to be extremely unhappy that you raised your weapon against me."

Bolthor laughed, but he stopped his approach less than ten feet away. "I don't know what your game is, boy, but I have a hard time believing your father put you up to this. He and I have had a business relationship longer than you've been alive."

Davyn shrugged. "What can I say? He's an evil wizard, remember? He's capable of doing anything to anyone at anytime—as long as it increases his power." Davyn wasn't lying about this part, and Bolthor knew it. A look of uncertainty came into the half ogre's eyes, and he started to lower his sword.

But then Bolthor grinned. "Your hand's shaking, boy."

Davyn's injured hand trembled. He wasn't sure how much longer he could keep his bow drawn.

"You're scared," Bolthor said. "If you really were here at your father's orders, you wouldn't be afraid."

Davyn wasn't afraid. At least, no more so than he ever was during a battle. But he knew better than to try to convince Bolthor that his hand shook because he'd been hurt. The outlaw chieftain would think that he was only bluffing.

Davyn risked a glance over Bolthor's shoulder and saw that

Catriona had been forced to her knees. Kuruk held his sword aloft, preparing to deliver a killing strike.

Davyn didn't hesitate. He took aim, willed his hand to be steady, and released his bowstring. Bolthor jumped when the arrow flew, but it sailed past the outlaw chieftain and struck the male Kagonesti in the shoulder.

Drat! Davyn thought. He'd been aiming for the elf's throat.

Kuruk hissed in pain and dropped his sword. Catriona immediately took advantage of the opening and swung one of her dragon claws at the elf's legs. With a howl of pain, Kuruk fell to the ground. Catriona stood and looked down at her opponent. Davyn knew that she wouldn't slay the elf unless she was forced to. A Solamnic Knight—or a squire, for that matter—didn't take a life unless it was necessary. It was against their Code.

Catriona turned to help Elidor, but before Davyn could see more, Bolthor charged.

"You should've killed me when you had the chance!" the outlaw chieftain roared.

Just as Davyn reached for another arrow, he heard the clop-clop-clop of horse hooves. Bolthor heard it too, and he turned to see Ayanti galloping toward them, a dagger held in her hand.

The outlaw chieftain turned to Davyn and grinned. "Looks like your old friend has come to say a last goodbye to you, boy."

Bolthor raised his sword, but before he could swing, Ayanti charged up and slammed the hilt of her dagger into the side of Bolthor's head. The outlaw chieftain dropped his sword, and fell to the ground, unconscious.

Davyn looked at Ayanti and smiled. "Thanks. And thanks for warning me earlier. That was you who yelled my name, right?"

The centaur nodded. "It's good to see you again, Davyn. I hoped you'd return, but I didn't expect your homecoming to be so eventful."

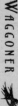

Davyn laughed. "Eventful is a good way to describe what my life has been like the last several months. I'll tell you all about it later after we get out of this mess."

He checked on his friends. Together, Catriona and Elidor had managed to drive off Shiriki. She cradled a wounded arm against her chest as she dragged Kuruk with her other arm. Davyn wasn't surprised to see her do this. Bolthor's bodyguards were cousins—one would never leave the other behind, no matter what.

Shiriki glared at Elidor and Catriona. "This isn't over," she said in a soft menacing voice before she and her cousin were obscured by the smoke drifting from the Pit.

Where was Nearra? The last time Davyn had seen her, she was by the Pit. Fear surged through him, and without a word to Ayanti, he ran to Sindri.

"Is Nearra . . . " He couldn't bring himself to finish the sentence.

"She's all right," Sindri said. "I've been trying to levitate her out of there, but I'm having trouble concentrating. I keep losing my grip on her, so to speak."

Davyn waved his hands to clear away the smoke so he could get a better look into the Pit. He saw the blackened carcass of the lizard-boar. So that's where the smoke came from, he thought. Not to mention the stink. But what had set the beast aflame? There had been no open fires in or around the Pit.

Then he saw Nearra. He was relieved to see that she appeared unharmed, but she just stood there, looking up at them with a strange smile on her face. The smile, which was so unlike Nearra, sent a chill through Davyn. If the Emergence—when the spirit of Asvoria assumed control of Nearra's body—had finally taken place, it would explain what had happened to the lizard-boar: Asvoria had cast some sort of fire spell at it.

"Are you all right?" he called out to her.

Nearra didn't answer right away, and Davyn began to fear the worst, but then she said, "Of course, though I'm going to smell like smoke for days after this."

Davyn smiled in relief. Perhaps Asvoria's spirit hadn't emerged after all.

"Just hold on for a few moments. We'll find a way to get you out."

He turned to Sindri and put a hand on the kender's shoulder. "Don't worry about using magic. Ayanti can get her out."

Sindri's brow smoothed as he stopped concentrating, and he let out a weary but grateful sigh.

Ayanti walked up and nodded toward Nearra. "A friend of yours?"

"Yes. Can you help us get her out of the Pit?"

By this time Elidor and Catriona had joined them. The elf looked down at the blackened remains of the lizard-boar and wrinkled his nose in disgust. "What a stench!"

"I'm not sure I *should* help her," Ayanti said. "Not after what she did to little Oshi."

"Little!" Elidor said in astonishment. "You mean that thing would've gotten even bigger?"

"Whatever Nearra did, she did in self-defense," Davyn said.

The centaur and the ranger looked at each other for a long moment. Finally, Ayanti nodded. "Of course, but we must be quick about it. I don't know how long Bolthor will remain unconscious—or how long it'll take Kuruk and Shiriki to see to their wounds and return to seek vengeance. Let's go and—"

Before the centaur could finish speaking, a shadow passed over them. They looked up, and at first Davyn thought a dragon was attacking. But the creature was too small, and he didn't feel a surge of dragonfear. Then he saw what the thing was, and he knew fear of a different sort. The creature was a collection

T I M   W A G G O N E R

of bleached bones held together with wire and leather straps instead of cartilage, tendons, and ligaments. Where in life it had possessed wings of muscle and feathers, it now had wings made of leather. Its skull had large round hollows where eyes had once been, and instead of a mouth it had a cruel curved beak of bone. The creature's front legs were avian, but its body and back legs were feline. Davyn knew that thing had been a griffin when it was alive, but now it was nothing more than an undead puppet, one whose strings were no doubt being pulled by Maddoc.

"Wow!" Sindri said. "I've never seen anything like that before!"

The skeletal griffin circled over the Pit. It opened its beak and produced an eerie, high-pitched shriek. The unnatural cry made Davyn shudder.

"What's that thing doing here?" Catriona asked.

"Maddoc sent it," Davyn said. "He must've sensed whatever magic Nearra used against the lizard-boar. If we can destroy the griffin's wings, it won't be able to fly. Then we can work on severing the straps that hold the bones together."

Davyn drew an arrow and nocked it. Elidor reached for a pair of throwing knives.

"Let me have your dagger," Sindri said to Ayanti. "I'll use my magic to send it flying at the griffin."

Ayanti looked at Davyn and raised a questioning eyebrow. There was no way Davyn could explain to Ayanti that Sindri's "magic" came from the enchanted ring Maddoc had given him long ago—a ring that Sindri now wore on one of his fingers. Even Sindri didn't know his ability to levitate things came from the ring; he truly believed he was a wizard. In the end, all Davyn could do was nod.

Evidently, it was good enough, for Ayanti bent down and handed her dagger to Sindri.

"I'll take the left wing," Davyn said.

"Then I'll take the right." Elidor nodded.

"I'll try to sever the skull from the neck," Sindri said. "Maybe it won't be able to function without its head."

"All right," Davyn said. "On the count of three. One, two—"

But before any of them could fire, the bone-griffin suddenly shrieked and dove into the Pit.

"Nearra, look out!" Davyn shouted.

4   TAKEN

Nearra flattened herself against the wall, but there was nowhere in the Pit to go. The bone-griffin reached out with its front legs, which ended in eagle talons, and grabbed her by the shoulders. Nearra struggled to break free, but the undead creature's grip was too strong. The bone-griffin flapped its leather wings furiously and lifted Nearra into the air.

"Don't attack!" Catriona shouted to her friends. "You might injure Nearra!"

And then the bone-griffin ascended into the sky and began carrying its prize toward its master's keep.

"Come on!" Davyn shouted. "We have to go after Nearra!" He started to run, but Catriona grabbed his arm and stopped him.

"Of course we will," Catriona said. "But we can't simply walk up to Maddoc's front door and knock. If we could, we wouldn't have come to Ravenscar in the first place."

Davyn knew his friend was right, but he couldn't stand the thought of Maddoc getting hold of Nearra. The wizard had already caused the deaths of Davyn's parents. Davyn didn't want to lose Nearra too.

Elidor put a hand on Davyn's shoulder. "We won't abandon Nearra. You know that."

Davyn shrugged off the elf's hand and glared at him. "This is *your* fault! If you hadn't bribed those two barbarians with counterfeit coins, they wouldn't have come after us, Sindri wouldn't have been forced to use his magic, and Maddoc wouldn't have become aware that we're in Ravenscar. The wizard wouldn't have sent his bone-griffin and most of all, Nearra would still be with us!" Davyn was almost screaming by the time he reached the end of his tirade.

Elidor took a step back, as if Davyn's words had dealt him a physical blow. "I didn't intend—"

"That's the problem!" Davyn interrupted. "You never *intend* anything, other than indulging your own need for excitement and riches, that is! They say that there's no honor among thieves. After getting to know you, I believe it!"

Davyn didn't wait for the elf to respond. He turned and walked away from the Pit in the direction of Maddoc's keep.

"Whoever wants to save Nearra, come with me," Davyn said. "We can think of a plan along the way."

But before Davyn could walk more than a few feet, Elidor said, "No honor? You have the gall to speak to me of honor? You, who lied to us about your relationship to Maddoc and who aided the wizard in his plan to restore Asvoria to life? If anyone here is responsible for Nearra's plight, it is you, my deceptive friend!"

Davyn stopped. He was so filled with fury that he started to reach for an arrow, but he didn't. He knew that Elidor was right, and the anger he felt wasn't directed at the elf but rather at himself.

He let out a long breath, and his anger drained away. He didn't start walking again, but neither did he turn around to face his friends. He couldn't bear to look into their eyes just then.

He heard soft hoof-falls as Ayanti walked up to him.

"I don't know what's going on with you and your companions, Davyn, but I do know one thing. You're a good person at heart, and I've always been proud to call you my friend."

Davyn looked at her smiling face and he smiled back.

"Now we should go somewhere safe," Ayanti continued. "You can fill me in on what's happening and maybe we can find a way to help Nearra. All right?"

Davyn nodded. He turned to look at Elidor. The elf was scowling, arms folded across his chest. But finally he nodded as well. "But only for Nearra's sake," he said.

Davyn knew he should apologize to Elidor, but he was too ashamed. "For Nearra," he agreed.

Davyn caught the concerned glance that Catriona gave Sindri but chose to ignore it. "Let's go," he said to Ayanti.

"Follow me, everyone," the centaur said, and then set off at a trot away from the Pit and toward the forest.

After helping Kuruk to the edge of the forest where he'd be safe, Shiriki returned to retrieve Bolthor. She dragged the unconscious bandit king to the dilapidated hut that served as his home and tossed him onto his straw-filled pallet. She then went back to Kuruk and brought her cousin to Bolthor's hut where she tended to his wounds while their employer slept.

Shirki was worried about her cousin. He'd taken an arrow in the shoulder and a sword blow to the left leg. His leather armor had prevented the arrow from penetrating too deeply, but his leg wound had bled quite a bit, and Kuruk's face was pale, especially for the normally swarthy-skinned Wilder Elves.

Shiriki treated his wounds as he lay on the floor of the hut. She removed the arrow from his shoulder, poured some of Bolthor's wine over the wound to clean it, and then bound it with a clean cloth. She then did the same for his leg wound. Kuruk hissed in pain.

"Hush," she said. "Don't be such an infant."

Kuruk gritted his teeth as she wrapped a bandage around his leg. When Shiriki was finished, she examined her work, then nodded in satisfaction. "They'll do."

"It's your turn, then." Kuruk attempted to sit up, but Shiriki pushed him back down.

"Lie still, my cousin. You lost more blood than I. I can tend to my own wound."

She tore the sleeve of her tunic to reveal the wound to her arm. She cleansed it then bound it in cloth. She flexed her arm and grimaced.

"Good enough," she pronounced.

"How's Bolthor?" Kuruk asked.

Shiriki glanced over at the pallet where their employer lay. "He'll live, but it's hard to say how long he shall remain unconscious."

"I can't believe those brats were able to wound both of us," Kuruk said bitterly. "And without so much as getting a scratch themselves!"

"It's that attitude which caused you to be wounded in the first place," Shiriki said. "You underestimated them just because they were young. Even the elf hasn't seen his first century yet."

Kuruk sneered. "The half-breed, you mean."

"Yes. But just because his blood is impure doesn't mean he is incapable of fighting."

Kuruk nodded at her bandaged arm. "It appears I'm not the only one who underestimated them."

"True," she agreed. "We were both overconfident. It is a common enough failing in our people." Elves, no matter what kind, were much longer lived than humans, had superior strength

TIM WAGGONER

and speed, and the ability to see in the dark. It was difficult for elves to remember that other races had strengths and skills of their own.

"We shall not be so foolish when we next encounter them," she said.

Kuruk smiled. "Does my beloved cousin have vengeance on her mind?"

Shiriki smiled back. "Of course. But even if I didn't, Bolthor is sure to send us after them."

Kuruk snorted. "Bolthor is scarcely more intelligent than the beasts he sends to their deaths in his loathsome Pit. If we had anywhere else to go we'd never have started working for him in the first place."

Shiriki glanced at Bolthor to see if he'd heard her cousin, but the bandit chieftain was still dead to the world.

Kuruk sighed. "If only the Dark Queen had succeeded."

"But she didn't," Shiriki said. "And because we served in her army, our own people shun us, and we are equally unwelcome in human lands. Only bandits like Bolthor and his ilk will have anything to do with us."

"We could always go into the wilderness," Kuruk said, "and live off the land, just the two of us."

"I've told you at least a dozen times before that if we are to continue to do Takhisis's work, to help prepare Krynn for the day of her return, we cannot isolate ourselves. We must continue to spread our Queen's darkness throughout Ansalon, even in our own small way."

Bolthor stirred on his pallet and sat up groggily. He put his hand to his head and winced in pain.

"I want to find those children," he growled. "Now!"

Shiriki nodded. "As you command, Bolthor." She held out a hand to Kuruk. "Rise, my cousin. The hunt begins."

Kuruk grinned as he took Shriki's hand and allowed her to pull him to his feet. "We'll find them quickly, then kill them slowly."

Shriki grinned back. "Exactly what I was thinking."

CHAPTER

5   CAIRNGORN KEEP

Nearra saw trees with new green leaves pass beneath her as the bone-griffin bore her away from Ravenscar. Her shoulders ached from where the undead creature's claws gripped her, but she didn't think the monster's talons had penetrated her flesh.

Nearra felt a surge of panic at being so high above the ground, but she fought it. She knew she would have to keep a calm head if she had any hope of survival. Her hands were free and she struggled to reach her dagger. But no matter how she struggled, she couldn't get her fingers on the blade. Not that it mattered; she doubted the weapon would do her any good. The bone-griffin was already dead and beyond pain. And even if she could've wounded it somehow and forced it to release her, she would fall to her death. All she could do was try to keep from surrendering to despair and let the griffin carry her where it would.

Before long, the forest thinned and a castle-like structure came into view. She didn't need Davyn to tell her that this was Cairngorn Keep. The main structure was a great stone tower that rose toward the sky. The tower ended not in a pointed spire but rather a flat surface surrounded by crenelations. Several smaller buildings were clustered around the central tower. The court-yard was covered with brick, as if whoever had built the keep had desired to seal it off completely from the rest of the world, including the earth upon which it was constructed. A twenty-foot wall surrounded the courtyard, but as this place was home to a wizard, Nearra doubted the wall was the only defense the keep possessed.

The bone-griffin stopped flapping its artificial wings and began gliding downward toward the top of the tower. As they drew closer, Nearra could see two figures awaiting her arrival. One was short and squat, his body wrapped in a gray cloak, his head and face hidden within the folds of a large hood. It was Oddvar, the dark dwarf who served Maddoc. And standing next to the Theiwar was the wizard himself, wearing the black robes of a mage dedicated to evil. It had been almost a year since Nearra had last seen Maddoc, but the wizard had changed a great deal in that time. He was thinner, his face drawn and haggard. There were dark circles around his eyes, and his beard, formerly a mixture of salt and pepper, now held far more white than black.

When Nearra was five feet above the stone surface the creature dropped her. She tried to land on her feet, but she slipped and fell onto her side.

One corner of Maddoc's mouth lifted in a cruel half-smile, but the wizard said, "Help our guest up, Oddvar."

The Theiwar took a step toward Nearra, but she held up a hand to stop him.

"Don't touch me."

Oddvar hesitated, and though it was difficult to make out the dwarf's features in the shadows of his hood, Nearra thought she detected a hint of fear in his large owl-like eyes.

He's afraid of me, Nearra thought with wonder. No, not me, she realized. Asvoria. Nearra had to keep from smiling. It seemed she had an unexpected advantage, if only she could figure out a way to use it. She rose to her feet, grimacing at the pain in her hip from where she had fallen.

Maddoc looked up at the bone-griffin who still hovered over them.

"I have no further need of you at this time. Go."

The bone-griffin squawked an acknowledgment and flew down to the courtyard, where it would presumably await its master's summons.

Nearra touched her shoulders. Though they hurt, her fingers didn't come away bloody, and she had no difficulty moving her arms. It seemed the creature hadn't seriously injured her.

Maddoc's eyes narrowed as he watched her self-examination.

"I see you've become something of a seasoned adventurer since last we spoke face-to-face," the wizard said. His voice was weak and breathy, as if it took great effort for him to speak. "Assuming, of course, that I am addressing Nearra."

"Who else would you be addressing?" she said.

Maddoc smiled thinly. "Who else indeed? Well, now that you're here, would you like a tour? Since this was once your home—or rather, Asvoria's—you might be interested to see what I've done with the place."

"Stop pretending that I'm your guest, Maddoc! We both know you brought me here by force!"

Maddoc smiled. "Perhaps I merely have an eccentric method of inviting people to my home."

"Davyn's told me everything. I know that you implanted the spirit of Asvoria within my body in hope of resurrecting and eventually controlling her. I also know that you suppressed my memories so that it would be harder for me to resist being dominated by Asvoria."

"A mistaken assumption on my part, I'll admit," Maddoc said.

"Even without your memories, you've proven to be strong and resourceful."

"Don't bother trying to flatter me, Maddoc. Ever since I awoke on the forest path without my memory, you've made my life a misery, and the lives of my friends, too! You've continuously orchestrated dangerous situations and steered me toward them." Nearra glared at Oddvar. "With the help of your servants, of course."

The Thiewar bristled when she said the word *servants*, but otherwise didn't react.

Nearra continued. "Davyn says it's because Asvoria's spirit didn't emerge the way you expected, and you've arranged various threats to try to force her to defend herself and take over my body."

"True," Maddoc admitted. "And while those efforts met with a certain amount of success, Asvoria always failed to emerge completely." He paused. "At least, she hasn't emerged before today."

Nearra didn't like the sound of that. "What do you mean?"

"Not long ago, I detected a burst of mystic energy from Ravenscar. The burst was so strong, it could only have been caused by Asvoria. And the sorceress could only wield that much power through you if she had finally emerged."

Nearra supposed it was possible. Her memory of what had happened once she fell into the Pit *was* somewhat fuzzy. Nearra had no love for the sorceress who shared her body, and she wanted nothing more than to be free of her. But she couldn't allow Maddoc to gain control of Asvoria either. As dangerous as Maddoc was now, he would be infinitely more so if he possessed Asvoria's knowledge of ancient magic.

"When I placed Asvoria's spirit into your body, I also cast a spell on the both of you: when Asvoria fully emerged, your body would

TIM WAGGONER

become completely paralyzed so that the sorceress could not work any magic, allowing me to gain absolute control over her."

"But I'm not paralyzed." Nearra held up her hand and wiggled her fingers. "See?"

"That proves nothing. It's possible that Asvoria has found a way to counter my paralysis spell in the months since I implanted her spirit within your body. I always knew there was a chance she might undo the enchantment. She is, after all, a powerful and cunning sorceress. I was reluctant to bring you here before now because I was loathe to risk harming you. If you were to perish, Asvoria's spirit would be released from your body and lost to me forever. However, after all this time, my patience has reached its end, and I'm willing to take that risk."

Nearra felt frost gather along her spine. Was there nothing she could do to fight him?

There was one thing, if she had the courage.

Though she knew there was no way Davyn would ever know her final thought, she nevertheless addressed it to him.

I'm sorry, Davyn. There was no other way.

She whirled and ran toward the edge of the tower. Nearra didn't want to die, but if that's what it took to stop Maddoc, it was a price she was willing to pay.

"Stop!" Oddvar shouted and ran after her. But her legs were longer than the dwarf's and she had a head start. Maddoc rapidly chanted alien syllables of power. Her limbs suddenly felt heavy, and it was all she could do to keep her eyes open.

She was almost to the battlements. All she had to do was get there and . . . climb . . . up onto them . . . and . . .

She stood upon the edge of a crenelation, swaying back and forth, wanting nothing more than to lie down, curl up on the stone, and sleep. But then a strong breeze wafted over her face. Cool and bracing, it roused her once more to alertness. She leaped out into space and spread her arms wide as she plummeted toward the stone courtyard below.

Ayanti led Davyn and the others to the edge of Ravenscar, where Bolthor's animals were kept. The main building was a barn-like structure with a wrought-iron gate in place of a wooden door and bars instead of shutters over the windows. Davyn hadn't been here for some time, but the rank smell of sour animal sweat mixed with manure was something he remembered quite well, though he wished he didn't. It was the stink of animals separated from nature, forced to live in squalor and boredom, their only excitement those few moments when they were released to fight in the Pit.

When Davyn had been younger, he'd found the smell disturbing. Now, it nauseated him. He knew what Maddoc would say about that if he were here.

Just shows you've grown soft, boy, feeling sympathy for a bunch of dumb animals.

Not soft, Davyn thought with a touch of pride and, surprisingly, sadness. Grown up.

Ayanti clopped up to the gate, removed a key from her vest, and unlocked the door.

"We should be safe enough in here, at least for a short time," the centaur said.

Catriona didn't look convinced. "You want us to go in there? With the animals? Are there any more creatures like that boar-thing inside?"

"I sure hope so!" Sindri said.

"The beasts are all locked in iron cages," Ayanti assured them. "Not even the most unnatural among them is strong enough to break through the bars."

"It's not the creatures I'm worried about," Elidor said, wrinkling his nose. "I fear the stench alone may kill me."

Davyn smiled. Sometimes it was a drawback to possess an elf's heightened senses.

"I don't care about that," Sindri said. "I just want to see the animals!" And without waiting for his friends to reply, the kender scampered inside.

Elidor sighed and followed, as did Catriona, though she kept her hands near her dragon claws, ready to draw them should trouble arise. Davyn went next, and then Ayanti walked in and closed and locked the gate behind them.

It was dim inside the barn and the dirt floor was covered with soiled straw. A narrow corridor ran down the middle of the building with animal cages in rows on either side. Most of the cages contained normal animals—dogs, wolves, bear, mountain cats—but a few held bizarre conglomerations of creatures: insect, lizard, amphibian, bird, mammal, and other unidentifiable monstrosities. One cage, however, was empty. Davyn knew this was where the lizard-boar had been kept.

The animals looked up eagerly as they entered, but Ayanti spoke in soft, soothing tones. "Hush, now. I know you're eager to fight—or better yet, be fed—but neither is going to happen right now, so it's best you all just settle down."

The animals did as their keeper suggested, lying back down in their pens and closing their eyes to rest.

As Davyn looked upon the unnatural hybrids created by Maddoc's fell magic, he thought how the wizard had used his power to transform Davyn's birth father into the monstrosity known only as the Beast. Not long ago, Davyn had been forced to deal the Beast a death blow. He only discovered it was his father when the man resumed human form as he lay dying. Maddoc had always led Davyn to believe that his experiments were mystical blends of natural animals, but now the young ranger wondered if the wizard had lied to him about that, as he had lied to Davyn about so many other things. What if these creatures, like his true father, had once been human?

"All right, Davyn," Ayanti said, "you've come home and stirred up quite a bit of trouble. I hope you have a good reason."

"It's Nearra," Davyn said. "Our friend who was taken by the bone-griffin. She's the reason we came to Ravenscar."

"She's been cursed by Maddoc," Catriona said. "We've all vowed to free her from the wizard's foul enchantment."

Ayanti looked to Davyn again. "You too?"

He nodded. "I originally helped Maddoc with his plans for Nearra, but I came to realize how truly evil he is. Now I want nothing more than to help Nearra and end Maddoc's evil once and for all."

Ayanti's eyebrow raised once more, even higher this time. "I don't suppose Nearra herself had anything to do with your decision to turn against your father?"

Davyn felt his face turn red, but he avoided Ayanti's question and said, "My *adoptive* father. And as far as I'm concerned, Maddoc is no longer even that to me."

"It seems you've returned with quite a tale to tell, Davyn," Ayanti said. "And since I won't be welcome in Ravenscar after knocking out Bolthor, I suppose I should hear the whole story."

"Very well," Davyn agreed. "It all began when—"

A booming voice from outside interrupted him.

"Davyn! Ayanti! I know you're in there!"

It was Bolthor.

Ayanti scowled. "I knew I should've hit him harder."

6   TRAPPED

"Bolthor won't stop until he's had his vengeance," Ayanti said. "The only way he can remain chieftain is if everyone else fears and respects him."

"And that means he has to deal with us first," Catriona finished.

Ayanti nodded. "And permanently." Her gaze darted back and forth nervously.

Elidor sniffed the air. "What's that smell?"

Davyn frowned. "This is hardly the time for you to complain some more about the odor in here."

"Not *that* smell!" Elidor replied. "It's—" His eyes widened. "It's smoke!"

Now Davyn thought he could smell it, too. Since Bolthor didn't have enough men to come in and get them, he was going to try burning them out. Or, if they didn't leave the enclosure, burn them to death. Either way, Bolthor won.

"The enclosure's wood is old and dry," Ayanti said, her voice trembling. "It'll be ablaze within moments!" She stepped back and forth restlessly, and her gaze darted around the enclosure as if she were looking for a way to escape. Though Davyn normally thought of Ayanti as human, she wasn't. It appeared that the

43

equine half of her nature was reacting to the possibility of fire the way any animal would, with sheer terror.

Bolthor's "pets" were reacting the same way. Some huddled at the back of their cages while others paced restlessly. Some growled, some whined, and others remained silent and shivering, eyes wide with fear.

The cage doors were all closed with padlocks.

Davyn turned to Ayanti. "Do you have the keys to open the cages?"

"There's only one key. It's the same one I used to lock the gate." Ayanti reached into her vest pocket, and held the key out to him.

Davyn snatched it out of her hand. "Elidor, you stay here with me. Everyone else, go to the back of the enclosure and stay close to the wall!"

Catriona nodded, and she and Sindri each took one of Ayanti's hands and led her toward the rear of the building. The centaur allowed the warrior and the kender to escort her, though her hooves rose and fell in a nervous, erratic pattern, as if she would bolt if there were only somewhere to go.

Davyn looked at Elidor. "How fast can you pick the gate's lock?"

Davyn didn't see Elidor's hand move, but suddenly the elf was holding one of his metal lockpicks.

"Just about as fast as you can blink. Why?"

"Get ready to open the gate when I tell you." He held up Ayanti's key and grinned. "I think it's time Bolthor's pets got a little exercise."

Shiriki watched in satisfaction as orange-red flames began to spread upward along the enclosure's walls. Tendrils of black smoke curled into the air, and she could hear the sounds of the animals inside howling in fear and throwing themselves against the bars of their cages.

Bolthor sighed. "It's a shame that we have to sacrifice my pets in order to deal with Ayanti and Davyn, but I suppose it can't be helped. And I *have* grown tired of seeing the same animals fight in the Pit time after time," he said, his voice brightening. "At least now I'll have an excuse to acquire some new ones."

Shiriki smiled. "Sometimes things have a way of working out for the best, my lord."

Kuruk scowled. "I'd rather have had a chance to pay them back personally for the wounds they gave us."

"You may yet get to, Cousin," Shiriki said. "*If* the fire drives them out. If they choose to remain inside and perish, their deaths well may be faster and more pleasant than what you would've done to them, but in the end, they will be just as dead. So—" Shiriki broke off as she saw a hand reach between the bars of the enclosure's gate, insert something into the lock, and give it a twist. The lock snicked open and the hand quickly withdrew.

"Prepare yourselves to have a bit of fun," Bolthor said to his bodyguards. "It looks as if our young friends can no longer stand the heat and are about the abandon the kitchen."

The gate swung wide, but what emerged wasn't the companions, but rather a gigantic monstrosity with a thin scaled serpent's body and six multi-jointed, insectine legs—and it wasn't alone. Davyn had released Bolthor's entire nightmarish menagerie.

Shiriki knew there was no way the two of them could hope to stand against all these monsters. She exchanged a quick glance with her cousin, and Kuruk nodded, as if he'd read her mind.

The two elves turned and ran toward the trees, abandoning their master.

"Stop! Come back!" Bolthor bellowed in fury. "I command—" His voice was cut off as the first of his pets fell upon him.

When the last of the animals had been released, Davyn and the others rushed out of the barn, coughing and rubbing at smoke-irritated eyes. Once outside, they saw that most of the animals had fled into the surrounding forest. But several of them crouched over Bolthor.

Davyn turned away. While he thought there was more than a bit of poetic justice to Bolthor's demise, he took no pleasure in it.

"At least we won't have to worry about him coming after us anymore," Elidor said, his voice weak with nausea.

"I'm glad the animals are free," Ayanti said. "I stayed on as their keeper only to make sure they were treated as well as possible. Now they'll never have to fight for someone else's entertainment again."

Davyn quickly scanned the area. "I don't see Kuruk or Shiriki."

"Maybe they've gone in search of a new employer," Elidor suggested.

"Maybe," Davyn said, "but I doubt it."

"So," Ayanti said, "you came to Ravenscar to find me. Why?"

"I thought you might be able to help us sneak into Cairngorn Keep during one of your regularly scheduled deliveries," Davyn said. "But that's no longer possible, obviously. Not only is Maddoc aware that we're here—"

"I won't be doing business at the keep anymore," Ayanti said. "Now that my boss is dead."

"So now what do we do?" Catriona asked.

"Good question," Davyn admitted. He'd given no thought to anything beyond escaping the burning enclosure.

"How about the Bottomless Lake?" Ayanti suggested.

Davyn smiled. "Perfect."

"Sounds rather ominous to me," Elidor said.

"That's just what we called it when we were children," Davyn said. "It's really more of a pond."

"But it's not easy to get to, so hardly anyone ever goes there," Ayanti said.

"As long as we're not bothered by *them*," Elidor said, nodding to the creatures crowded around Bolthor, or rather what was left of him.

"Let's get going," Davyn said. "Before these creatures finish with Bolthor and begin to look for new playthings. The sooner we get moving, the sooner we can start working on a new plan to get into Cairngorn Keep and rescue Nearra."

Davyn led them away from the burning enclosure, Ayanti walking beside him, the others following close behind.

"Do you think it would be possible to tame one of those things?" Sindri asked of no one in particular. "A wizard such as myself can always use an interesting familiar."

"Why don't you give it a try?" Elidor said. "We'll wait for you here."

Sindri looked back. The creatures were just about finished with Bolthor and were starting to fight over what was left.

The kender's face paled. "Never mind."

7
Soft Beds and Bottomless Lakes

t's time to get up, honey."

The voice was kind, but insistent. Nearra did her best to ignore it.

She felt a hand take hold of her shoulder and begin to shake her, gently at first and then, when she didn't respond, more firmly.

"There's work to be done, Nearra. You can't lie around in bed all day."

Nearra moaned and tried to hide her head beneath the covers, but they were snatched away before she could do so.

"I hate to do this, but you leave me no other choice."

Fingers moved along Nearra's ribcage, sides, and stomach, tickling her. Nearra's eyes flew open and she shrieked with laughter. She sat up and pushed the hands away.

"All right, all right!" she said, laughing. "I'm awake!"

"It's about time." Standing at the side of Nearra's bed, looking down at her with amused affection, was a blonde-haired woman in a simple brown dress. Nearra had no memory of ever seeing her before, but nevertheless, a single word came to her lips upon seeing the woman.

"Mother?"

The woman smiled. "And who else would I be? I know you tend to be groggy when you first wake, but you've never failed to recognize me before."

Nearra stared at the woman. Though she still had no memories of her, Nearra was suddenly filled with overwhelming love. It seemed that while Nearra's mind didn't recognize her, her heart had no such trouble.

Nearra jumped out of bed and threw her arms around the woman's—around her *mother's*—neck and hugged her tight. She had no idea how she had come to be here but for now it didn't matter. She was home!

"It's so good to see you again!" Tears started to roll down Nearra's cheeks, and for a few moments, she couldn't speak.

Her mother pulled Nearra down to sit on the edge of the straw-filled mattress. She then held Nearra and rubbed her back gently while she cried. After a bit, her mother said, "Nearra? Sweetheart? Are you all right?"

Nearra pulled away from her mother and wiped her eyes as she tried to get control of herself. "I'm fine. I just . . ."

Images and sensations flooded her mind. Falling toward gray stone . . . a creature of lashed-together bone with wings of stitched leather flying up toward her . . .

"I just had the strangest dream." She frowned. "At least, I think it was a dream. It couldn't have been anything else." She looked into her mother's loving eyes. "Or maybe *this* is the dream?"

Mother took her hand and chuckled. "You really are having a hard time waking up today, aren't you? Do you feel my touch?" She gave Nearra's hand a squeeze.

"Yes."

"Does my hand feel like something from a dream?"

Mother's grip was warm, firm, and comforting. Nearra smiled. "No, it feels real."

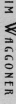

"All right. At least we have that settled." She paused. "Tell you what: It's just you and me here today. If you want to lie back down and sleep a bit longer, it's all right with me. But don't tell your father. You know how he feels about slugabeds."

"Where is Father?" Nearra struggled to remember his face.

"Your father and your sister have already left with a wagonload of wood bound for Ravenscar," Mother said.

"I have a sister?" Nearra sat up.

Mother furrowed her brow. "Are you feverish, girl?" She bent down and felt Nearra's forehead. "You feel cool. Maybe you just need some more sleep. Lay down now. Father and Jirah will be home soon."

With a last smile, Mother left the room and closed the door behind her.

Nearra was sorely tempted to take Mother's suggestion. It felt as if she hadn't gotten a good night's rest in months and months! But there was work to be done. There always was. And if her father and Jirah had already left for Ravenscar, then Mother would expect Nearra to help her with chores around the cottage. Nearra was grateful she'd overslept. She didn't like going to Ravenscar. She understood that her father was a woodcutter and, as he'd said on numerous occasions, "Outlaw money spends just as good as any other kind." Still, she never felt comfortable or safe there. She—

Nearra's thoughts came to a sudden halt as she realized she'd remembered something! She'd remembered that her father was a woodcutter, and she'd remembered how much she disliked going to Ravenscar! She'd also remembered what her father had said about taking outlaw money for his wood . . . she could almost hear his voice as he spoke the words! For the first time in nearly a year, she'd remembered specific details about her past!

She was so excited that she hopped off the bed and ran toward her door, intending to share this wonderful news with Mother.

The "lake" was even smaller than Davyn remembered. It was so small, he wasn't sure it even deserved to be called a pond. "Hole in the ground with some water in it" seemed more fitting. Even so, Elidor stood a couple feet off shore, leggings rolled up to his knees. He held a tree limb that he'd turned into a spear by sharpening an end with one of his throwing knives. The elf scanned the water for fish, trying to procure lunch "in the manner of my father's people," as he'd put it.

The others had similar ideas, it seemed. Sindri sat at the pond's edge, dangling his bare feet in the water while he watched Elidor. Catriona was busy sharpening her dragon claws with a whetstone. Every now and then she'd look off toward the east, in the direction of Cairngorn Keep, with a worried frown.

Davyn stood talking with Ayanti.

"I can't believe we used to climb three steep hills and go through a rock-filled ravine to get here," Ayanti said.

"Traveling here was part of the fun," Davyn said. "The trip made coming here seem more like an adventure."

"From what you told me, you're adventuring for real these days."

"If you can call it that," Davyn said. He looked at the Bottomless Lake just as Elidor stabbed his spear into the water. But when he lifted the spear tip to inspect it, there was nothing there.

"Did you see a fish?" Sindri asked, excited.

"Of course I did," Elidor said, sounding offended that Sindri would even ask such a question. He returned to standing still.

"Is he . . ." Ayanti began.

"Crazy? Sometimes I think so." Davyn sighed. "I didn't really mean that. Elidor just isn't good at sitting around and doing nothing—especially when one of his friends is in danger."

"From the tone of your voice, it sounds as if you're used to being in danger."

"Unfortunately." Davyn sighed. "And it's all to do with Maddoc, of course. If he'd never discovered that Asvoria had transferred her spirit to that tapestry."

"But he did," Ayanti said. "I don't know your father . . . excuse me, I mean *the wizard* well, but I know that, like all his kind—even those who wear robes or white or robes of red—he cannot resist an opportunity to increase his power. All that has happened to Nearra and the rest of you has been his doing, Davyn. You mustn't blame yourself."

Davyn smiled. "What makes you think I'm blaming myself?"

Ayanti returned his smile. "Because I know you. You always take too much upon yourself. You blamed yourself for being unable to master the magical skills Maddoc tried to teach you. Now you're blaming yourself for what has happened to your . . . friend."

Davyn didn't fail to notice the pause Ayanti placed before the word *friend*.

"But I *am* responsible—at least in part. I started off helping Maddoc with his scheme to revive Asvoria."

"Yes, but now you seek to stop him. And from what I can see, your friends do not hold your earlier actions against you."

Davyn looked at Elidor, Sindri, and Catriona. They'd all been through so much together that they were more than just friends. They were family.

"That's true," he admitted.

"And what of Nearra? Does she still blame you?"

"No. She has such a kind and forgiving nature that she's incapable of holding a grudge. Even when perhaps she should."

Ayanti looked at him for a moment, her gaze penetrating, as if she were trying to see into his mind, or perhaps his heart.

"You care for her very much, don't you?" Ayanti asked softly. Davyn nodded.

Ayanti smiled. "Then we will have to do everything we can to help her, won't we?"

Elidor made another stab at the water, again without luck.

"Are you sure you're doing that right?" Sindri said. He stood and waded into the pond to help his friend. As the elf and the kender began to argue about the proper technique to spear fish, Catriona watched them, shaking her head, an amused grin on her face.

"I'm sorry about all this," Davyn began. "I've really messed things up for you, haven't I?"

"Hush. Don't blame yourself because I no longer have a job. I've been meaning to leave Ravenscar for a while now. I told myself that I stayed because of the animals, but the truth is I didn't have anywhere else to go." She smiled. "Now I do. And believe me, I am *not* going to miss working for Bolthor."

Catriona finished sharpening the dragon claws, put away her whetstone, and tucked the claws into her belt. She then joined Davyn and Ayanti. "So, what next, boss?" she said.

Davyn scowled and Ayanti gave him a questioning look, but he ignored it.

"We can't go with our original plan," he said, "and we can hardly make a frontal assault on Cairngorn Keep."

"Not unless one of you is hiding an army in his or her backpack," Ayanti said.

"I wish," Davyn replied. "We need to find a way into the keep that won't immediately alert Maddoc to our presence."

"Maybe you could disguise yourselves," Ayanti offered. "Dress up like servants or something."

Davyn shook his head. "Too risky. Not only does Maddoc know we're already in the area, the other servants would betray us to him rather than risk his wrath."

"Elidor should be able to unlock any door and disarm any traps," Catriona said.

"Physical traps, yes," Davyn admitted. "But not magical ones. Maddoc has placed wardspells on every possible entrance."

Ayanti nodded toward Sindri. The kender had taken hold of Elidor's fishing spear and was trying to pull it out of the elf's hands.

"Let me have a turn!" Sindri shouted.

"What about him?" Ayanti asked. "He's some sort of wizard, isn't he? Maybe he can nullify Maddoc's wards."

Davyn and Catriona exchanged looks.

"Let's just say he's not the right sort of wizard for the job," Davyn said.

Ayanti shrugged. "Then I'm out of ideas—unless you want to go through the tunnels underneath the keep."

Elidor and Sindri stopped fighting and turned to look at the centaur. Davyn and Catriona both stared at her.

"What did I say?"

Davyn grew thoughtful. "I'd forgotten all about those tunnels."

Sindri and Elidor left the pond and came over to join their companions. Both of them still held onto the spear.

"Are you serious?" Elidor asked. "Are there really tunnels beneath Cairngorn Keep?"

"When we were kids, we were playing near the keep's outer wall one day," Davyn explained. "The ground collapsed beneath Ayanti's forelegs."

"I was lucky I didn't break one," she added.

"We examined the hole she'd made and widened it some more. We kept at it and eventually we got it large enough that it began to look like the entrance to a tunnel. Before long it got dark and we had to stop digging. We agreed to continue our excavation the next morning, but that night Maddoc came to the kitchen where

I was eating my dinner. He often took his meals in his study or one of his work rooms, so I was surprised to see him. But he hadn't come to eat. Instead, he told me that he was aware that Ayanti and I had found a 'subsidence,' as he called it. He said that he was going to have it filled in and that I was to stay away from it from now on, and that I should do no more digging on or near the keep grounds.

"He said that Cairngorn Keep was more than just the tower, the buildings, the courtyard, and the wall. He said that a labyrinth of caves and tunnels extended far beneath the keep. This labyrinth was so complex and dangerous that Maddoc himself had explored only a small portion of it. He made me promise never to go near the tunnels, no matter what, and like the dutiful son I was, I obeyed. Even when I later learned that Maddoc was secretly repairing and extending the tunnels."

"Do you think we might be able to get into the keep through this labyrinth?" Catriona asked.

"Perhaps," Davyn said. "If so, it won't be easy."

"Of course it won't," Elidor said. "People don't normally use the word *labyrinth* to describe a simple basement."

"But if it's the only way we can have a chance of reaching Nearra, then we have to try it," Sindri said. Then he smiled. "Besides, it sounds like fun!"

"Are we all agreed?" Davyn asked, and everyone nodded.

"It's too bad you two didn't catch any fish," Catriona said. "We could've used a good meal to build up our strength before we set out."

"Well, if we don't have time to catch them the fun way . . ." Sindri stretched his hand toward the pond and a beam of sunlight struck his silver ring in such a way that for an instant, it shone with the multicolored light of a rainbow. Then the surface of the water began to bubble in a half dozen places and then six medium-

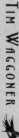

sized fish rose into the air. One by one, the fish floated over to the companions and landed flopping at their feet.

When he was finished, Sindri lowered his hand. His brow was beaded with sweat and he was breathing more heavily than normal, as if he'd just ran a fast sprint.

"Could one of you start a cooking fire?" the kender asked. "I haven't quite mastered flame spells yet."

8 Dragonstorm

I see my daughter finally managed to drag herself out of bed."

Nearra sat on a stool in front of the cottage, peeling potatoes for stew. She looked up to see a horse-drawn wagon approaching across the grassy field, its wheels traveling along well-worn ruts. Sitting in the front and holding the reins was a black-haired man with a curly beard. Next to him sat a thin young girl with shoulder-length black hair.

Though she had no memory of seeing either of them before, she still knew who they were: her father and younger sister, returned from delivering wood to Ravenscar. Her father was a tall, broad-shouldered man with thick arms and large hands that were perfect for chopping wood. Her sister was shorter than she, and slighter of build, and her hands were thin, with long delicate fingers. They were more the hands of a musician or an artist, Nearra thought.

Her father gently pulled back on the reins and the piebald mare pulling the wagon—whose name was Grania, Nearra suddenly recalled—slowed to a stop.

"Here, Jirah." Father handed the reins to his daughter. "Take 59 the wagon around back and unhitch Grania. Rub her down and give her food and water."

He climbed down from the wagon and Jirah, grinning from ear to ear, gave the reins a flick and Grania began plodding forward.

Father doesn't usually allow Jirah to take the reins, Nearra thought. So this is something special for her.

"*You* could've driven the wagon to Ravenscar and back if you'd gotten up in time," Father said as he walked toward Nearra.

Nearra dropped a peeled potato into the wooden bowl at her feet. She stood, laid the paring knife on the stool, then wiped her hands on the rag tucked beneath her belt.

"That's all right. I'd rather stay home and help Mother anyway."

Her father frowned. "I understand when you asked not to ride along to Cairngorn Keep anymore, but now you won't even go to Ravenscar."

"Leave the girl alone, Eric." Mother stepped out of the cottage, a stern expression on her face. "You can't blame her for not wanting to go to either of those godsforsaken places."

Eric sighed. "I suppose you're right, Lanni." He stepped to his wife's side, put an arm around her shoulders, and gave her a kiss on the cheek. "I just want Nearra and Jirah to learn the trade. We won't always be around to provide for them, you know. And if Nearra won't ride along—"

Fear bordering on panic suddenly gripped Nearra. "Don't say that!"

Both Eric and Lanni turned to look at her, concerned.

"Don't say what?" Eric asked.

"That you won't be around someday!" Tears blurred her vision. "It's an awful, horrible thing to say!" She knew she was overreacting, but she couldn't help it.

Eric came over and hugged Nearra. "Hush, child. Everything is all right. Your mother and I might not be youngsters anymore, but I'll wager we still have quite a few good years left in us. If you don't want to travel to Ravenscar, you don't have to, and that's that."

Her father's voice was kind and soothing, but there was also a core of strength in it that always reassured her as nothing else could. When her father told her that everything would be all right, she believed it. Though she felt safe and protected in her father's arms and would've liked nothing better than to remain standing like this for the rest of her life, she pulled free from Eric's embrace and took a step back.

"Father, Mother, I need to talk with you about something."

Her parents exchanged a quick glance.

"You sound so serious," her mother said. "Is something wrong? Are you in some kind of trouble?"

Nearra couldn't help laughing. "Sometimes it seems as if trouble is all I've ever known." She took a deep breath. "Almost a year ago, Maddoc cast a spell on me. He—"

An ear-splitting roar cut through the air, drowning out the rest of Nearra's words. A shadow fell over the cottage, and Nearra and her parents looked skyward. Descending toward them, wings spread wide, sunlight glittering off its iridescent scales, was a blue dragon.

Terror slammed into Nearra, so strong and intense that it was almost a physical force. Dragonfear, she realized, and though she'd experienced it before, it was all she could do to keep from screaming.

"Get inside, both of you!" Eric shouted. He started running toward the back of the cottage, presumably to find Jirah. Filled with dragonfear, he moved haphazardly, body trembling.

"We won't be any safer in there than we are out here!" Nearra said. "The dragon can tear our home apart as easily as if it were a pile of sticks!"

The dragon swooped low over them, and Nearra and her mother were knocked to the ground by a blast of air. The dragon arced upward and began gaining altitude once more. Nearra helped her mother stand.

"We need to make for the forest!" she said. "A creature that size will have a hard time getting between the trees!"

"How do you know this?"

"Believe me, Mother, I've had some experience with dragon attacks." Nearra glanced upward and saw that the dragon was slowing in its upward climb, that meant it was going to come driving down toward them any moment.

"C'mon! We can't stand around here talking!" Nearra tried to tug her mother along after her, but she resisted.

"We can't leave your sister and father!"

Nearra felt the same way, but she knew they'd all stand a greater chance of survival as two pairs instead of one foursome.

Just then Eric and Jirah came running around to the front of the cottage. Both gripped axes used for cutting wood. They were tools, not weapons, but even if they had been battle axes forged from the finest steel in Ansalon, they would've been useless against a creature the size of the blue dragon.

"Are you mad?" Nearra shouted. "You can't fight a dragon with those! We have to run!"

Eric stared up at the dragon. His gaze was filled with terror, but his jaw was set in a determined line. "This is our home. I built it with my own two hands, and I'd sooner die than let it be destroyed without a fight! Take your mother and your sister and run! I shall deal with the beast!" Eric's voice quavered, but his grip on the axe remained sure and steady.

Jirah wasn't managing her fear quite so well. Her face was

chalk-white and her eyes were wild, like those of a trapped animal desperately looking for escape. Nearra tugged at her sister's arm. But Jirah wouldn't move.

The blue dragon paused at the apex of its flight. The gigantic beast was so far above them that it looked no larger than the small lizards Nearra found in the woods as a child. The sky around the dragon suddenly grew dark and storm clouds began to form. They were dark, angry clouds colored a pure, deep black. If it was possible for something like a cloud to be evil, then these were.

The dragon flapped its wings and hovered in place. Great gusts of wind buffeted Nearra. So strong was the sudden gale that she was forced to huddle against her mother and sister to keep from being knocked to the ground.

The blue dragon peered down at them, arcs of blazing white energy crackling from its eyes. And then the monster opened its mouth and a sizzling burst of lightning shot from its tooth-filled maw.

Nearra screamed as the bolt raced to earth and struck the roof of their cottage. The dry thatch caught fire instantly and flames rose into the air.

"No!" Eric shouted. "Come down and face me, and I'll show you what a woodsman's axe can do!"

The wind was howling so loudly now that Nearra could barely hear her father's words. The dragon must have heard Eric, though, for the beast stopped flapping its wings, folded them against its scaly sides, and dived toward them.

"Come on!" Nearra still had hold of her mother's hand and now she grabbed Jirah's as well. She pulled as hard as she could, and they allowed her to lead them away from the blazing cottage—perhaps because they'd realized the foolishness of staying where they were, but more likely because they were too overwhelmed with dragonfear to resist her.

As she pulled her mother and Jirah away, Nearra called back to her father.

"Run!"

But Eric just stood there, axe held high, looking up at the rapidly approaching dragon. Perhaps he stayed because he was paralyzed with fear, or perhaps out of determination to strike back at the monster that had destroyed his home and now threatened his family. Perhaps a bit of both.

At first, it appeared that the blue dragon intended to crash into Eric, but at the last instant before it reached the ground, the dragon spread its wings and halted its dive. For a moment, Nearra hoped that the dragon had decided for some reason to spare her father, but then the beast opened its mouth and once again a bolt of lightning blasted forth. But this time the blue-white energy arced downward to strike Eric.

The flash of light was so intense that Nearra had to avert her eyes. When she opened them, she saw a glowing purple afterimage of her father holding aloft his axe. But that image was no longer a reality. Her father—or what remained of him—was a steaming, blackened husk lying on the ground.

Lanni wailed and Jirah began to weep.

"No!" Nearra screamed. She had only just found her father again . . . now to lose him in such a horrible fashion . . . "Maddoc!" she shouted to the heavens. "This is your doing! It has to be!" She clutched her hands into fists and felt a warm tingling sensation of power begin to build within them.

She let go of Jirah and Lanni and stepped forward to confront the blue dragon. Tendrils of lightning shot back and forth between its sharp teeth, making them glow an eerie blue-white.

She willed the power of the dark sorceress within her to come forth, to take her over completely if that was what she had to do to destroy the monster that killed her father. She looked into

TIM WAGGONER

the blue dragon's eyes. They were two pits of darkness, cold and absolute, just like the storm clouds that now covered the sky from horizon to horizon.

Though Nearra's hands felt as if they were on fire and she ached to release the power she'd summoned, she hesitated, though she wasn't sure why. There was something bothering her, a thought that seemed to drift upward from somewhere deep in her mind. Maddoc's greatest desire was to obtain the secrets of Asvoria's ancient magic . . . He *wanted* Nearra to wield the sorceress' power, *wanted* Asvoria's spirit to take her over. And she couldn't allow that, no matter what.

Nearra took a deep breath, then concentrated on allowing the warm tingling in her hands to diminish. It did so, slowly fading until her hands felt perfectly normal once more.

The dragon looked at her with its awful black eyes.

"You'll regret that, girl," the beast growled in Maddoc's voice, and then it yawned wide and a burst of lightning came for her so swiftly that she didn't have time to even think about screaming, let alone begin to do so.

9   MADDOC'S OFFER

"They've gone," Shiriki said.

"My cousin, you have an absolute genius for stating the obvious," Kuruk replied.

Kuruk and Shiriki had picked up the trail of the companions after the beasts had finished with Bolthor and dispersed. The two elves had followed the trail to the bank of a small pond. Between them were the blackened remains of a fire, along with a pile of fish bones.

Ignoring her cousin's sarcasm, Shiriki knelt down and touched her fingers to the soot. She rubbed a bit of black between her thumb and forefinger then held it up to her nose and sniffed.

Kuruk crouched low and picked up a fish bone. He touched it to the tip of his tongue and considered.

"They left an hour ago," he said.

"Closer to one and a half." Shiriki wiped her fingers clean on the grass then stood. She knew Kuruk's analysis was the more accurate of the two, but she didn't like to acknowledge that his senses were superior to hers.

Kuruk dropped the fishbone back onto the pile and stood. Shiriki waited for him to challenge her assessment, but all he did was lick fish oil from his fingers and smile.

"Where do you suppose they're headed?" he asked.

While Kuruk's senses were keener than hers, Shiriki was the superior tracker of the two. She stepped away from the burnt-out fire and walked around the area, keeping her graze trained on the ground, reading bent blades of grass and depressions in the soil as easily as a child deciphering an alphabet.

"They went east," she said at last. "And the centaur was with them."

Kuruk harrumphed though he didn't seem especially surprised by the revelation. "What lies in that direction?"

"Depending on how far one travels, the whole of Krynn could be said to be east," Shiriki said. "But if you mean what's to the east *near* here, I can only think of one thing: Cairngorn Keep."

Kuruk frowned. "What could they want there?"

Shiriki shrugged. "The human male is Maddoc's adopted son. Perhaps the boy is leading his companions there in search of sanctuary."

"And they have an hour, I mean, one-and-a-half hour's head start on us," Kuruk said.

"They will be forced to avoid certain routes because the centaur is with them," Shiriki pointed out. "Her equine legs will prevent her from climbing some of the steeper hills between here and the wizard's keep. They will be forced to detour around them."

Kuruk groaned. "I can see where you're going with this, and my wounded leg is already throbbing."

Shiriki punched him on the arm, far harder than necessary. "You are a Kagonesti warrior and a servant of Takhisis. What's a little climbing to one such as you?"

"A gigantic pain in the posterior, my cousin," Kuruk said, then sighed. "Let us waste no more time. The sooner we resume our pursuit, the greater chance we will have of arriving at Cairngorn Keep before our quarry."

"And then?" Shiriki said, grinning.

Kuruk grinned back.

"And then."

Nearra opened her eyes and looked around. She sat cross-legged on the floor of a small, unfurnished room lit by candles set into brass wall sconces. A dozen paintings hung on the walls, each encased in elaborate gold frames. The paintings were blank, save the one directly in front of her. It was a rendering of a blue dragon attacking a woodland cottage. Huddled near the cottage were four people and though the figures were so small that it was difficult to make out the details of their features, Nearra knew that she was looking at a painting of herself and her family. She stood to examine the image more closely, but before she could, it began to fade until the painting was blank like all the others.

A door opened and Maddoc shuffled into the room, followed by Oddvar.

"As you've no doubt guessed by now, your little dive off the tower was interrupted, thanks to my griffin," Maddoc said. "Did you really think you could escape me that easily?"

Nearra sighed. "I had rather hoped." She looked back at the blank painting. "What is this place?"

Maddoc smiled. He trembled all over, as if he were so weak he could barely stay on his feet. "Merely a place where you could rest and recover from the sleep spell I cast upon you." A sly tone crept into his voice. "Why do you ask?"

Nearra knew that whatever had happened in this chamber had been the result of another of the evil wizard's spells, but if Maddoc wanted to play games, so be it. However, she wasn't about to play along.

"Has the sorceress' spirit emerged?" the Theiwar asked his master.

Maddoc fixed Nearra with a penetrating gaze, and she had the feeling that he was somehow peering into her mind.

"Well?" the wizard asked Nearra. "Did she?"

Nearra thought rapidly. If Maddoc were able to tell which personality was in control of her body, then he wouldn't need to ask. She gave the wizard what she hoped was an enigmatic smile.

"You tell me."

Maddoc scowled. "This isn't amusing anymore. There are spells I could cast that would allow me to determine the truth, but they are somewhat involved, and take a certain amount of time to perform adequately."

"Right," she said. "And you looking like you've got one foot and a couple extra toes in the grave."

Maddoc's eyes narrowed, but he didn't deny Nearra's charge. "I admit that I am not currently up to my full strength. But that's due in large part to the last enchantment I worked."

"The sleep spell, you mean," Nearra said.

Maddoc shook his head and Oddvar laughed.

"No, I cast another spell while you were sleeping," the wizard said. "I reapplied the paralysis spell, the one that will completely immobilize you if Asvoria emerges and wields her powers. And she won't be able to counter it so easily this time; I've had months to research ways to make the spell much stronger than when I last cast it upon you."

Maddoc hobbled forward and gazed deep into Nearra's eyes.

"If you are in there, Asvoria, if you work even the simplest of magics, you shall be paralyzed. And then you'll be mine at last!" The evil wizard chuckled, the sound more like a raspy cough than a laugh.

He turned turned and shuffled toward the door. "Follow me,"

he said without turning back to look at her. Maddoc walked out of the chamber, Oddvar following close on his heels. Nearra hesitated for a moment longer, but realizing she didn't have any other options, she did as Maddoc commanded.

The wizard led them down a gloom-shrouded corridor. They walked past a number of wooden doors, and Nearra wondered what dangers might lurk behind them.

Before long they came to an open entrance that led to a spiral stairway. They ascended the stone steps and stepped off to walk down another corridor, Maddoc stopped before a door. He made a small gesture and the lock clicked open, and the door swung inward of its own volition. Maddoc then indicated that Nearra should go in first. She didn't want to, but she *did* want to keep Maddoc in doubt as to whether she or Asvoria was in control, and she knew Asvoria wouldn't hesitate to go into the room. So Nearra stepped inside, hoping that she wasn't walking into another trap.

Maddoc and Oddvar came in after her, and then the door swung shut, though it didn't lock this time.

Nearra looked around. Lining the room were shelves filled with books, scrolls, and stacks of loose vellum. A large fireplace was set into the wall opposite the door, in which a fire was blazing away, though it did little to dispel the room's chill. In front of the fireplace was a carved wooden and leather chair and a polished mahogany side table. Several feet from the chair stood a full-length wardrobe mirror, the glass surface spiderwebbed with cracks.

But the feature that dominated the room was the large tapestry hanging on the wall above the fireplace. It portrayed a striking woman in a green dress trimmed with red fur. She had long raven-black hair and intense violet eyes. Around her neck hung a medallion shaped like a sun, and at her feet rested a silver sword.

Nearra knew at once that the woman was Asvoria.

"I don't know what the sorceress used this room for," Maddoc said. "When I first discovered Cairngorn Keep nearly twenty years ago, the room was empty, except for the chair and that tapestry. It took me more years of research to discover that Asvoria had placed her spirit into the tapestry in a last desperate attempt to escape a group of so-called heroes that had come to the keep to capture her. And it took even longer for me to discover a way to free her spirit from the tapestry and implant it into the body of a living person." Maddoc looked at Nearra. "In case you're not following along, that would be you."

She turned to Maddoc. She knew that by saying what she was going to say next, she would destroy any illusion that Asvoria was in control, but she didn't care. "In the chamber with the paintings, I had a vision of my family being attacked by a blue dragon. Was it true? Did that really happen? Are they . . ." She couldn't bring herself to say *dead*.

"Perhaps what you experienced was a vision of the past, or maybe a vision of a future that might come to pass—*if* you don't cooperate with me. "

She should've known better than to ask: Maddoc lied as easily and naturally as he breathed.

"Why did you choose me? Why not use one of your goblin servants . . . or Oddvar, for that matter?"

The Theiwar looked suddenly startled, as if it had never occurred to him that he could possibly be the subject of one of his master's magical experiments.

"There were a number of reasons," Maddoc said. "Most of them having to do with magical factors too esoteric to concern you. But I suppose the main reason was simply that you were close at hand. A keep of this size doesn't run itself, you know. I maintain a staff of servants, drawn from the peasantry that live in the surrounding area. Few of them wish to work for me voluntarily,

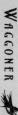

so I'm forced to use various methods of persuasion. Sometimes all it takes is money. Other times my agents in the field, such as Oddvar here, must resort to more physical means. In your case, money was sufficient."

"My case?"

"You worked as a servant for me, Nearra. Your family was so poor that when Oddvar came to your cottage one day and offered you a bag full of steel coins in exchange for ten years' service, you jumped at the chance."

Oddvar grinned. "Your parents were against your coming here, even through your father sold us firewood. But you said something to them . . . let me think . . . ah, yes! You said, 'Maddoc's money will spend just as good as anyone else's,' and you let them keep the steel and accompanied me back to the keep."

Nearra was stunned. "That means I used to live and work here, that I knew you and Oddvar and . . . Davyn."

"I wouldn't say you *knew* us," Maddoc said. "You were a servant, after all."

"Why didn't Davyn ever tell me?"

"Because he's a liar. Don't you see that, girl? He's been working for me all along. Whose idea was it to come here, eh? Who brought you to Ravenscar?"

Nearra knew that Maddoc was just trying to break down her defenses and destroy whatever hope she had left. Davyn had long ago admitted helping Maddoc and he'd repented his actions. In the year since she'd come to know and care for Davyn, he'd made up for whatever transgressions he'd committed against her a dozen times over.

"It's most ironic, isn't it?" Maddoc said. "You first came to Cairngorn Keep only because you wished to help your family. A noble, one might say heroic motive. And now your body is host to one of the wickedest beings ever to plague Solamnia. What's the old cliché? No good deed goes unpunished? In your case, I'd say the sentiment fits, wouldn't you?"

Oddvar chuckled with dark mirth.

Nearra felt a surge of anger. If she could access Asvoria's magic, she'd blast both of them to cinders on the spot! But she forced herself to remain calm—or at least as calm as she could, given the circumstances.

Maddoc continued. "While I would of course prefer to gain total control of the sorceress, after a year of trying to force the Emergence, I am willing to accept a lesser prize."

Nearra felt a stirring deep inside her mind and she knew that Maddoc had peaked Asvoria's interest.

"Go on," she said.

The wizard pointed to the tapestry. "See the amulet around her neck and the silver sword that lies at her feet? From my research, I've learned that the amulet is called the Daystar and the sword is called the Aegis. Both are objects of incredible mystic power. Asvoria will help me obtain them, and once both objects are in my possession, then I shall release her."

Nearra could sense that Asvoria was intrigued, but the girl didn't like the sound of Maddoc's offer. "What do you mean by 'release'?"

"I shall remove the paralysis spell that I placed upon you. Asvoria will be free to assume complete control of your body."

Nearra felt a stab of fear at Maddoc's words. "And then what happens to me?"

The wizard shrugged. "Perhaps you will be but a passenger in your own body, still thinking and feeling but unable to actually do anything. Perhaps it will merely seem as if you go to sleep, and Asvoria will be in command of your body while you slumber. Perhaps you will simply cease to exist. What does it matter, so long as I get the Aegis and the Daystar?"

Nearra felt the spirit of Asvoria begin to rise upward from the depths of her mind, as if the sorceress was a swimmer who had been submerged too long and was desperate to return to the surface for air.

"Do you really think you can be trusted, Maddoc? Why would you be satisfied with only two magical objects when you could have all of Asvoria's knowledge?"

Nearra sensed the spirit of Asvoria hesitate, and then withdraw once more deep into the mind of her host.

Nearra looked at Maddoc and smiled. "No deal."

The wizard's lips tightened and his face reddened with anger. But when he spoke, his voice remained calm. "Very well. We'll just have to do this the hard way. It shall take me several hours to make the necessary preparations. In the meantime, Oddvar will escort you to quarters where you can rest until I am ready for you."

Maddoc turned toward the dark dwarf. "You know where to take her. If she shows the slightest sign of resistance, prick her with your knife."

The Theiwar grinned at her as he drew a dagger from his belt. "Don't worry, girl. The blade's not coated with poison this time. It's smeared with a fast-acting sleeping potion. One nick and you'll be instantly rendered unconscious." The dwarf's eyes gleamed. "Of course, there's always the chance that my hand might slip and I'll cut you more deeply than I intended."

Nearra had to keep herself from shuddering. "I won't give you any trouble."

Maddoc opened the door and gestured for Nearra to walk through. She obeyed and Oddvar, holding the dagger tight in his stubby fingers, followed.

But just as Nearra reached the door's threshold, she detected movement from the corner of her eye. She turned her head and saw a small brown mouse sitting atop a large book on one of the shelves. The tiny animal seemed to be gazing at her intensely with the most remarkable blue eyes. Their color was so clear and piercing that they almost seemed to glow.

"No trouble, remember?" Oddvar said, and Nearra realized she'd stopped walking to look at the mouse. She turned to the dwarf, nodded, and Oddvar marched her down the corridor to whatever prison awaited her.

When the girl was gone, Maddoc glanced over at the bookshelf where she had been staring before she'd departed. He saw nothing but books and scrolls. But whatever had caught Nearra's interest didn't matter now. He had a problem—a big one.

Since he'd removed Asvoria's spirit from the tapestry that had been its home for centuries and implanted it within Nearra, he'd continued to research spells dealing with spiritual transference. After experimenting on countless animals and combining elements of several different rituals, he believed he had finally developed the spell he needed. But conducting the enchantment would've demanded a lot of him when he'd been healthy. Now, suffering from the aftereffects of his familiar's death, the ritual would take even more out of him. Worse, he hadn't anticipated needing to recast the paralysis spell upon Nearra, and he feared he wouldn't have even the strength to conduct the Rite of Emergence. This was why he'd offered to make a deal with Asvoria, but unfortunately, Nearra and the sorceress hadn't accepted it.

He needed to find a way to restore his strength within the next few hours. And then it came to him. There was one way. It was dangerous and might very well have serious consequences for him. But Maddoc was willing to take any risk to increase his knowledge and power. And if all went as he hoped, after tonight he'd be the single most powerful wizard in Solamnia—perhaps in all of Krynn!

His cold dark heart momentarily warmed by dreams of power, Maddoc left his study and closed the door behind him. He didn't see the fly that buzzed out into the hall just before he pushed the door shut, a fly whose multifaceted eyes were a most striking color of blue.

10 HIDDEN DANGER

"Tell me again . . . why we couldn't . . . take the main . . . road." Ayanti spoke though gritted teeth as she struggled to maneuver her equine half through a tangle of brush. In the forest, green leaves were just beginning to peek out from their buds, though the undergrowth was already well developed, too well for Ayanti.

Elidor tried not to smile at the centaur's plight, though it wasn't easy. Horses—or beings that were half-horse—were simply not designed for woodland travel.

"Maddoc expects us to attempt to rescue Nearra," he said. "He's sure to have his agents patrolling the road to his keep."

Elidor and Ayanti led the others. Elidor so he could watch for traps, and Ayanti because if they came to a section of the woods she couldn't pass, they'd all have to turn back and find another route more conducive to centaurs. Ayanti had made it so far, but not without much struggling and even more complaining.

"We have more to worry about than Maddoc's two-legged servants," Davyn said. He, Catriona, and Sindri followed behind the elf and the centaur. "The land around Cairngorn Keep is protected by savage attack hounds."

"Like the lizard-boar back in Ravenscar?" Sindri asked eagerly.

"These animals are far larger and more vicious than normal hounds. Still, they're only dogs," Davyn said.

"Aw," Sindri said, clearly disappointed.

"I'd forgotten about them," Ayanti admitted.

"During the time I spent with my father's people, I came to know the ways of the forest and the animals that dwelled there," Elidor said. "I am completely comfortable with what humans think of as 'wild' animals. They act only according to their natures. But attack dogs are trained by humans to act unnaturally—to hunt and kill not out of hunger but simply because their master commands them to. Beasts such as these are far more dangerous than their forest brethren."

Elidor turned to look at Davyn. "Please tell us that since you grew up in the keep, the hounds will recognize you and wag their tails, happy to see an old friend come home."

"I wish I could," Davyn said. "But the hounds are trained to attack anyone who trespasses on Maddoc's land. Only one of his guards can call them off."

"I can vouch for that," Ayanti said as she carefully detoured around a patch of poison ivy. "Whenever I would deliver supplies to the keep or pick up a new beast Maddoc had created for the Pit, one of the guards would have to ride out and escort me into the keep so the hounds wouldn't come after me."

"So how do we defend ourselves against these animals?" Catriona asked.

"There aren't really that many of them," Davyn said. "About four or so. Just their presence is usually enough to deter most trespassers. They're most dangerous when they're given specific orders. So as long as we aren't spotted by any guards, we should be all right."

Should. Elidor knew from hard experience that there was a world of difference between that word and *will.*

There was something else on the elf's mind, though, something that, in its own way, disturbed him as much as the prospect of being attacked by Maddoc's dogs. Back at the so-called Bottomless Lake, he hadn't really been trying to catch anything. He'd been engaged in a Kagonesti ritual he learned from his father called Mind Cleansing. When an elf was troubled, he or she would carve a fishing spear and wade into the nearest body of water. The elf would then imagine the worries and fears were fish swimming just beneath the surface of the water and then spear them one by one. When the ritual was completed, the elf would feel calmer and could then deal more effectively with the problems that had prompted the ritual in the first place.

Elidor had thought Mind Cleansing was nothing more than an exercise in lunacy the first time his father had convinced him to try it, but he'd been surprised by how well it worked. He continued to use the ritual ever since, whenever he needed it, like today.

But this time, the ritual hadn't left him feeling cleansed. Instead, he was more confused and disturbed than when he'd started. For the "Bottomless Lake" wasn't even a pond, more like a depression in the ground that trapped rainwater. And he was certain of one thing, before Sindri worked his magic, there were no fish in the water.

Elidor glanced back at the kender. Sindri kept turning his head this way and that, as if he were determined to take in every sight, sound, and smell that the forest had to offer. The kender presented himself as a wizard, but Elidor knew that in truth his friend had no magical powers. Elidor wasn't exactly sure why Davyn had decided to aid Sindri in his pretense of being a wizard. For that matter, he wasn't sure why any of them did unless of course, it was simply out of affection for their small friend.

But now it appeared that perhaps Sindri Suncatcher had somehow developed the ability to work true magic, and as much as Elidor cared for him, the idea of the childlike and impulsive kender possessing—and using—real magical power scared him. When he got the chance, he'd have to tell Davyn of his suspicions and—

"Oh, by the gods' all-seeing eyes!" Ayanti swore. Before them lay the partially rotted remains of a fallen oak tree. Jagged, broken limbs jutted out all around, preventing the centaur from simply jumping over the downed tree.

"Wait," Catriona said. She moved past Sindri and Davyn and drew her sword. "Let me cut away some of the branches, then you should be able to get over without much difficulty."

But as Catriona stepped forward to begin her work, Elidor had a sudden feeling that something was wrong.

"Hold a moment, Catriona," the elf said.

Catriona frowned, but she did as he asked.

Elidor swept his gaze over the fallen tree and the ground around it. Something was out of place. If he could just . . . ah! There it was! Hanging in the branches of a nearby elm was an oak branch. In and of itself, this wasn't suspicious. When the oak had fallen, any number of branches would've snapped off and flown through the air to land in various places, including the limbs of other trees. But there was something too neat, too deliberate about this branch. It was perfectly straight, as if any smaller offshoots had been cut off. And it sat precisely balanced in the Y where two of the elm's limbs branched out. It would take only a mild gust of wind to knock the oak branch off. And then there was the way it was angled to point directly at the half-rotted oak, as if it were a marker of some . . .

Then it hit him. The oak branch *was* a marker. It was a marker indicating where a trap had been set.

"What's wrong?" Davyn asked.

"There's a trap here," Elidor replied. "Set up by Bolthor's bodyguards." He gave his companions a small smile. "It appears as if they hold a grudge against us. While Kagonesti prefer to hunt their prey, matching skill against skill and strength against strength, they aren't above laying traps when necessary." Elidor pointed. "That balanced oak branch is a Kagonesti signal that says, 'Watch out, trap ahead.' And since it is a Kagonesti signal, it could mean two things. There are new Wilder Elves in the forest and the signal is meant to keep others of their kind from blundering into their trap. Or Kuruk and Shiriki somehow guessed where we're going, got here before us, and set this trap along the most likely route we'd take to Cairngorn Keep. To cover all their bets, the two might well have set traps along other potential routes as well."

"But if Kuruk and Shiriki are responsible, why would they leave a signal?" Catriona asked.

"To taunt me," Elidor said, a bitter edge to his voice. "To see if the half-breed has enough wits about him to recognize such an obvious sign."

Elidor stepped cautiously toward the fallen log, carefully testing the ground with each foot before putting his full weight down. He looked for telltale signs of trip wires, branches that had been lashed together with tiny strips of leather, a smear of partially dried mud that had been applied to conceal the bodyguards' handiwork. But he saw nothing.

He looked closer at the tree and examined its corrugated gray bark. Just when he thought there was nothing to see, he detected a thin seam where a section of the tree roughly the length of broom handle and a hand-span wide had been cut away and then put back. It was held loosely in place with—he sniffed—pine resin. If anyone in their party stepped on that section of the tree, and the odds were good that at least one of them would, that section of the tree would collapse inward. As for exactly what the trap was designed to do . . .

It took Elidor a few more moments, but now that he knew what he was looking for, it wasn't that hard to find. He straightened and stepped away from the tree.

"Once the wood falls inward, the trap is tripped." He nodded to the right of the tree and then to the left. "Branches of some of the smaller bushes have been bent back and tied down with bits of vine. When the trap is activated, the vines are torn and the branches released, flinging dozens of poison-coated thorns at those attempting to cross the tree." Elidor smiled grimly. "Namely, us."

"It sounds complicated," Sindri said. "But I don't see any bent branches or poison thorns." The kender started forward, obviously intent on seeing for himself. "Are you sure—"

Elidor gripped his friend by the shoulder and stopped him. "So sure that I'm not even going to make a joke about it."

Sindri looked impressed. "That sure, huh?" When Elidor removed his hand, the kender didn't try to move closer to the tree, though he did continue examining it from where he stood.

"So what do we do about it?" Ayanti said. She looked upset, and Elidor had a good notion why. As the largest and heaviest member of their group—not to mention the least graceful in the woods—she most likely would've been the one to set off the trap.

"We have three options," Elidor said. "We can turn back and find another way through the forest to Cairngorn Keep—through there's no guarantee that any other route we choose won't be booby-trapped as well."

"Or that Kuruk and Shiriki themselves won't be lying in wait to ambush us," Catriona added.

Elidor nodded. "We could purposely set off the trap before attempting to cross—"

"Which would still be dangerous," Davyn said.

"Or we can simply go around," the elf finished. "Personally, while I'd love to set off the trap just to see how it works, detouring around the tree would be the smarter move." Elidor waited to see what Davyn would say.

After a moment's thought, Davyn said, "All right, let's go around. It'll only take a bit of time, and we can hardly help Nearra if we get pierced by poison thorns, can we?"

Elidor smiled. "You're the boss."

Davyn gave a long-suffering sigh.

"Which way?" Elidor asked. "Right or left?"

Davyn shrugged. "Right."

So, with Elidor in the lead, followed by Ayanti, and then the others, they began their detour around the fallen oak. They walked toward the base of the tree and soon reached the spot where it had once been rooted to the ground. The earth was a mass of loose black soil, and the roots rose into the air, looking more like the tentacles of some strange water creature than part of a tree.

As they walked around the roots, Elidor caught a whiff of musky animal scent, and out of the corner of his eye, he noticed that one of the smaller roots had been tied into a knot. A knot, he instantly knew, that Kuruk and Shiriki had wanted him to see.

A cold pit of fear opened in his stomach as he realized he'd been tricked. The first trap, while real enough, had been meant as a decoy to distract him from detecting this second trap in time.

He opened his mouth to warn his friends, but before Elidor could speak, he detected movement above their heads, and he looked up to see a dozen objects tied with vine ropes swing from the trees. He understood then where the musky animal scent had come from, for each of the objects was a different small forest creature—a rabbit, a squirrel, a fox, a weasel, a stoat. They were all dead, their bodies criss-crossed with dagger slashes. The dead animals swung toward one another, collided, and a rain of blood spattered down onto the companions. There wasn't enough to soak them thoroughly, but their clothes and hair were dotted with liberal amounts of gore.

For a moment, they all stood there, stunned and disbelieving.

"What sort of disgusting trap is this?" Catriona said. She removed her metal helmet and ran her fingers through the back of her red hair, trying to get the blood out of it. "Is this some kind of sick Kagonesti joke?"

"I'm afraid not," Elidor said. He wiped a smear of blood from his face and flicked the warm liquid off his fingers. "It seems that Kuruk and Shiriki are more angry with us than I thought. They don't want to merely kill us: they want to make us suffer."

"How?" Ayanti said. She shook the equine portion of her body, trying to fling the blood off her brown coat. "By making us need baths?"

Davyn's eyes suddenly widened in fear, and Elidor knew his friend understood.

"Maddoc's dogs are trained to kill whenever they smell blood," Davyn said.

An instant later, from somewhere not so far off in the distance, they heard the baying of hounds.

CHAPTER

11 FOUR HOUNDS AND A ROCK

The companions quickly came up with a plan to deal with the hounds, and then plunged out of the forest at a run. Sindri struggled to keep up, but his legs were shorter than the others and he began to lose ground. Ayanti reached down, grabbed the kender, and swung him onto her back.

Dusk was drawing near, and dim light filtered through the trees, casting long shadows on the ground. Still, Davyn had no trouble making out the ominous shape of Cairngorn Keep looming less than a half-mile away. Almost exactly at the halfway point between them and the keep lay a large slab of rock the size of a small hut. Maddoc had used his magic to transport a hunk of stone and placed it over the tunnel entrance to seal it up after he learned of Davyn and Ayanti's excavation of the tunnels. Maddoc had probably never considered that in doing so he'd created the perfect marker that his adopted son would one day use in an attempt to break into the keep.

"Any sign of hounds?" Davyn called to Sindri.

The kender, who looked as if he were enjoying his centaur ride immensely, took a quick glance around.

"Not yet!" he answered.

A howl echoed through the air, sounding uncomfortably close despite Sindri's words.

Before fleeing the forest, the companions had all rolled in the dust to wipe off as much blood as they could and to cover the scent of what remained. But from the sound of it, Davyn feared their precautions had been wasted. The hounds already had the scent. He wouldn't have been surprised if Kuruk and Shiriki had left blood trails all over the keep grounds to stir up the hounds and lead them to the companions.

They ran straight for the rock, weapons drawn. Though Ayanti could run much faster than the rest of them and could've reached the stone first, she matched her pace to theirs. They'd decided they all would have a better chance against the hounds if they remained together.

"Over there!" Sindri pointed northward. "I see three, no, four of them!"

Blast! Davyn had hoped they'd only have to deal with one or two at the most.

"Ayanti, Catriona! Keep going! Elidor and I will stay back and try to hold them off!"

"We will?" Elidor said, sounding skeptical. But the elf stopped running and instantly fell into a fighting stance. Davyn stood by his side and together they faced north.

Four large black dogs bounded across the grassy plain, tongues lolling, jaws flecked with foam. These beasts weren't just eager to close in for the kill, Davyn realized, They lusted for it.

The ranger drew an arrow from his quiver and nocked it.

"Uh, remember what I said back at Ravenscar, about all this being your fault?" Davyn began. "I just want you to know that I didn't mean anything by what I said. I was just upset about Nearra."

TIM WAGGONER

"Don't worry about it," Elidor said. "You were right. I should've behaved more responsibly." The elf twirled his knives in his hands. "Do you think I should use my bow instead?"

"Not if you want to hit anything," Davyn said. Despite being an elf—and half Kagonesti at that—Elidor had yet to gain skill with a bow, which was something of a sore point with him.

The largest of the four hounds came running at Davyn. The young ranger took aim at the beast and fired. The arrow struck the dog in its left shoulder, and although it yelped in pain and stumbled, it did not go down.

"Blast!" Davyn swore. "Maddoc's hounds are bred and trained to resist pain, but even so, I'm amazed it can take such a wound and keep coming." He readied another arrow and released it at the same animal. This time the dog dodged to the right at the last instant, and the arrow thunked into the ground.

"I understand the dogs are well trained," Elidor muttered, "but I can't believe they're *that* well trained."

The hounds were closing fast and would be upon them in moments. They hadn't managed to disable a single one.

Elidor nervously juggled his throwing knives. "Perhaps once they get close enough, they'll be so intimidated that they'll turn tail and slink back to their kennel."

"I wouldn't count on it." Davyn fired a third arrow. The shaft caught another hound on the flank, but it caused only a grazing blow and the point didn't stick. The dog didn't slow down, didn't so much as yelp. Davyn doubted the beast even knew it had been hit.

"Perhaps you need to spend a little more time at archery practice," Elidor said.

"I hope I live long enough to take your advice." Davyn didn't think he could get another arrow off in time. He dropped his bow to the ground and drew his hunting knife.

As the four hounds came near, two of them suddenly broke away and angled off to the right. At first, Davyn thought the pair intended to attack from two different sides. But as the gap between the two pairs of hounds widened, Davyn realized with horror that the hounds had split into separate attack groups. One pair continued toward Elidor and him, while the other pair ran toward Ayanti, Catriona, and Sindri.

Davyn risked a glance over his shoulder and saw that the others had reached the stone. Sindri had dismounted and now stood before the boulder, hands raised in a mystic gesture. Catriona gripped her dragon claws and stood ready to defend Sindri. Ayanti stood at the warrior's side, holding Catriona's sword. Davyn knew that Ayanti wasn't trained to wield the weapon, but it was better than trying to face the hounds armed with only a dagger and her hooves.

Davyn turned forward again just in time to see the hound with the arrow jutting out of its shoulder leap for his throat.

He raised his blade, intending to gut the animal, but the dog was too fast and Davyn too slow. The hound crashed into the ranger and they fell to the ground in a tangled mass of arms, legs, fur, and gnashing teeth.

Sindri really wanted to turn around and watch the hounds attack—not only because he'd never seen a pack of hounds in action (especially a *wizard's* hounds!) but because he wanted to know if his friends needed his help. But he restrained himself. He had a job to do, and his friends were counting on him.

Sindri stretched his hands toward the rock and concentrated on shutting out the barking and growling of the approaching hounds. He extended his awareness toward the mass of stone before him, and he pictured it rising into the air. At first nothing happened and Sindri became aware of a great heaviness pressing down upon him as if he were trying to physically lift the rock instead of levitate it with his magic. But then his hands began to grow cool, as if they were immersed in cold water, and he felt the sensation of heaviness begin to diminish.

As Sindri watched in amazement, tendrils of multicolored mist curled from his fingers and drifted toward the stone.

"Well, this is something new!" he said in delight. Strands of red, blue, green, violet, orange, and yellow wrapped around the rock and suddenly the feeling of heaviness was completely gone. Sindri felt so full of power, it was as if he could not only levitate the rock, but he could send it soaring up into the heavens if he wished.

It seemed that he had reached a new level in his development as a wizard, though he had no idea how or why.

Time enough to sort it out later, he told himself. Right now you've got a great big rock to move!

Sindri concentrated harder. He felt energy pouring out of him, as if he were a dam that had just sprung a leak. The boulder began to shudder and then rise upward. Only a few inches at first, but then a few more, and a few more, until the great stone hovered three feet above a dark opening in the ground—the tunnel entrance Davyn and Ayanti had discovered years ago.

Sindri could hear fighting behind him, dogs snarling and snapping, his friends yelling and grunting with effort as they defended themselves.

Don't turn around, Sindri warned himself. Your friends can take care of themselves. It's your job to move the rock off to the side so that we can get into . . .

The kender's thoughts trailed off. Now that the rock hovered above the ground, he could see two pairs of deerskin-booted feet on the other side. And he knew exactly whom those feet they belonged to.

He turned and shouted over his shoulder. "It's an ambush! Kuruk and Shiriki are hiding behind the rock!"

Sindri was so surprised by the two elves, and too intent on warning his friends to maintain his concentration. The misty tendrils began to fade, and the stone wobbled in the air. It listed right, then left, and then the tendrils vanished and the boulder came crashing back down to the ground. The impact of the boulder slamming into the tunnel entrance knocked Sindri off his feet. He landed on his back and felt the air whoosh out of his lungs. But that wasn't all he felt. The ground shuddered and bucked, and then he felt it begin to subside beneath him. And though kender don't experience the emotion of fear, he came very close to something like it as he realized the stone's impact had weakened the earth above the tunnels. There was a phrase for what was about to happen. A terrible, awful phrase.

Cave-in.

Sindri scrambled to his feet and turned to run. He felt tired, drained of energy, and the dirt was slipping from beneath his feet as he struggled to get away. The ground began to shake more violently, and a low moaning sound issued from deep within the tunnel depths, as if the earth itself were in pain.

Unable to resist, Sindri glanced back and saw that the boulder was sinking as the ground around it collapsed.

Kuruk and Shiriki had been coming at him, swords drawn, but realizing that something was horribly wrong, they turned and began to run in the opposite direction.

Sindri looked forward and saw his friends doing their best to remain on their feet. Two of the four hounds lay wounded or dead upon the ground, while the remaining two were bounding away, their instinct for survival overriding their training.

Sindri wished he knew a spell to stop a cave-in, but he didn't. Maybe he could try to levitate his friends so that when the ground collapsed beneath them, they wouldn't fall. Of course, he'd never attempted to levitate so many objects at once—and never when the earth was falling out from under his feet—but maybe he could do it using his newfound power. Provided he could maintain his concentration this time.

So as he ran, he focused his thoughts on summoning the strange new magic that dwelled within him. Once again he felt the cool sensation of the multicolored mist coalescing around his fingers. Good. Now all he needed to do was picture—

A loud roaring filled his ears, and he felt the world fall away beneath him. As Sindri tumbled down into darkness, his last thought was for his friends. He wished there was some way he could protect them. And as he fell, tendrils of mist snaked from his fingers.

CHAPTER

12   BENEATH THE SOD

My lord!"

The voice was muffled, distant, as if the speaker had a mouth full of cotton.

"Be silent," Maddoc mumbled, squeezing his eyes shut even tighter. "Or I'll turn you into . . . I don't know what. Something nasty." He put his pillow over his head and tried to return to sleep. He was so weary. But then he always was these days. Not for the first time he wondered if power truly was worth the price that it demanded from those who sought it, and as always, he decided that it was.

"I apologize for disturbing you, but you must wake up!"

Maddoc recognized the voice then. It was Oddvar. The normally calm, composed dwarf sounded almost panic-stricken.

Maddoc pushed the pillow off his head and sat up. He scooted to the edge of the bed, threw aside the bed curtains, and saw the dim outline of Oddvar in the gloom of his bedchamber. The Theiwar never used a candle or a lantern if he could avoid it.

"What is it?" Maddoc demanded. "Is something wrong with Nearra?" Excitement surged through him. "Has Asvoria fully emerged at last?"

95

"No, my lord. The girl remains locked in the chamber where I took her. Drefan, Fyren, and Gifre are standing guard outside her door."

"Wait a moment." Maddoc glanced around the room. "Where's Kaz'un? He's normally the only being I will permit in my bed chamber."

"He and I had a bit of a disagreement. And I—" A vicious grin spread across Oddvar's face. "Well, you could say I sent him home."

"What have you done with him, you bloodthirsty fool?" The wizard lunged for Oddvar's throat, but Oddvar threw up his hands.

"Stop! Don't you want to know what has happened? The ground outside the keep walls has collapsed!"

Maddoc sat back down on the bed. "What? Has one of the tunnels given way?"

"More than one from the extent of the destruction, I'd say."

Theiwar lived underground, and the dark dwarves understood the ways of stone and the movements of rock and soil as no other race did. If Oddvar said several tunnels had collapsed, Maddoc believed him.

"This seeming disaster might end up working for our benefit. Once we've cleared away the debris, we might be able to gain access to sections of the cave system that we've never been able to explore."

"There's more," Oddvar said. "Just before the cave-in the hounds went berserk and ran toward that area as if they had caught the scent of trespassers."

Maddoc frowned. "Did you see these intruders?"

"No," Oddvar admitted. "But two of the four hounds are missing, presumably lost during the cave-in. But while the remaining two survived, they suffered serious wounds. Wounds caused by edged weapons."

A suspicion began to grow in Maddoc's mind. "Where exactly did this cave-in take place?"

"On the grounds to the west side of the keep, where that large boulder rests. I mean, *used* to rest. It was swallowed by the collapse."

Maddoc's lips curled into a slow smile, and despite himself, he couldn't keep a touch of pride out of his voice as he said, "Clever boy." He looked at Oddvar. "I believe Nearra's friends have come to the fair maid's rescue and plan to steal into the keep using the tunnels beneath it. Though it seems as if things didn't quite go as planned when they attempted to find their way into the tunnels."

"If you're talking about the cave-in, then they're all dead," Oddvar said. "Nothing standing on the surface could've survived such an extensive collapse."

"Perhaps," Maddoc said. "But over the last year I've learned not to underestimate Davyn and his companions. Take several guards and investigate the area of destruction more closely. If you find their bodies, do your best to recover them. Despite our differences, I would give Davyn a proper burial. As for the others, I can always use more raw material for my work. But if you discover no bodies, try to find a way into the tunnels and search for the young ones. If you find them alive, make certain you don't leave them that way."

"What about Nearra?"

"I'll tend to her myself. Now go."

Oddvar bowed. "As you wish." The Theiwar straightened then turned to leave. But before the dark dwarf could reach the door, Maddoc called after him.

"And Oddvar, if you find Davyn alive, bring him to me. I would have words with my son."

The dark dwarf bowed one last time and then left the room. **97**

RETURN OF THE SORCERESS

Neither the Theiwar nor his master noticed a small blue-eyed mosquito that accompanied Oddvar out.

Davyn opened his eyes, but all he saw were strange swirls of softly glowing multicolored light. I must be asleep and dreaming, he thought, and closed his eyes again.

Funny, it didn't feel like he was dreaming. The air was cool and damp and the ground beneath was hard and rocky. There was a dull pain in his lower back, and when he felt around to see what was causing it, he discovered he was lying on top of his bow.

Feels awfully real for a dream.

He opened his eyes and once again saw only undulating colors. He'd seen something like this before, but he couldn't recall where.

Then he remembered: the hounds attacking, fighting the beasts alongside Elidor, risking a quick glance to see how Sindri was doing, seeing the boulder floating in the air, wrapped in colorful tendrils of magic power that extended from Sindri's fingers . . . but then something happened and the tendrils vanished and the giant rock fell to the earth. Davyn recalled the loud booming sound of its impact, the feel of the ground trembling beneath his feet, beginning to give way. And then he was falling . . . no, *floating*, swaddled in a cool mist of roiling colors. Colors like those that surrounded him now.

He knew then that this was no dream.

He sat up. The colored mist was so thick that he couldn't see anything else. "Is anyone here?" he called out. His voice sounded strange, as if the mist swallowed up his words before he finished speaking them.

"I'm here," Catriona said. Her voice was muffled as well.

"Me, too," Ayanti said.

"I wish I weren't here," Elidor said.

Davyn waited for Sindri to answer, but the kender didn't respond. Davyn pictured the little wizard crushed beneath tons of earth, but he pushed the image from his mind. This mist, whatever it was, had to have been caused by Sindri. If the mist was still here, then there was a good chance that Sindri was too.

"I can't see any of you," Ayanti said. She sounded frightened, and Davyn didn't blame her. He was more than a little frightened.

"It's this confounded mist," Elidor said. "It's so thick you can't see a thing."

"Everyone keep talking so we can find each other," Catriona said.

"Move carefully," Davyn warned. "From the feel of the ground, I'd say we've fallen into one of the tunnels, and after the cave-in, there's no telling how stable it is."

"What a cheerful thought," Elidor muttered.

The companions continued speaking, mostly saying variations on "I'm over here, where are you?" and making their way through the mist until at last they found one another. They took a quick headcount and discovered that only Sindri was missing.

"Oh no," Catriona breathed.

"That idiotic kender!" Elidor said, his voice on the verge of breaking. "If he's dead, I'll drag his body to a cleric, have him resurrected, and then I'll kill him!"

"I . . . not dead . . . yet." The voice was so soft they could barely hear it, but it was unmistakably Sindri's. "But if I . . . lose concentration again . . . tons of soil and rock will . . . fall on us and we'll . . . all be killed."

Davyn couldn't understand what was happening. They seemed to be wrapped in the protective embrace of magic, and the multicolored mist prevented the earth above from collapsing down on them. Sindri said the magic was coming from him, but how could that be? Kender don't have *real* magic powers. Was the ring he'd given Sindri powerful enough to levitate the earth above them?

Davyn shook his head to clear it. For now it didn't matter. "We have to find a way out of here—now."

He thought quickly. "Sindri, try to keep talking. Elidor, the rest of us will remain quiet while you attempt to locate him. When you do, lift him carefully and bring him over to Ayanti. Set him gently upon her back, and then we'll all try to find a way out this mess."

"All right . . . Davyn," Sindri said. He sounded as if he were close to total exhaustion. Davyn knew they'd have to hurry.

Sindri continued to mumble, and Davyn couldn't make out the words, but he hoped that Elidor's elf ears could. He strained to hear Elidor's movements, but even without the sound-suppressing effect of the mist, the elf moved so silently that Davyn wouldn't have been able to hear him anyway.

Moments passed with agonizing slowness, each one seeming to last several eternities. Davyn expected the colors swirling before their eyes to fade and tons of earth come crashing down upon them. But then Sindri's voice began to get louder, and Davyn knew Elidor had found the kender and was carrying him to Ayanti.

A few moments later, Elidor said, "It's done."

Davyn felt like cheering, but he knew they weren't out of danger yet. "We need to move farther down the tunnel. If we can get far enough away from this section before Sindri's, uh, spell ends, we should be unaffected when the ground collapses."

"There's that word again," Elidor said with a sigh. "*Should.*"

"Which direction?" Catriona asked. "One way might lead toward Cairngorn Keep, but the other might lead away from it."

Davyn had no way of knowing. He'd gotten all turned around during the first cave-in, and the mist was still clogging the tunnel, making it impossible to see.

"Elidor, can you see through this mist?" Davyn asked.

"No, not even my eyes can penetrate this murk," the elf answered.

"Straight ahead," Ayanti said with conviction.

"Are you certain?" Elidor asked.

"Yes. Centaurs have a highly developed sense of direction. The keep lies before us."

"That's good enough for me," Davyn said. "Everyone stand close to Ayanti and let's go."

"Better hurry," Sindri said.

There was a soft patter like raindrops falling, and Davyn felt tiny objects pelting him. Sindri's spell was beginning to fade and bits of rock and soil were starting to fall though the mystic barrier.

If they'd been able to see, Davyn would've shouted for them to run, but with their vision obscured by the same mist that protected them, they could all too easily run straight into a tunnel wall. Despite the rain of rock and dirt coming down, they had no choice but to move forward at a slow walk.

It was like something out of a nightmare, as they took one torturous step after another. Now clumps of soil and fist-sized rocks came down. Once Ayanti stumbled and a torrent of soil fell upon them. Davyn was terrified that Sindri's concentration had been broken, but then the flow of earth diminished and they were able to continue on.

Eventually the rain of dirt began to slacken and the colors of mist started to grow dull. Davyn realized they were reaching the boundaries of the protective zone the kender's magic had created. They were going to make it!

"That's far enough."

The voice came from behind them, but not nearly far enough behind to suit Davyn. It was Shiriki.

"My cousin and I appreciate your leading us to safety, but I'm afraid we can't allow you to go any farther. You wounded us and killed our employer. Now it's time to pay."

"You talk when instead you should strike," Catriona said. "Run!" she shouted.

Davyn heard the cloppata-cloppata-cloppata of galloping hooves as Ayanti surged forward. Davyn ran to keep up with the centaur, one hand on her flank to guide him. He hoped that Catriona and Elidor were managing to keep up as well, for he had a good idea what Catriona had in mind next.

"Let it fall, Sindri!" the warrior shouted. "Let it all fall!"

Just like that the mist vanished and there was a deafening roar, as if the world collapsed behind them. The vibrations of the falling rock and soil knocked them off their feet, and they lay on the ground, feeling the earth shudder and buck beneath them. The tunnel was filled with dust, and they all coughed as they struggled to breathe.

Then it was over.

The earth grew still, and the roar of falling rock became nothing more than a ringing echo in their ears. Slowly, the dust began to settle, and though breathing wasn't comfortable, it became easier.

Davyn sat up. "Is everyone all right?" He could barely hear his own voice though the ringing in his ears. They all answered that they were unharmed, if shaken up.

Sindri moaned. "I'm so weary, I feel as if I haven't slept for a year."

"You'll be fine," Davyn said. I hope, he added mentally. "You've got the mystic equivalent of physical fatigue. It used to happen to Maddoc all the time when he overextended himself."

"If you say so, Davyn. All I know is this feeling"—Sindri yawned—"isn't much fun."

The rest of the companions got to their feet and dusted off. Davyn took a lantern out of his pack, but it was broken, so he tossed it onto the ground. Catriona's lantern, however, was intact. She lit it and shone the light onto the tunnel behind them. A mound of rock and soil blocked the tunnel less than twenty feet behind them. If they'd run any slower, they would've been buried.

Ayanti looked at Davyn. "Do you think Kuruk and Shiriki . . . ?"

As if in answer, a moan came from the mound of rubble, and a hand pushed its way free of the debris. It was a slender, feminine, elf hand.

Shiriki was alive.

13 REUNION

"D id you hear something?" Fyren asked, a quaver in his voice.

"No," Drefan said.

"Me neither," Gifre said, but then added, "well, maybe."

The trio of goblins stood in front of a large oak door on the lowest level of the keep. They held short swords at their sides, ready to use them at the first sign of trouble.

"Why so nervous, Fyren?" Drefan asked.

"Me nervous?" Fyren forced a laugh. "Why should a mighty goblin warrior such as myself be afraid of a tiny slip of a girl?"

"That's right!" Gifre echoed.

Drefan raised a skeptical eyebrow. "I ask, because this is the eighth time in the last hour that one of you *didn't* hear anything."

Neither Fyren nor Gifre replied.

"The door is locked," the goblin leader said. "Besides us, only Maddoc and Oddvar have keys. And Maddoc placed protective wardspells on the door so that if anyone on the outside *or* the inside even tries to touch the handle without the right key in their hand, they'll regret it. As guard jobs go, this is as good as it gets. We're not really needed. We're just here for show."

105

Fryen sighed. "I know."

"So what's your problem?" Drefan demanded.

Fyren glanced at the door with a fearful expression, as if he thought the girl inside might come bursting out any moment. He lowered his voice to a whisper.

"What if she's . . . you know . . . *changed*."

"Maddoc is a wizard," Drefan said. "And despite his recent weakness, he still wears the black robes. Not only isn't it my place to question what he does or why he does it, I know I'm likely to live a longer and happier life if I mind my own business."

"A very sensible attitude."

The three goblins froze as Maddoc came walking down the corridor toward them, holding a small lantern to illuminate his way.

Drefan's red face turned a pale pink and he began to stammer. "My-my lord, I-I didn't mean any dis-disrespect—"

Maddoc waved a hand to silence him and Drefan flinched, as if he thought the wizard intended to strike him down with a bolt of mystic energy.

"Has our guest been behaving herself?" Maddoc asked.

"Yes, my lord," Drefan said. "She hasn't made a sound."

"We can attest to that!" Fyren added nervously. "We've been checking! Eight times this hour alone, or so Drefan tells us."

Drefan glared at Fyren but said nothing.

Maddoc smiled. "Really? Eight times, you say? Then you must be quite weary after so much effort. It's a good thing then that I've come to relieve you of your posts."

Drefan frowned in confusion. "My lord?"

"There's been an incident outside the walls of the keep. A section of ground has collapsed, creating a substantial pit. I've sent Oddvar to investigate, and I'd like you to join him."

Drefan suppressed a sigh. So much for their cushy assignment.

"Of course, my lord. At once."

"My lord?" Gifre suddenly asked. "Are you well?"

Maddoc frowned. "Why do you ask?"

Drefan motioned for Gifre to shut up, but the goblin ignored him. "It's your eyes. They're . . ."

"What?"

"Blue," Gifre finished.

Maddoc chuckled. "They've always been blue."

"Yes, but not like this. They're *extremely* blue, and they almost seem to . . . well, to glow."

"Oh, that. I've been preparing all day to cast a very demanding spell. What you notice is merely a side effect of those preparations."

"Oh." It was clear from the blank expression on Gifre's face that he didn't understand, but at least he didn't say anything more about their master's eyes.

"I apologize for the feeble-minded fool, my lord," Drefan said. "We'll be on our way now."

But before any of the three goblins could move, Maddoc held up a hand, indicating they should pause a moment.

"First give me the key to this chamber."

Drefan blinked. "Pardon, my lord?"

"The key." Maddoc held out his hand palm up. "Give it to me."

"But you already have a key," Fyren said.

Maddoc gave the guard a scowl and his extra-blue eyes seemed to flash with an angry light.

"Since when do my guards make it a habit to question their master?"

Drefan swallowed and both Fyren and Gifre looked as if they might cry.

"If you must know," Maddoc continued. "I left the key in my bed chamber and I do not feel like walking all the way back to get it. Now give me the key or I'll use the three of you as subjects for an extremely nasty mystical experiment."

"Yes, my lord," Drefan pulled a ring of keys from his tunic pocket and held it up. "Of course, my lord, our most sincere apologies, my lord, we—"

"Are beginning to annoy me to no end." Maddoc snatched the key ring out of Drefan's hand. "Well? What are you three waiting for? Go assist Oddvar!"

With quick bows, the goblins hurried down the corridor.

The being that held Drefan's keys watched until the three were out of sight. Then its form shimmered and a moment later a dark-haired girl with intense blue eyes stood in place of the wizard. She selected the proper key and gently inserted it into the lock.

Nearra was wakened by the sound of the lock clicking open. The air in front of the door rippled for an instant, and she knew the wardspell had been deactivated.

It must be time, she thought. During the hours she'd been in the small, unlit cell, she had searched every nook and cranny, looking for some possible means of escape, but she'd found none. There was no window, and the ceiling, walls, and floor were all stone. The only object in the room was a wooden bed without a pallet. As it was marginally more comfortable than the floor, Nearra had lain down on it to consider her predicament, and she must've dozed off. She'd wasted her time in sleep, and now it was too late. Maddoc had come for her.

But when the door opened, it wasn't the wizard who stood there holding a lantern. It was . . .

"Jirah!" Nearra leaped to her feet and ran to embrace her younger sister.

Jirah held the lantern at arm's length so she wouldn't get burned and laughed as her sister hugged her.

Nearra released Jirah and took a step back. The younger girl looked exactly as she had in the dreamlike vision Nearra had experienced in the chamber with the blank paintings. It was as if her sister hadn't aged a day.

"Your eyes," Nearra said. "They're such a bright shade of blue."

Jirah smiled. "So? My eyes are blue, silly."

Nearra struggled to remember.

Jirah continued to smile as Nearra looked at her questioningly. Nearra shook her head. "Never mind. What are you doing here?"

She grinned. "I'm happy to see you, too, Sister." She held up a hand before Nearra could apologize. "Don't worry, I understand. You must have many questions. Close to a year ago Father and I brought a wagonload of wood to Cairngorn Keep. We expected you to come greet us, as you usually did. But that day you did not. When you again failed to greet us during our next two deliveries, Father, Mother, and I became suspicious. We knew we couldn't confront Maddoc and demand to know if you were all right, so I hired on as one of the wizard's servants in the hope that I could see you or, failing that, if I could at least find out what had happened to you. It took me a long time to put together all the bits and pieces of information I learned. From what I understand, you are host to the spirit of an ancient sorceress called Asvoria."

"It's true," Nearra confirmed. "Though Paladine knows I wish it wasn't."

Jirah nodded. "And the sorceress can see what you see and hear what you hear?"

"Yes, I believe so."

Jirah's eyes narrowed and a corner of her mouth rose upward in what seemed to Nearra to be a sly half smile.

"How did you get the key to the cell?" Nearra asked. "And how did you manage to get past the guards?"

"I stole the key ring when Maddoc left it lying on a table in his study," Jirah said. "As for the guards, it was a simple matter to trick them. But that's not important now. We need to get you out of here."

Nearra felt new hope rising within her. "Can you really help me escape?"

"During my stay here, I've explored a great deal of the keep," Jirah said. "At times, it almost feels as if it is the only home I've ever known. I've discovered a series of hidden passageways within the keep that I believe not even Maddoc knows about. These passageways lead down to a network of caves and tunnels that run beneath the keep and beyond. I believe that we can use them to get you out of here."

Nearra didn't like the idea of traveling underground—she and her friends had done too much of it over the last few months. But then, this was Jirah, her little sister. If she couldn't trust her, who could she trust?

She linked her arm with her sister's. "All right. Let's go before Maddoc discovers what we're up to." Despite the fact that they were still in Cairngorn Keep and still very much in danger, Nearra couldn't help laughing as they headed arm in arm for the open doorway.

"It seems like old times, doesn't it?" she said. "You and me, going off on our own to get into mischief."

Jirah smiled. "Old times indeed."

It was strange, but for an instant Nearra had the impression that Jirah wasn't speaking to her. But then they were through the doorway and into the hall. Jirah closed the door behind them and locked it. The air rippled as the wardspell reactivated, and then they began heading down the corridor, toward freedom.

14   Into the Underworld

For a wizard, Maddoc can be awfully stupid at times, Oddvar thought.

The dwarf stood at the edge of the newly created pit. The three goblin mercenaries stood behind him nervously. The sun was on the verge of setting, and the light was dim enough that Oddvar could wear his hood down.

"Maybe we should take a few steps back from the edge," Drefan said.

"Say perhaps two or three hundred," Gifre added.

"There's nothing to worry about," Oddvar said. "The ground is stable enough here. We're in no immediate danger of falling in."

"Um, not to question your judgment," Drefan said, "but how can you tell?"

Oddvar fixed the goblin leader with a hard stare. "I am Theiwar," he said, as if that were the only explanation anyone could need.

"We know that," Fyren said. "What does that have to do with us standing way too close to the edge of this great big hole?"

Oddvar sighed. "My people live beneath the ground. We understand the ways of earth and stone." The goblins wore expressions that were blanker than usual. "It means I can tell where it's safe to stand."

"Oh!" Drefan said, understanding at last bringing a smile to his face.

Oddvar turned his back on the trio and examined the pit once more. He recalled when the tunnel here had first shown signs of collapse—when Davyn and that centaur were playing around and happened to stand in the wrong place at the wrong time. Neither had been hurt, but Maddoc had been determined to discourage them from playing near the opening they'd created. But a simple warning hadn't been enough for the mage, oh no. He'd had to levitate a boulder from one place or another and use it to plug up the hole. Oddvar had tried to explain to his master why placing several tons of rock on top of unstable ground wasn't the wisest decision Maddoc had ever made, but the wizard wasn't one to entertain suggestions from subordinates, and he'd ignored the Theiwar's advice.

And here was the result: a pit sixty feet in circumference and thirty feet deep. No tunnel opening was visible at either end of the pit. There was too much rubble. If they were lucky, this would be the full extent of the damage. If not, it was possible that the entire cave system running beneath the keep and the surrounding land had been seriously destabilized. And if that were the case, Cairngorn Keep itself might well come tumbling down like a tower made of children's blocks.

"Do you think *they* caused this?" Drefan asked.

"Davyn and his friends? Yes, I do. It's too much of a coincidence that this should happen so soon after the girl's capture—and the hounds were attacking intruders when the collapse took place. We need to find out if those intruders were killed in the collapse or if they managed to survive and are even now making their way toward the keep."

"And how are we going to do that?" Drefan asked.

Oddvar grinned and gestured toward the rubble that filled the bottom of the pit.

"Start digging," he said.

"You don't need that lantern, you know."

Elidor didn't respond to Shiriki's statement. Leather strips bound her hands and a rope was tied around her wrists for good measure. Elidor held the other end of the rope, his captor walking behind him as if she were some sort of trailing pet. They'd disarmed her, and Elidor wore her sword along with his own. Both elves hung back from the rest of the party. For one thing, being too close to the lantern light hurt their eyes. For another, Davyn wanted to keep the others out of Shiriki's reach to discourage her from trying to attack them. Just because she had no weapons didn't mean she still wasn't dangerous.

Elidor got the job of guarding her because he was the only one whose reflexes were fast enough to match hers. Besides, Shiriki had said that she would only submit to a fellow Kagonesti. "Even if he is a half-breed," she'd added.

"Our vision allows us to see in the darkness," she continued. "I don't understand why you permit yourself to be limited by the others' weaknesses."

"And I don't see how you could ever work for scum like Bolthor."

Shiriki shrugged, and even this simple movement was made graceful by her elf nature. Her lips formed an amused half-smile, and her eyes shone with wary intelligence mixed with mischief. Strange, but he hadn't noticed how attractive she was until now. Perhaps that was because she'd been trying to kill him the last two times he'd seen her.

"Bolthor paid us," Shiriki said. "It's as simple as that."

"That's not a good reason, not for a Kagonesti. Money is an invention of the civilized world."

"Which of course is why you're a thief," Shiriki said with a smile. "Because money means nothing to you."

"How did you know I was a thief?"

Another shrug. "I guessed. You fight like one who is used to relying on stealth and speed instead of brute strength. Besides, what honest work is there for a half-breed such as yourself?"

Elidor's jaw clenched at her use of the word *half-breed*. All elves found the idea of interbreeding between clans to be distasteful at best and obscene at worst. Only in human lands could Elidor ever be just an elf, instead of half Kagonesti and half Silvanesti.

"My 'stealth and speed' were enough to get the better of you in battle," he said.

"You are not without some measure of skill, but do not delude yourself. If I hadn't needed to go to my cousin's aid, I would have defeated you in the end."

Elidor glanced ahead to see how the others were doing. Surrounded by the gauzy halo of lantern light, they continued walking, Catriona and Davyn in the lead with Ayanti following, still carrying Sindri on her back. The kender was so exhausted from the enchantment that he'd worked that he could barely sit upright.

Elidor turned back to Shiriki. "Speaking of your cousin, you don't appear particularly bothered by his demise."

Shiriki's lips twitched, but when she replied, her voice remained cool and even. "We both fought in what some have come to call the War of the Lance. As warriors, we accepted that death could come to use at any moment. I'm sure that Kuruk would've preferred to die on the battlefield rather than in a rockslide, but who among us has the luxury of choosing the exact time and method of our end?"

"I'm certain your cousin's ghost is comforted by your detached philosophic view of his death," Elidor said wryly.

"I am Kagonesti. To our people, death is as natural a part of existence as birth. If we do not fear the latter, why should we dread the former?" Her eyes narrowed. "Though you are but half Kagonesti, I am surprised you do not know this."

"I spent only a short time with my father's tribe. While he was . . . tolerant of me, the other members of his tribe were not. Eventually, in order to preserve the peace among his people, he asked me to leave."

Shiriki snorted. "If you were truly Kagonesti within your heart, you would've fought for your blood-right to stay."

"Perhaps." Elidor fell quiet for a time as he contemplated unpleasant memories. Eventually, he looked at Shiriki once more. "You said that you and your cousin fought in the War of the Lance. I take it from your association with Bolthor—not to mention your less-than-sunny disposition—that you didn't battle for the Light."

"I serve Takhisis, the Dark Queen."

Elidor had guessed as much, yet it was still a shock to hear her admit it. Even more shocking was the pride in her voice.

"Whatever on Krynn for? I may not be an expert on the ways of the Kagonesti, but I know they revere life and strive to live in harmony with the natural world. Why would one of—" He'd been about to say "our people" but he caught himself. "Why would you ever serve the Dark Queen?"

When Shiriki answered, her tone was defiant. "Because the Dark is just as much a part of the natural world as the Light. Because Paladine and the other so-called gods of Good are intent on controlling our world and forcing us to live by their laws. Takhisis wishes only for us to have the freedom to choose how we shall live. 'Do as you will' is the whole of her law. What could be more natural than that?"

"What if what *your* will is to kill *me*? Is it not evil to deprive one of life for no reason?"

"What if *your* will is to steal something that belongs to *me*?" she countered. "A lesser evil than murder, I grant you, but still an evil nonetheless, no?"

Elidor was confused and more than a little ashamed, though he wasn't certain why. He was saved from having to come up with a reply to Shiriki's point when Davyn held up a hand and said, "Hold, everyone."

Davyn glanced back over his shoulder. "Elidor, come join us. And bring our prisoner, too."

The others parted to make room for Elidor. When he stepped to the front, he saw that they had come to a chasm thirty feet across. He peered down into complete darkness. Who knew how many feet it was to the bottom? The tunnel resumed on the other side of the cavern, but the entrance was blocked by rubble.

"Did we cause this?" Ayanti asked as she gazed upon the chasm.

We? Elidor thought. You mean Sindri, don't you? He glanced at the kender. Sindri sat upon the centaur's back, his hands around her human torso to help steady him. He looked bleary-eyed. Elidor wished they could take the time to allow Sindri to rest and recover, but they couldn't. Nearra needed them.

"This looks old," Davyn said. "My guess is it was created by the Cataclysm. That's one of the reasons why Maddoc has had such a hard time exploring the tunnel system. Too many of the passages were damaged or destroyed during the Cataclysm. Others are blocked, sealed off by wardspells placed by Asvoria. Maddoc has been able to nullify some of her spells, but most have proven too strong and complex for him."

"I never thought I'd say this, but good for Asvoria," Catriona muttered.

"So what do we do now?" Elidor asked.

"We saw no side tunnels along the way," Davyn said.

"And we can't go back to where we started," Catriona added.

Sindri spoke for the first time since they'd started traveling through the tunnel. "I'm still too weary to attempt to move those rocks on the other side, let alone levitate anyone over." The kender slumped against Ayanti's back.

"I might be able to jump that far if I got a running start." Ayanti eyed the chasm more carefully. "But even if I did, I'd still have to find a way to deal with all those rocks blocking the tunnel entrance."

Elidor looked at his companions. He had the sense that they were trying to tell him something, but he wasn't sure what.

"Oh, for oblivion's sake!" Shiriki said. "You can't possibly be that dense! You're an elf, stronger and more agile than any of them. They're hinting that they want you to climb down into the chasm and see if there's another tunnel farther down below. They're reluctant to ask you straight out because they're your friends and they know it could be dangerous."

"I hate to admit it," Davyn said, a sheepish look on his face, "but she's right. If these tunnels are artificial—and Maddoc believes they are—then perhaps they line up. If so, there might be another tunnel below us, one that's not blocked by rubble."

Elidor didn't relish the notion of climbing into the darkness. Even with his elf eyesight, he couldn't see very far down. He looked at Shiriki. She had a mocking grin on her face.

"Afraid?" she asked.

Elidor knew better than to do something because of what someone else—even a very beautiful someone else—might think of him. Especially when that someone would slit his throat in an instant if the opportunity presented itself.

Nevertheless he handed the other end of the rope that bound Shiriki to Davyn.

"Watch her closely," he said, though he knew he didn't have to.

"Let me get a safety line for you," Catriona said. She slipped off her pack and began rummaging around in it, but Elidor saw the derision in Shiriki's eyes.

"My thanks, but I won't need it," he said. "It would only get in my way."

Catriona frowned. "I really think—"

"I'm an elf," Elidor said. He hoped that would prove enough to forestall further argument.

It did. Catriona nodded and slipped her pack back on again, though she didn't look at all happy about it.

"I'll be back shortly," Elidor said. I hope, he added mentally. Then he knelt at the chasm's edge, swung his feet over, and began his downward climb.

CHAPTER 15

WHAT GOES DOWN

Elidor was glad to discover that the surface of the rock wall was hard. He wouldn't have to worry about chunks falling off as he climbed. But on the other hand, the same hardness had kept the surface relatively smooth, and there were few hand and footholds to choose from.

Elidor took his time, gingerly testing each depression in the rock before putting his full weight on it. In this fashion, he slowly descended the chasm wall, feeling like a blond-haired spider with pointed ears.

If only Mother could see me now, he thought. Hanging here in the darkness, trying to find an underground passage into the keep of an evil wizard. She'd disown me all over again.

His mother was a Silvanesti elf. The Silvanesti tended to be conservative and traditional. Seeing her son behaving like a common adventurer would've dismayed her to no end.

And his father, he would've berated Elidor for taking such a foolish risk just on the chance there might be another tunnel opening close by. But inwardly he'd be proud of his son for rising to the challenge.

But more than mere distance prevented his father from being here. He had fought with the armies of Light during the War of the Lance, and he had paid for helping preserve Krynn's freedom with his life.

Elidor's left foot slipped and he nearly fell. He cursed himself for allowing his thoughts to distract him. After all the dangers he had faced since joining Nearra and the others, it would be a cruel irony if he died as the result of simple carelessness.

He couldn't believe he'd been stupid enough to forego using a safety line *and* that he'd done so solely to win Shiriki's approval. The woman was evil, and she'd kill them all if she could. But then again, even though he knew it was impossible to win Shiriki's respect, let alone desirable, he hadn't been able to keep himself from trying.

Elidor felt around with his left foot, but he couldn't find any purchase, just empty space. A thrill of excitement ran through him. Perhaps he'd found another tunnel entrance! Then again, perhaps the chasm wall merely curved inward. He climbed down far enough to confirm that it was an opening, and one large enough for them all to fit through, including Ayanti. Still, just because there was an opening didn't mean the tunnel was intact.

He climbed into the tunnel and followed it for several dozen yards. The tunnel showed no signs of blockage, and structurally it seemed sturdy enough. It appeared to curve around to the right and angle downward. Elidor didn't know if this tunnel would eventually take them in the direction of Cairngorn Keep, but they would have to give it a try.

Of course, with our luck, the tunnel will probably take us straight down to a nest of demons, or something equally as nasty.

Elidor turned around and headed back to the mouth of the tunnel so he could tell the others what he had discovered. He decided it might be better not to mention the nest of demons, though.

"Mind the steps. There's an underground river not far from here, and the dampness tends to make the stone a bit slick," Jirah said.

Nearra looked at her sister. "How could you know such a thing?"

They were walking down a narrow stone passageway built into the outer wall of the keep's main tower. The uneven, cracked steps curved downward and, true to Jirah's word, they were indeed slick here.

"I told you, I've explored these passages. As for the river, the other servants talk, and I listen. Simple as that."

Jirah led the way, holding the lantern up so that Nearra could better see where to place her feet. They kept their hands on the wall to steady them as they went.

"You never told me what your duties are," Nearra said.

Jirah stopped and turned around to face her. She smiled easily enough, but there was a hard, calculating look in her eyes. "You sound as if you're suspicious of me."

Nearra was, actually. There was something not quite right about her sister, though she wasn't certain what it was. She was beginning to wonder if Maddoc had placed some manner of spell upon her, too.

"I'm sorry. I just . . . can't remember much . . . " She trailed off, hoping that would be enough to get her to answer.

Jirah looked at her a moment longer before turning back around and continuing to descend the stairs. Nearra followed.

"I started out as an assistant to the stablemaster. I spent my time shoveling horse dung, mostly. Since then I've managed to improve my status, and now I assist the cook in preparing Maddoc's meals." She glanced over her shoulder at Nearra. "Satisfied?"

"Of course." Jirah's explanation sounded good, but that was the problem. It sounded *too* good. She gave too many details and spoke too formally. The sister she remembered would've just said, "I work in the kitchen." Still, maybe she was being too suspicious. After all, Jirah was her sister, and she was helping her. She decided to try to put her suspicions aside and concentrate on escaping.

After a time, the air grew cooler and Jirah said, "It's not much farther."

The stairs ended and a large iron door loomed in front of them. The surface was thick with rust and Nearra thought how the door was centuries old, at least.

"This door leads to a system of tunnels that runs beneath the grounds surrounding the keep," Jirah said. "We can use them to escape."

Nearra caught a wisp of memory, but she didn't think it was hers. Perhaps it was Asvoria's. The cave system was the reason the sorceress had built Cairngorn Keep here. She'd spent decades—or rather her servants had—digging tunnels to connect the caves.

"How is it possible that Maddoc doesn't know about the tunnels?" she asked.

"Uh, he does," Jirah said. She held the lantern out to Nearra. "Could you hold this a moment?"

She took the lantern and Jirah stepped up to the door.

"Maddoc has long explored the tunnels, searching for whatever secrets Asvoria might've hidden away there. But despite all his efforts, he's never located this door."

Jirah reached into her tunic pocket and brought out a large iron key. It might have been a trick of the lantern light, but it seemed to Nearra that the key wasn't clasped in Jirah's hand. It appeared that the key somehow *protruded* from her hand, as if the iron had grown from her flesh.

Jirah inserted the key into the lock. The inner mechanism resisted her at first, so she turned harder. Finally, the lock made a slow grinding sound as it yielded to the key. Jirah removed it from the lock, and Nearra stepped forward so she could get a better look at it, but Nearra blinked and the key was gone. Jirah's hand looked completely normal again.

She decided she was just seeing things. After all, it was dark down here and the lantern cast strange shadows.

Jirah looked at her sister and smiled. "Behind this door lies your freedom." She pressed her shoulder against the rusted iron and shoved. The door didn't budge and then, right before her eyes, Jirah seemed to grow. She was suddenly taller, with broader shoulders and thicker muscle. Hinges groaned in protest and rust fell to the ground in large flakes, and the door slowly swung open.

She bowed and gestured to the darkness that filled the now open doorway.

"You have the lantern, milady. After you." Jirah laughed as if she were enjoying a private joke and could barely contain her glee.

Nearra felt a chill run up her spine. "What's so funny? You're scaring me."

"Don't you want to"—Jirah stifled another laugh—"escape?"

Nearra stared at the gaping tunnel beyond the doorway, trying to decide what she should do. But the only other option was to go back up the stairs and take her chances with Maddoc.

In the end, it wasn't that hard of a decision.

She walked into the darkness.

"Hey, I think I've found someone!"

Oddvar made his way over to Fyren, walking across broken stones as easily as someone else would walk across a smooth tiled floor. It was dark now, and the goblins worked by the light of lanterns set on top of poles. The light wasn't that intense, but Oddvar was still forced to squint as he drew near the spot where Fyren had been clearing away rock. The goblin crouched near the wall of the pit, where Oddvar guessed the opening to a tunnel lay buried beneath the earth and stones.

As the Theiwar approached, Fyren pointed to a hand. "See?"

At first Oddvar thought the hand wasn't attached to a body, but then he saw the wrist and forearm sticking up from the rubble. Oddvar's lips formed a dark smile. It seemed as if one of Davyn's friends, or perhaps even Davyn himself, hadn't survived the collapse. But when the dwarf was close enough to take a better look, he saw that the hand was adorned with an intricately tattooed design. Oddvar sighed with disappointment. Whoever this was—or rather, had been—it wasn't one of the accursed brats.

"Let's see who it is. Uncover the body."

As Fyren went to work, the other two goblins came over to watch. They'd made good progress in clearing away the debris blocking the tunnel entrance, primarily due to Oddvar's ability to always pinpoint the best places to dig. But Fyren needed no direction to uncover the body beneath the rocks, and within moments, a Kagonesti male garbed in leather armor was revealed. Oddvar recognized the elf. His name was Kuruk, one of Bolthor's bodyguards.

"He doesn't look too good, does he?" Gifre said.

"What do you expect?" Drefan snapped. "Several tons of rock landed on top of his head!"

Oddvar could tell that the goblin leader's estimate was way off. Given the size and type of rocks and the position of the pit, as well as their proximity to the wall, Oddvar judged that only a few hundred pounds of stone had fallen on Kuruk. The elf had very likely been near the edge of the cave-in. A dozen feet or more in the other direction and he might well have escaped unscathed.

The elf's hair was crusted with blood from a head wound. One leg was broken, and one arm was a shattered ruin. Oddvar had to suppress a shudder. To his people, dying in a rockslide was a real and most feared danger, the sort of thing that parents talked about to frighten naughty children into behaving.

Oddvar was about to tell the goblins to carry the corpse of the elf back to Cairngorn Keep so Maddoc might make use of it later. But before he could speak, the elf's eyelids flickered and he let out a soft moan.

Fyren jumped back in alarm. "Undead!" he shouted.

"*Not* dead," Oddvar corrected. "In other words, still alive." It looked like Maddoc would have to wait a bit longer before he got this one, but at least Oddvar had a survivor to question.

The Theiwar knelt down next to the elf's head.

"Kuruk, this is Oddvar. Can you hear me?"

Kuruk didn't say anything, but he opened his eyes and gazed up at Oddvar. He frowned.

"Odd . . . var?"

Kuruk's voice came out in a gurgling wheeze and Oddvar guessed that the elf had broken ribs and one of more of them had punctured a lung.

"That's right. You were caught in a cave-in. Can you tell me what happened?"

"Cousin and I . . . were following younglings . . . Davyn and others. They . . . wounded us and killed . . . Bolthor. Wanted . . . revenge."

Oddvar shook his head in disgust. In his view, elves were arrogant, and because of this they were prone to overestimating their capabilities. Such arrogance had probably led Kuruk and Shiriki to underestimate Davyn and the others. For Kuruk, it had almost proven fatal—and judging by the elf's condition, it still might.

"Was anyone else caught in the rockslide?" Oddvar asked.

Kuruk closed his eyes, and for a moment Oddvar thought the Kagonesti had died, but then he opened his eyes again.

"Don't . . . think so. I was the . . . last one still . . . under rocks when . . . mist vanished."

"What mist?" Oddvar said, but the elf didn't answer. Oddvar decided Kuruk was likely in so much pain than he wasn't thinking straight.

"My thanks for your help. Oddvar stood and turned toward the three goblins. "We need to get the tunnel entrance open as quickly as we can. While it's highly unlikely that Davyn and the others will reach Cairngorn, it is our job to do everything we can to make sure that they don't."

Kuruk's fingers twitched as he attempted to reach out to Oddvar.

"Help me . . . up. Must . . . find cousin."

Oddvar ignored him. "Why are you three standing around? Get to work!" He pointed toward a mound of rubble less than ten feet from where Kuruk lay. "If you start there, you should be able to clear away a large enough space for us to fit through in a short time."

The goblins exchanged glances, as if they all wanted to say something, but none of them could find the courage to do so. Finally, Drefen said, "Uh, what about the elf?"

"What about him?" Oddvar shot back. "Just let him lie there. With any luck, he'll be dead before sunrise." The Theiwar gave the others a cold grin. "Especially if he's discovered by a night predator."

Drefan nodded and turned toward the section of rubble that Oddvar had indicated. He began to clear away stones. A moment later, Fyren and Gifre joined him.

As they worked, Oddvar kept a close eye on the surrounding rocks, watching to make sure a small landslide wasn't going to result from their efforts. He didn't give Kuruk another thought.

After the four of them were gone, Kuruk, moving slowly and painfully, began to free himself from the rubble.

16   CAVERN OF DARKNESS

The companions continued slowly down the dark tunnel.

"You look worried," Catriona said in a low voice so the others couldn't hear.

"I am," Davyn admitted. "Sure, we managed to get into the tunnel system, but we almost got ourselves killed doing so, and the resulting cave-in has undoubtedly drawn Maddoc's attention. And the only reason we didn't perish was Sindri." Davyn glanced at the kender. While he sat upright on Ayanti's back, his eyes were half closed, as if he were dozing.

Catriona gave Sindri a quick look. "Who'd ever have thought a little kender could be so powerful?"

"Who indeed?"

"I'm not thrilled to be stuck with Shiriki," Catriona said. "It would've made things simpler if we'd just killed her. After all, she'd do the same to any of us if our situations were reversed."

"You're not serious, are you?" Davyn asked.

"Not really." She sighed. "After all, we're the good guys, right?"

"I'm most worried that we might be lost," Davyn said. "Now that we're in the tunnels, I realize how foolish it was to come here. There's no way to tell if any of these tunnels leads to the keep. We might end up trapped down here, while Nearra suffers whatever fate Maddoc has planned for her."

Thinking of Nearra made Davyn's heart ache. Though he'd done his best to make up for originally aiding Maddoc in his plan to resurrect Asvoria, he still felt responsible for her situation. Nearra was too kind, too sensitive, too *good* a person to deserve everything that had happened to her over the last year.

And now, just when she needed all of them the most, it looked as if they were going to fail her.

"Dead end," Ayanti said, and they all came to a halt.

Davyn expected the tunnel to be blocked by rubble left over from a cave-in, but it ended in a wall of rock, as if whoever had dug this tunnel had, for some unknown reason, decided to stop here.

"Elidor?" Davyn called over his shoulder.

The elf came forward, bringing their prisoner with him. He handed the rope that bound Shiriki over to Catriona, and then stepped up to the craggy gray wall. He spent several moments standing and staring at the wall. He then reached out and ran both of his hands across the wall's rough surface. He touched it here and there, seeming to feel no need to cover the entire wall. But how he chose which specific section to examine, Davyn had no idea.

Finally, after what seemed a long time but probably couldn't have been more than a quarter hour, Elidor stepped away from the wall.

"There are no hidden catches, no seams, nothing but solid rock."

The elf sounded disappointed, and Davyn wondered if it was because he thought he'd let down his friends or because he'd found no locks to pick or traps to disarm. Probably both, Davyn decided.

Ayanti frowned. "It doesn't make sense that whoever went through all the trouble to carve these tunnels would just stop here."

Catriona shrugged. "There are many reasons why such a project might be abandoned. The most obvious one is that Asvoria's servants stopped digging after she was defeated and her spirit was trapped in the tapestry. Without their mistress around to force them, why would they keep working?"

"Maddoc has had some tunnels enlarged and extended, but not many," Davyn said. "This may be one he's never gotten around to—assuming he knows about it at all."

"So what do we do now?" Elidor asked. "Turn around?"

Davyn looked at the wall once more. While it had been difficult to keep track of the progress underground, he thought there was a good chance that they were close to Cairngorn. He hated to back up and start again. The longer it took them to reach Nearra, the more time Maddoc had to do whatever he planned to do with her. But Davyn could see no other option. Not only didn't they have the tools or the skill to continue digging the tunnel, even if they had, it would be long, slow work. They'd never—

". . . color of stone . . ."

The words were little more than a whisper, but they immediately caught everyone's attention. Sindri had spoken them.

The kender still looked exhausted, but his eyes were open and his lips had formed a faint smile.

"What did you say?" Catriona asked.

"The stone of the wall. It's not the same color as the rest of the tunnel." The kender's voice was stronger now. "It's a subtle difference, but you can see it if you look closely."

Elidor frowned, but he stepped up to the wall again and peered at it intently. After a moment, his eyes widened and he turned to look at Sindri. "You're right! I guess I was so busy looking for locks or traps that I didn't notice the color."

Davyn didn't see any difference in the wall's color, but then he didn't have kender or elf eyes.

"What does it mean, Sindri?" he asked.

The kender motioned for Catriona to come over. She placed the lantern on the ground, handed the rope that bound Shiriki to Elidor, and lifted the diminutive wizard down from the centaur's back. Sindri walked to Davyn's side and the ranger saw the lantern light reflected in the kender's large brown eyes. The light had a multicolored cast, just like the tendrils of mystic energy Sindri had conjured earlier.

"It's a spell, of course." Sindri grinned. "What else could it be?" He stepped up to the wall and pressed his palms flat against its surface. There was a strange look on the kender's face, as if he were listening to a voice that only he could hear.

For a moment, nothing happened. But then the stone began to change color as threads of blue, red, green, yellow, purple, and orange spread outward from Sindri's hands. The hues mixed, swirled, and roiled until the wall was a mad riot of color. Then, just like that, the colors winked out. And when they were gone, so was the wall. Beyond, the tunnel opened up into a large cavern.

Sindri's strange new magic once again took its toll. The kender slumped, exhausted, and Davyn grabbed him by the arm and helped him remain standing.

"What was it?" Catriona asked with an awe-filled voice. "Some kind of illusion?"

"It's hard to explain," Sindri said. "The wall was both there and not there at the same time. I just sort of gave it a push so now it's completely not there."

Catriona scowled. "You're right. It *is* hard to explain." She came forward without waiting to be asked. She lifted Sindri, carried him to Ayanti, and set him down once more upon the centaur's back.

Elidor gazed into the cavern, his eyes gleaming. "There must be something especially good in there for Asvoria to go to such trouble to hide it."

"Perhaps," Davyn said. "But don't forget, what might be good to an evil sorceress like Asvoria is bound to be something we'd find very, very bad."

Elidor sighed. "Point taken."

"Is it possible the wall hid an underground entrance to the keep?" Ayanti asked.

"Let's hope," Davyn said. But even if it did, he was certain that wouldn't be all they'd find in the cavern. If he'd learned anything in his last year of adventuring, it was that anything rarely was simple.

"Weapons out, everyone," he said. "Elidor, keep a close eye on our friend. If anything happens, the first thing she'll do is attempt to escape."

Shiriki said nothing, but her grin confirmed Davyn's assessment.

"Let me hold the lantern," Sindri said. "I'm too weak to do much else, and the rest of you will need your hands free in case there's trouble."

"What do you mean, *in case*?" Elidor said. "You mean *when*."

Davyn ignored the elf. "Good idea, Sindri."

Catriona lifted the lantern off the ground and handed it to the kender.

Davyn took a deep breath, and not for the first time wondered exactly what danger he might be leading his friends to.

"All right. Let's go."

Davyn and Catriona took the lead, Ayanti following behind with Sindri on her back. Elidor brought up the rear, pulling Shiriki along after him.

The cavern was huge—at least seventy feet in height, maybe even a hundred. Stalactites hung down from the ceiling, looking like stone teeth, as if they weren't entering a cave but rather the mouth of some gigantic monster that might devour them any moment. Stalagmites rose from the cavern floor, but not so many that they made passage too difficult. It was hard to estimate how wide the cavern was since the walls were uneven, curving in here, curving out there. Maybe an average of two hundred feet wide, Davyn guessed.

"It's cold in here," Catriona said.

"It's your armor," Davyn replied. "Metal doesn't retain body heat the same way that leather armor does, so it gets cold faster."

"I know that," she said, sounding irritated. "Just as I know that caves are supposed to be cool and damp. But it's more than cool in here. Haven't you noticed our breath?"

Davyn hadn't, but now that Catriona had pointed it out, he saw that their breath was misting in the air. Davyn knew that the temperature below the earth remained constant, the equivalent of a cool autumn day.

"This isn't a natural cold," Sindri said.

Shiriki looked at the kender. "No! Do you *really* think so?"

Everyone ignored the elf's sarcasm.

"Let's just keep going," Davyn said. "The sooner we find our way out of here, the better." He didn't bother telling them to be quiet. It would be pointless. The glow of the lantern had already announced their presence, and he wasn't about to ask Sindri to close the hood. Trying to make their way though the cavern in total darkness wouldn't be stupid, it'd be suicidal.

As they wound their way around the stalagmites, they saw no signs of life. No bats, no rats, no insects, not even any molds or lichens. Davyn told himself that this wasn't necessarily an ominous sign. If the cavern had been sealed off from the outer world, how would any creatures get down here, and even if they did, how would they survive? Still, some instinct told him that wasn't the reason for the absence of life. There was no life here because this was a place of death.

Davyn felt a crawly-cold sensation in the pit of his stomach, and he was about to suggest that they turn around and try to find another route to Cairngorn, when from behind, Elidor said, "What's that?"

Davyn gripped his hunting knife, but the elf's voice sounded excited, not alarmed. He scanned the area in front of them and saw what Elidor was referring to. A metallic glint came from a stalagmite thirty feet away.

"Do you think it's some forgotten treasure?" Elidor said. Davyn didn't turn around to look at the elf, but he could imagine him nearly drooling as he spoke.

"More like a mineral deposit," Shiriki muttered.

"Probably," Davyn agreed. "Still, we should—"

Davyn was interrupted by an eerie sound, a whispering-clacking noise, as if a leather bag stuffed with splintered bones was being dragged across stone. Strangest of all, the sound seemed to be coming not from in front of them, but rather from *above* them.

Davyn looked up and saw that something was detaching itself from the shadows between the stalactites. It was huge, and it looked like a—

"Dragon," Catriona whispered in fear and awe.

"No," Shiriki corrected. "It's a dracolich."

The undead creature turned its fleshless reptilian head toward them. Glowing points of baleful yellow-green light blazed from deep within its shadowy sockets.

Davyn experience a wild urge to laugh as he realized he'd been right earlier. There *was* nothing alive in this cavern.

And then the dracolich spread its half-rotted wings, dropped from the ceiling, and swooped toward them.

CHAPTER 17

ATTACK OF THE DRACOLICH

Nearra sensed that something was wrong before she felt the drop in temperature. There was an itchy-tingly feeling at the base of her skull, as if a colony of ants had suddenly decided to nest there. She looked at Jirah and saw that her so-blue eyes appeared to be glowing with a soft inner light that had nothing to do with the lantern she carried.

"Almost there," Jirah said. Her voice sounded different now. It was still Jirah's voice, and yet it wasn't. The tone and inflections were wrong, and there was a dark anticipation underlying her words that sounded nothing like her sister.

"I'm getting scared, Jirah," she said, her breath coming out of her mouth in wisps of white fog. "And I'm cold. I want you to take me back to the keep—now."

Jirah stopped walking and turned to her. When she spoke, her voice was kind and concerned, but her eyes remained empty of feeling.

"But we're so close. You're freedom is almost at hand."

Her eyes narrowed. "*My* freedom? Or Asvoria's?"

Jirah recoiled, and Nearra wished she had her dagger, or a good **137** strong staff to defend herself with, but she didn't. The best she could do was take a step backward to get out of Jirah's reach.

"Who are you?" she demanded. "And where are you taking me?"

The being who wore Jriah's face opened her mouth to speak, but before she could say anything, a sound echoed from farther down the tunnel. It was a cross between a roar and a scream, and Nearra felt a jolt of fear upon hearing it. Not ordinary fear: dragonfear. But the cry wasn't exactly that of a dragon. It sounded like a dragon, yes, but it was higher-pitched and reverberated in a way that had nothing to do with the tunnel's acoustics.

The impostor's head jerked in the direction of the sound. "Blast! Someone's gotten there before us! We must hurry, before they get the Daystar!"

The being grabbed Nearra's hand and pulled the girl along. At first Nearra tried to tear free from the being's grip, but then she realized that it wasn't holding her hand. Instead, its fingers had curled around hers like serpents, and its flesh had fused together, completely encasing her hand. It was as if they were joined at the wrist.

The impostor ran down the tunnel in the direction of that awful cry, with Nearra struggling to keep from stumbling and falling. It seemed as if the thing's legs had grown longer so that it could run faster.

It's a shapeshifter, she thought. And then she wondered how she knew this. But then she had no more time to wonder about the imposter, for the tunnel suddenly opened into a huge cavern, and Nearra saw a half-rotted dragonish thing hovering above her friends— Davyn, Catriona, Sindri, Elidor, and Ayanti. standing beneath it. They'd come to rescue her!

But Nearra's joy instantly gave way to horror at their predicament.

The imposter continued to pull her forward, but Nearra grabbed hold of a stalagmite with her free hand. The shapeshifter tugged and pain shot through her arm and up into her shoulder, but she refused to let go.

If that monster is some kind of dragon, then maybe my friends need another dragon to fight it! Nearra thought.

Nearra concentrated on tapping into the magic power of the sorceress that dwelled within her. She could feel Asvoria trying to stop her, but Nearra redoubled her efforts, and she began to feel the familiar warm-tingling sensation in her hands that meant she was channeling Asvoria's magic. She had to be careful, though. If she summoned too much power, she risked triggering Maddoc's paralysis spell.

Nearra formed a mental message and then sent it flying as if it were an arrow and she an archer.

Tarkemelhion! We need you!

But something didn't feel right. She was certain the message had been sent, but . . .

"Come on!" The impostor gave one last yank and Nearra couldn't hold onto the stalagmite any longer. She let go, and it pulled her toward the center of the cavern where her friends were busy fighting for their lives.

Caravan wagons circled around a campfire. Men and women sat before the flames, singing along as a man played a sprightly tune on a wooden flute. Horses were tied to wooden stakes to keep them from wandering off as they grazed. And less than a dozen yards away from the campsite a dragon sat and listened.

Raedon had taken a position that was not so close that he'd be noticed, but not so far away that he couldn't hear, either. To avoid detection, he'd disguised himself as a large clump of bushes covered with tiny copper-colored flowers. It was dark, and he was far enough away from the firelight that the humans in the caravan wouldn't notice him no matter what form he wore. But their horses would pick up his dragon scent if he remained in his natural shape, and while it might be amusing to watch the animals' reaction as they realized a honest-to-Paladine dragon was near, Raedon didn't want to disrupt the camp—at least not yet. He'd never heard the song the traders were singing, and he wanted to memorize both the tune and the words.

Copper dragons belonged to the order of Chromatic—or Good—Dragons. Unlike their brethren, coppers lived for songs, stories, riddles, and jokes—especially practical jokes. Like others of his particular hue, Raedon loved to seek out travelers and have a little good-natured fun with them. He'd originally intended to trick the traders into believing that they'd chosen to camp in a haunted clearing. He was going to cast a spell to make dancing lights appear in the air above their campfire and then throw his voice so it sounded as if the lights were moaning. But when the traders began singing, Raedon decided to postpone his prank until they were finished.

As the song continued—and began to take a rather bawdy turn—Raedon became aware of another voice speaking over the music.

Tarkemelhion! We need you!

It was a voice he hadn't heard for some time, summoning him by his True Name, and he knew that the words were being spoken directly into his mind.

It was Nearra.

Accompanying her words was a strong sense of urgency, and Raedon knew that his friend and the little ones who were her companions were in serious danger. Without another thought, he cast off his floral disguise and assumed his true shape. The traders' horses immediately began to whinny in fear and the humans stopped singing. Raedon didn't have time to worry about them, though. He had to get to Nearra!

He spread his wings, coiled his powerful leg muscles, and launched himself into the night sky. He heard the humans in the camp shriek with terror and he called out, "Sorry! I didn't mean to scare you! At least, not this much!" And then he beat his wings and ascended toward the clouds.

Raedon didn't fully understand the bond he shared with Nearra. He was rather young as dragons went, and though like all of his kind he could cast spells, he was by no means an expert when it came to human magic. He knew that a great mystical power dwelled within Nearra, and that somehow the girl had used this power to reach out to him and create a link between their minds almost a year ago, when she and her friends had been threatened by an ogre and needed help. But whatever the true nature of the bond between them, it existed, and Raedon could not ignore her plea, even if he'd wanted to.

Raedon wasn't sure where Nearra was, but he had a feeling that he was supposed to head southeast. It was odd because he had two mental pictures: one was a shadowy stone keep and the other was a grove of twisted, tangled trees. The more he concentrated on the images, the more the first one faded and the stronger the second became, until the keep vanished from his thoughts and only the sinister grove remained.

That's where he was supposed to go—he was sure of it. If only he could get there in time.

The dracolich spread its rotted wings as it gazed down upon its prey.

Waves of fear pounded into Elidor. He couldn't take his eyes off the monster hovering over them. In life, the thing had been a white dragon, judging from the color of the flesh that clung to the beast's skeletal frame. Its skull was bare, and its wings were little more than leathery tatters. Elidor knew that those wings were too damaged to work and only magic kept the hideous thing aloft.

The hollows of its eye sockets glowed with a hypnotic yellow light that seemed to bypass Elidor's eyes and shine directly into his mind. He could feel his arms and legs becoming stiff and heavy, as if they were becoming coated with thick ice. The dracolich was using its power to paralyze him, and if he didn't resist it, he would be frozen in place like a statue, easy prey for the undead monstrosity.

Elidor felt a tug, and he realized that it came from the rope that he still held in his hands. With great effort, he turned his head and saw Shiriki rubbing her bound wrists against the rough surface of a stalagmite, trying to cut herself free. Shiriki seemed unaffected by the dracolich's presence, and Elidor wondered if that was because she served the dark goddess Takhisis.

He dropped the rope and began to string his bow. He wasn't very skilled with it, but he doubted his throwing knives would have much effect on an undead dragon. And at least the beast was large enough that he stood a decent chance of hitting it.

Davyn was already firing arrows at the dracolich, one after the other in rapid succession. Some of the shafts lodged in the monster's hide, but a number of them passed through its frame, tearing holes in its desiccated skin, but doing nothing to slow it down.

After a bit of fumbling, Elidor finally managed to get his bow strung. But before he could nock his first arrow, the dracolich opened its skeletal mouth and released a blast of frigid air.

Davyn ducked behind a large stalagmite to shield himself, while Catriona darted out of the range of the dracolich's frost breath. Ayanti still had Sindri on her back, and the centaur whirled and galloped off, weaving around stalagmites with equine grace.

Elidor was so busy messing with his bow that he didn't have time to seek cover from the dracolich's wintery blast. He saw it coming at him, a rolling cloud of white, accompanied by a soft crackling sound as if the dragon's arctic breath was freezing the air itself.

Then Elidor saw a rope pass over his head and chest and tighten around his waist. Just as the wave of frost was about to engulf him, he was yanked backwards. He landed on his side and fiery pain shot through his ribsElidor saw Shiriki a few feet away. Her hands were free and she held the end of the rope that had bound her.

"Lucky for you I have good aim," she said with a grin.

Shiriki knelt down and looked deep into Elidor's eyes. "You know something? You're kind of cute for a halfbreed." She leaned forward and planted a kiss on his lips. Then, swifter than he would've thought possible, even for one of his kind, she looped the rope around his wrists, then around his ankles and he was bound tight as a pig destined for market.

Shiriki gave him a wink, took back her sword, and then slipped away into the darkness.

"Stop!" Sindri shouted to Ayanti. "I want to get a good look at the dracolich!"

"Are you crazy? We're about to get frozen!"

"I wanted to see something." Sindri was upset. Not only was Ayanti taking him away from the dracolich, but also that intriguing metallic glint he'd spotted. There was something about that glint that called to him, more strongly even than interesting objects usually did. He wanted—no, he *needed*—to get closer, to investigate whatever caused the glint, to touch it, pick it up, to *handle* it in the fullest sense of how his people used the word. But he could hardly do so while sitting on the back of a centaur who was galloping in the wrong direction.

He was still weak from the enchantments he had performed earlier, but he sensed that if he didn't act now, he would never get a chance to take a look at whatever-it-was. So, without any further consideration of whether or not it was wise—and indeed, what kender worth his salt would waste time on something so unnecessary as looking before they leaped?—Sindri pushed off Ayanti's back.

"Hey!" Ayanti called. "What are you doing?"

As Sindri fell, he remembered the lantern that he held, and he tried to angle his body so that it wouldn't break and deprive his friends of the light they needed to battle the dracolich.

He struck the stone floor and the air shot out of his lungs. As he lay there trying to catch his breath, he realized he hadn't heard glass breaking and there was still light glowing around him. He'd managed to keep the lantern intact. He rose to his feet, ignoring the wobble in his legs and the ache in his hip where he landed.

"Sindri! Wait!" Ayanti shouted. "I'm coming back for you!"

Sindri wasn't about to wait. He'd explain to Ayanti later. He hurried off, moving the lantern until the whatever-it-was caught the light and reflected it. Sindri grinned. Gotcha! he thought, and started toward the center of the cavern.

As if it came from a great distance, he heard the sounds of his friends battling the undead dragon—the twang of Davyn's bowstring, and the *chuk-chuk* of Catriona's dragon claws cutting into the dead flesh of the beast, the roar and *whooooosh* as the dracolich released another gust of frost breath. But Sindri's attention was so completely focused on the marvelous whatever-it-was that he forgot about his friends and the monster they fought, and continued across the cavern floor toward the metallic glint. The atmosphere in the cave had turned as cold as the air in Icereach, and Sindri shivered as he walked.

Moments later the kender stood before the stalagmite where the glint came from, and his mouth hung open in amazed delight. Looped around the top of the stalagmite was a golden medallion embossed with the shape of a stylized sun. With fingers that trembled only partially due to the cold, Sindri reached out and gently, almost reverently, lifted the medallion off the stalagmite. As soon as his fingers touched the metal, he felt warmth flow into his hand, and he thought he heard a chorus of voices whispering, though he couldn't make out what they were saying.

"Sindri! Look out!" Catriona shouted.

Irritated at being distracted from the whispering voices, Sindri absentmindedly slipped the medallion into one of his cape pockets and then turned to see what Catriona was making such a fuss about.

The dracolich still hovered in the air, though its feet dangled low enough for Catriona to have gotten in a few good strikes with her dragonclaws. The beast's flapping wings spread the chill created by its frost breath. The baleful light that served the dracolich in place of eyes were trained on Sindri, and the kender had the feeling that he'd done something to anger the undead monster, but he couldn't imagine what it had been.

"You're very interesting," Sindri called out to the dracolich, "but one of my friends is being held captive in Cairngorn Keep, so we really need to be moving on."

The half-rotted abomination stared at Sindri for a moment. At least, he *thought* it was staring—it was rather difficult to tell since it didn't have physical eyes. Then the dracolich let out an angry hiss and reared back its head, preparing to unleash another blast of its frigid breath.

"Sindri, watch out!" Catriona shouted.

Even in the face of his own death, Sindri still experienced the endless curiosity that lay at the core of a kender's being. He wondered how an undead creature could still produce the same frost breath that it had it had in life. After all, it was dead and didn't need to breathe anymore. It was magic, of course, but what was the precise nature of the enchantment? That was the truly fascinating part.

"You fool!"

Suddenly Catriona was at Sindri's side. She snatched the lantern out of his hand and hurled it at the hovering dracolich. The lantern arced through the air and struck the creature's chest. Glass shattered, oil spilled, and the part of the dracolich that was still flesh caught fire. The thing's dead dry skin was better than kindling. The flames spread quickly and within moments the undead dragon was a gigantic torch that lit the entire cavern.

Sindri turned to Catriona, a hurt look on his face.

"Why did you call me a fool? That wasn't very nice."

The Chase is On

Nearra huddled silently behind a large stalagmite. On the other side of the cavern,
her friends battled for their lives. The shapeshifter still held
Nearra's hand encased in the malleable flesh of its hand, and it'd
wrapped the other hand around her mouth so she couldn't call
out to her friends.

"Curses! The kender got to the Daystar before us!" the shapeshifter said in a near whisper.

Nearra thought it didn't need to keep its voice low. The burning dracolich was screaming loud enough to shake the stalagmite
they hid behind. Nearra doubted the loathsome creature was in
pain. After all, it was already dead. The dracolich didn't sound
hurt. It sounded *mad*.

She struggled to pull free from the shapeshifter, determined
to go to her friends' aid, but its grip was like iron.

"Perhaps we should sneak up on the kender and try to take
the Daystar from him," it mused. "A burning dracolich certainly
makes an effective distraction."

The dracolich hovered in the air despite its wings burning
in flame. It shook its huge body like a wet dog. But instead of 147

water drops, bits of burning flesh flew off and rained down upon Nearra's companions. "But on second thought, perhaps it would be better to allow Frostclaw to finish them off. Then if it is still functional, I'll be able to speak its true name and command—"

Nearra couldn't stand it any longer. Before the shapeshifter could finish its sentence, Nearra bit down on its palm as hard as she could. Whatever the true nature of the creature's form, its palm was soft as any human's, and Nearra felt skin break and blood well forth.

It cried out in pain, and the voice that erupted from its throat sounded nothing like Jirah's. It was a disturbing amalgamation of human, animal, and creatures impossible to name. As the shapeshifter yanked its bleeding hand away from Nearra's mouth, she jammed her elbow into its ribs. At least, she aimed for the place on its body where the ribs should be. But when her elbow came in contact with its side, it sank into the flesh as if its chest were nothing more than a leathery pouch filled with fluid. Whatever it had in its body in place of human organs was still sensitive, for it gasped and drew away from Nearra and released her wrist.

She was free! She ran toward her friends, all of whom had taken cover from the rain of fire.

"Davyn!" she shouted. "Catriona, Sindri, Elidor! It's me!"

Her companions remained crouching behind their meager shelter, but they turned their heads in her direction.

"Nearra!" Davyn called, a sudden grin of happy surprise on his face.

The sight of his grin sent joy pulsing through her heart.

He looks happy to see me, she thought, almost as happy as I am to see him.

But Davyn's grin vanished as suddenly as it had appeared. "Watch out for the dracolich!" he shouted.

TIM WAGGONER

Nearra realized that Davyn's first thought was always for her safety. It was at precisely this moment that she realized how much she truly loved him. As difficult as it was, she forced herself to put all thought of Davyn out her mind and concentrate on summoning Asvoria's power. But as she began to concentrate, she felt a strange sensation, as if a wall had sprung up in her mind. It was almost as if the sorceress was trying to stop her. Nearra tried to push her way though the psychic barrier, but it was no use. The mental blockade was too strong.

A hand clamped down on her shoulder. Talons sprang from fingertips and dug into her flesh. Nearra cried out in pain as the shapershifter tightened its grip. She stumbled and would've fallen if it hadn't held her.

"I need you alive, but I don't necessarily need you unharmed," the shapeshifter hissed in her ear. "Keep that in mind."

It kept his grip on her shoulder and turned her around. She tried to resist but the creature was too strong, and its talons were beginning to pierce her skin.

"The odds are no longer in our favor, so we're going back to the keep," the shapeshifter said. "Fast as we can, understand?" And then it started running and Nearra had no choice but to try and keep up with it.

She glanced back over her shoulder, trying to catch one last glimpse of Davyn, but all she saw was the fiery blaze of the dracolich. The shapeshifter squeezed her shoulder and growled for her to look forward. With her captor's claws digging painfully into her shoulder, she ran out of the dracolich's cavern and into the tunnel beyond.

"Nearra!"

Davyn forgot about the dracolich, he forgot about his friends.

149

His only thoughts were for Nearra. He hadn't come this far only to lose her again.

He stood, forsaking the shelter of the stalagmite, and ran after Nearra.

"Davyn!" Ayanti shouted. "Stay down!"

But Davyn barely heard her. He ran around stalagmites, leaped over burning bits of dracolich flesh, and when he couldn't jump over them, he ran through the flames as fast as he could, ignoring the heat and the pain. His companions shouted again and he felt a wave of intense heat at his back and realized what was happening. He'd drawn the dracolich's attention and the undead breast was coming for him. He didn't look back. If he slowed down even a fraction, it could prove fatal. All he could do was keep running as fast as he could, and hope that the dracolich didn't unleash a blast of ice or rain blazing gobs of flesh on him.

Davyn ran for all he was worth. Behind him, the dracolich finally succumbed to the flames and crashed to the cavern floor. Davyn felt hot sparks singe his back, but he ignored them and kept running.

"Come on!" he shouted to his companions. "We have to follow Nearra!"

Shiriki waited several moments before emerging from the dark corner of the cavern where she had been hiding. She sent a prayer of thanks to the Dark Queen for providing her an opportunity to escape. For some reason, though, Takhisis had allowed the companions to escape as well. It didn't occur to her that another god might have been protecting them, or that their escape might have had more to do with luck than divine intervention. Perhaps, she thought, the Dark Queen had spared their lives so that Shiriki herself could find them and avenge her cousin's death. If so, she wouldn't let her goddess down.

She felt a pang of reluctance at the notion of slaying Elidor, though. After all, he was Kagonesti, if only by half. And she had to admit that he *was* rather cute.

As the last of the dracolich was devoured by the flames, Shiriki thought she saw a dark shadowy form rise up from its body and merge with the murky gloom of the cavern ceiling. Had she just witnessed the dracolich's foul spirit being released, or had it simply been an illusion created by smoke and flickering firelight?

Just then she heard a shuffling, scraping noise over the hiss and pop of dying flame. She withdrew once more into the shadows and looked toward the sound. Shiriki saw a figure walk out of the tunnel and into the cavern. It was man-shaped and walked unsteadily, as if it might fall over any moment. The light cast by the remains of the burning dracolich interfered with her elf night vision, but she squinted and held up a hand to block to the light. Her eyes focused and she saw that the figure was Kuruk.

Elation welled up inside her, for despite the words to the contrary that she'd spoken to Elidor, she loved her cousin and, though she had fought not to show it, she'd been devastated by his loss. But she hadn't lost him. He was here and alive!

She ran across the cavern toward her cousin, grinning with delight that he'd been returned to her. But before she could reach him, Kuruk collapsed to his knees and slumped over on his side.

"No!" Shiriki shouted. She felt a frigid blast of air shoot past her and for an instant Kuruk's body was cloaked in shadow. But then it was gone, so quickly that she wasn't certain she'd seen it.

She reached her cousin's side and knelt, placing two fingers against his neck. She felt no pulse. She removed her fingers and stroked her cousin's blood-matted hair. The injuries he'd suffered during the cave-in had been too severe. Only his fearsome will had allowed him to make it this far. But no matter how strong a will one has, if the body can no longer function, there is nothing that can be done.

Tears streaming down her face, Shiriki stood. She would find rocks to build him a burial mound, and then she would commend his soul unto darkness and continue on her quest to avenge him.

But as she turned to begin looking for rocks, she heard a sound. She turned back and saw Kuruk sitting up, his eyes open.

"Takhisis be praised!" she said.

Kuruk looked up at her and slowly smiled. "Yes, Takhisis be praised, indeed."

A wave of cold seemed to emanate from Kuruk's mouth and Shiriki shivered. She reached out to help him up, and when he took her hand, she found his flesh was ice cold.

It's just the cavern's temperature, she thought. He'll warm up when we finally get out of these blasted caves.

She began to suspect something was wrong, but she didn't care. She had her cousin back, and that was all that mattered.

CHAPTER 19

ONCE MORE TO THE KEEP

The shapeshifter and Nearra burst into the cell where Maddoc had imprisoned her. Nearra's heart raced and she gulped for air, but the shapeshifter appeared not to have been affected in the slightest by the exertion of running from the cavern, through the tunnel, and up all those steps. But then, it wasn't human, was it?

"Who are you?" she demanded.

"My name is Ophion." The creature looked around the cell, as if unsure what to do next.

Ophion looked deeply into Nearra's eyes. "I humbly beg your forgiveness, Mistress. You made me to be a creature of stealth, not of action."

"Mistress? What are you talking about? *I'm* not your mistress!"

"I wasn't speaking to you, girl, but rather the spirit that is trapped inside you," Ophion said. "Your friends will be here soon, so we can't stay in here. But if I take you out into the hall, I risk Maddoc seeing us." The shapeshifter pondered a moment longer, looking increasingly indecisive.

"How is it that you knew to take the form of my sister? Is Jirah really one of Maddoc's servants?"

"One of my gifts is the ability to pluck images out of people's minds so I can assume the best form to trick them. I can take on the shape of any of your relatives, friends, acquaintances, any animals you've ever seen—but that's not important right now. We have to make our escape!"

"You'll never get away from Maddoc," Nearra said. "If you truly want to serve your mistress, you should release me and let me leave with my friends. At least that way Asvoria's spirit will be out of Maddoc's reach."

Nervous sweat beaded on Ophion's forehead, surprising Nearra. She didn't think such a creature could do something so human as sweat.

For a moment, she thought the shapeshifter was going to do as she suggested, but then it shook its head. "Your friends have seen what I am capable of, so I will have a difficult time deceiving them with my powers. But Maddoc does not know of my existence. So there is still a good chance that I can trick him."

As Nearra watched, Ophion's form shimmered and shrank. It no longer resembled Jirah. Now it looked exactly like Oddvar—if the Theiwar had possessed large blue eyes.

One detail hadn't changed, though. Ophion's hand still had talons but because of its new size it could no longer grip her shoulder with them, so it pressed them to her side instead.

"Make no noise or sudden moves," Ophion said in Oddvar's voice. Then without another word it led Nearra to the cell door and out into the hallway. She had no choice but to follow.

Ophion didn't run down the hall, and for that Nearra was grateful. She guessed it didn't want to draw unnecessary attention. What had it said to Asvoria? It was a creature of stealth. Oddvar wouldn't run through the keep with her unless it was an emergency, so Ophion wouldn't either, though it was walking at a faster pace than the dark dwarf usually set.

Their speed could work to her advantage, Nearra thought. While the effectiveness of Ophion's disguise depended on going unnoticed, her friends had no such limitations. They would keep running as fast as possible, and hopefully would catch up with her soon.

She tried to drag her feet to slow them down even more, but Ophion jabbed his talons into her side, making her yelp with pain.

"Keep moving," Ophion growled.

As she once again matched his pace, she saw that his gaze kept darting back and forth, as if he were desperately looking for some way of escape. They passed numerous closed doors, but Ophion didn't slow down, let alone stop to open any of them and see what was inside. Either he already knew or he didn't care.

"Stop!"

It was Davyn! Nearra looked back over her shoulder and saw Davyn pounding down the hallway toward them. Not far behind him were Catriona and the others. Sindri rode on Ayanti's back, arms clasped around the waist of the centaur's human half.

Ophion, of course, had no intention of stopping. Instead, it coiled its arm around her middle as if it had become a serpent, and started to run, pulling her along with it.

Nearra heard a clang as Davyn dropped his knife, and she knew what he would do next. In her mind, she saw him stop running, ready his bow, draw an arrow from his quiver, nock it and—

She heard the twang of his bowstring.

Evidently, Ophion had too, for its back was suddenly covered in armor plating that reminded her of a turtle's shell. The arrow struck the shell and bounced off without leaving a mark.

"Blast!" Davyn swore, then picked up his hunting knife and started running again.

Ophion and Nearra came to the end of the hall. The entrance

to a flight of stairs lay before them. Ophion pulled her up onto the stairs and Nearra knew this was her chance. She let her legs collapse beneath her—which didn't take much effort considering how tired she was. She hoped to drag Ophion down, making it stumble. If only she could delay the shapeshifter long enough for her friends to catch up.

But as she began to fall, Ophion's forms blurred again. No longer did it resemble Oddvar. Now it was a long, sleek, blue-eyed mountain cat with a thick tawny coat. The arm that had encircled her waist became a band of fur, and it shifted and pulled her onto the cat's back. Ophion continued bounding up the stairs.

Ophion carried her up two flights before exiting into another hallway. It kept running, its large padded paws making no sound on the stone floor. It passed one door, two, then stopped before a third door. Nearra recognized this door. She started to shout a warning to her friends, but a strip of fur-covered flesh wrapped around her mouth, silencing her.

Ophion reached up, its paw becoming a human hand so that it could open the door.

Davyn was still in the lead when they entered the hallway. But though he was certain this was the floor they'd gotten off on, Nearra and the creature that held her captive were nowhere to be seen.

What is that thing, anyway? he wondered. He didn't remember Maddoc having any servants who could shift form like that. But he'd been away for almost a year. Perhaps Maddoc had recruited or created some new servants in that time.

As Davyn ran, he was struck by a sudden realization. He was within the keep where he had grown up. This used to be his *home*, He doubted he'd ever think of it as home again.

TIM WAGGONER

Plenty of time for nostalgia later, he thought. Right now he had to focus on rescuing Nearra.

He saw a door ahead that was cracked open.

He reached the door, threw it open, and dashed inside, knife in hand, ready to plunge it up to the hilt in the chest of Nearra's abductor.

But the room was empty.

No, he realized. It wasn't completely empty. A number of blank paintings hung on the walls.

He suddenly had a bad feeling about this room.

He whirled around to warn the others to stay outside, but it was too late. Catriona, Elidor, Ayanti, and Sindri all pushed inside.

"For Paladine's sake, don't shut the door!"

But even though none of them were near it, the door suddenly slammed closed.

The paintings began to glow as the chamber came to life.

Across from the chamber, a long arm emerged from the stone wall opposite the door. From the end of the arm sprouted the hand that had shut the Gallery's door. But then an even stranger thing occurred. A section of stone flowed away from the wall, revealing a young woman that it had covered. The stone contracted and reformed until it resembled a dark dwarf named Oddvar.

Ophion grinned at Nearra. "I trust you're none the worse for having to go without air for a few moments?"

Nearra glared at the shapeshifter. "I've been in that room. It's a terrible place. If you open the door and release my friends, I'll go with you and do whatever you want."

Ophion looked at her for a moment, considering her offer. "You know, I think you just might. But even if I believed you, your friends would never agree to such a deal. No, I'm afraid they'll have to remain inside while I help you—and therefore my mistress—escape the keep."

"I wouldn't speak so soon if I were you, *brother*."

Nearra and Ophion turned toward the voice. The real Oddvar approached them, accompanied by Drefan, Fyren, and Gifre.

Ophion's blue eyes narrowed as they came, and Nearra guessed that it was sizing up the situation and calculating its chances for success. Finally, it turned to look at Nearra.

"I'll be back for you," it whispered, and then Nearra blinked and the ersatz Oddvar was no more. In his place buzzed a tiny blue-eyed fly. She made a grab for it, but the insect avoided her hand easily and flew off down the hall.

Nearra darted toward the chamber door, intending to open it and free her friends, but before her hand could touch the knob, Oddvar's fingers wrapped around her wrist. The Theiwar jerked her away from the door.

"I think we'd better speak to Maddoc first before we do anything so rash as attempting to release your friends, don't you?"

The dark dwarf pulled her down the hallway, the goblins following behind.

"And the being just disappeared?" Maddoc sat up in his bed, curtains pulled back, blankets drawn up to his waist. Before him stood Oddvar and Nearra. The goblins waited out in the hall as befitted their stations, or lack thereof.

Oddvar nodded. "One moment he was standing there, looking like the twin I never had, and the next he was gone."

"I suppose it's possible," the wizard mused. "A teleportation spell wouldn't be beyond the abilities of one who could change shape. But if this being were an accomplished spellcaster, I doubt it would've fled from you. It's more likely that the creature's abilities are confined solely to adopting other forms. It probably transmogrified into something very small to get away without being seen." Maddoc fixed Nearra with his gaze. "You were standing next to the creature. What did it become?"

Nearra didn't answer right away, and Maddoc began to think that she had no intention of doing so. But then she said, "A fly."

Maddoc allowed himself a small smile. If he gloated too much, Nearra might decide to go back to being silent. She'd always been a stubborn, spirited girl, and she'd only become more so during the months since he'd implanted Asvoria's spirit within her. At the time, she had seemed a perfect choice for the procedure. Now he wondered how he ever could've been so foolish as to select someone with so strong a spirit.

"What can you tell me about 'him'?"

"Its name is Ophion. It first appeared to me in the form of my sister, Jirah."

"That must mean you remember who Jirah is."

Nearra nodded. "Some of my memories have returned since my experience in the chamber of paintings."

Maddoc nodded as if such a revelation was only to be expected, but the truth was he had no idea the Gallery of Despair would have such an effect on her. A wise wizard never admitted ignorance. "Go on."

"From various things Ophion said, I believe it was one of Asvoria's servants."

Another surprise and a most unwelcome one. Maddoc wondered where this shapechanger had come from, but he supposed it didn't matter. Ophion *was* here and still at large within Cairngorn Keep. Maddoc suspected the shapeshifter would try to free its mistress. That meant he would have to take precautions to see that Ophion didn't interfere with tonight's ritual.

"I told you what you wanted to know," Nearra said. "Now I have a request of my own."

Maddoc raised an eyebrow. It seemed there was no end to the surprises this evening.

"I promise that I won't resist when you cast the spell to give Asvoria control over my body . . . *if* you release my friends from the Gallery of Despair and allow them to depart the keep unharmed."

Maddoc laughed. "How noble of you! But I'll have to decline your generous offer. As long as your companions are in the grip of the Gallery's enchantment, they cannot interfere with my plans. And I have other ways of ensuring your cooperation. Grab hold of her, Oddvar."

The dark dwarf did as his master commanded, and though Nearra struggled, the Theiwar was stronger than he looked and she couldn't break free.

Maddoc reached over to his nightstand, grimacing as his frail body protested the maneuver. He removed a small leather satchel from a drawer and settled back onto the bed with a weary sigh. Inside the satchel were a number of ingredients necessary for casting spells. No mage beyond the first year of his apprentice-ship was ever far from the materials necessary to ply his trade. Maddoc removed the physical components for a sleep spell: a pinch of white sand mixed with powdered nightshade. He sprinkled the mixture into the air and moved his hand in a mystic pattern, chanting liquid syllables of power that escaped his memory the moment they were spoken.

The sand-and-nightshade powder vanished before it could fall onto the wizard's sheets and the spell was cast. Nearra's eyes closed and her chin drooped to her chest. She would have slumped to the floor if Oddvar hadn't been holding her.

Maddoc felt suddenly dizzy, and he lay his head back on his pillow and closed his eyes for a moment. Even a simple sleep spell took so much out of him since the demise of his beloved familiar.

"My lord?" Oddvar asked. "Are you all right?"

The concern in the dwarf's voice infuriated Maddoc. He was a master wizard. He didn't need sympathy from a mere underling!

He opened his eyes and forced himself to sit up. He took a deep breath and then put his feet on the floor and stood. He was pleased and more than a bit surprised that he hadn't fallen back onto the bed.

"She should sleep until it is time to perform the ritual. I have already made most of the preparations. Nearra can remain here in my bedchamber until all is ready. I placed the wardspells on this room myself and I doubt Ophion will be able to bypass them. But in case he tries, I want the goblins to stand guard outside, and I want you to remain inside the room and not take your eyes off Nearra until I call for her. Do you understand?"

Oddvar inclined his head. "Yes, my lord."

"Good. Well, don't just stand there. Bring her over to the bed. After all, we want to make sure that Asvoria's new body will be rested and ready for her when she takes control of it."

Maddoc shuffled over to his wardrobe closet while Oddvar placed Nearra on the bed. The wizard slipped off his nightshirt and donned a fresh black robe.

Oddvar said, "If I might ask, what will you be doing until it's time to work the spell?"

Maddoc wanted to slap Oddvar. But he was too close to obtaining his ultimate goal, and he didn't want to risk angering Oddvar. He needed the Theiwar's full cooperation, at least for the next few hours.

"I plan to check on the final preparations and then have a little something to eat." He smiled. "I dislike working major enchantments on an empty stomach."

Oddvar nodded. "Very well. I shall keep watch on the girl and await your summons."

"One last thing," Maddoc said. "If anyone enters the room and approaches you—including myself—before midnight, assume that it is Ophion and kill the creature."

Oddvar drew a poison-coated dagger and smiled grimly. "I shall not hesitate, my lord."

"Good." Maddoc turned and then shuffled toward the chamber's door. He hadn't told Oddvar the complete truth about what he planned to do until midnight. He was going to make a stop first—at the Gallery of Despair. Now that Davyn had returned, Maddoc intended to give his adopted son a proper welcome home.

CHAPTER

20

RAEDON'S DILEMMA

Raedon soared through the night. The sky was free of clouds, and the stars above looked like finely wrought crystals set into rich black velvet. The crimson moon Lunitari was half full, while Solinari was a mere crescent hanging close to the horizon. Something about the moons' configuration bothered the copper dragon, but he couldn't say what it was.

Normally Raedon enjoyed flying at night. It was quiet and peaceful, and he always felt as if he were the only being in the world and all of creation existed for him alone. But he felt no such joy this night. Nearra needed his help and while he knew he was in the vicinity of where she had been when she'd contacted him, he was having a terrible time pinpointing the exact location. The image in his mind was clear enough: a grove of twisted, bare trees. He had flown in the direction he sensed the grove lay and had passed near a large stone keep. He'd seen the structure once of twice before but only from a distance. He had no idea who lived there. Besides, dragons—both Good and Evil—hadn't been back in Ansalon very long, and even good dragons could inspire enough fear in humans to provoke them into attacking. And as far as Raedon was concerned, anyone who lived in a keep was probably of a warlike turn of mind and best avoided.

But this time when he'd flown past the keep, he'd felt a powerful tug, as if the stone structure were calling to him. A keep had been one of the two images that had accompanied Nearra's cry for help, a keep like this one.

Raedon had almost flown closer, but then the image of the grove of twisted trees flashed through his mind and the keep's pull lessened, though it didn't completely diminish. Raedon had continued on toward the grove, but now he was beginning to have second thoughts. Both the keep and the grove called to him equally, but how could that be possible? Nearra couldn't be in two places at once. He didn't fully understand the mystic power that dwelled within her or how it worked. But regardless, it was hardly unheard of for a telepathic message to be vague, unclear, or difficult to interpret. But this indecision was driving him mad! The longer he hesitated, trying to decide where he should go—the keep, the grove, the keep, the grove—the longer Nearra was in danger.

The copper dragon growled in frustration. Instead of wasting time trying to decide, he should just check both locations and be done with it. With that much decided at least, he felt a little better. Now he had only to choose which location to investigate first.

He looked down and spotted a grove of bare, twisted trees surrounded by normal, healthy forestland, exactly like in his vision.

He grinned. It seemed this latest choice had been made for him.

Raedon lowered his head, stopped flapping his wings, and angled his body downward. As he glided toward the grove, he scanned the area for signs of human life but saw none. He sniffed the air, but he was still too high up and the breeze was too strong for him to pick up any scent trails.

He began to think the grove wasn't the place he was supposed to go after all. But then again, just because no one appeared to be here didn't mean they *hadn't* been. Perhaps Nearra had sent her message from here, and then for some reason had to move on. He'd know for sure once he was on the ground and could sniff around for Nearra's scent. If he couldn't find it, that would mean she hadn't been here and he'd be free to head to the keep. But if he did find her scent trail, then he could follow it to wherever she was now.

As Raedon drew closer to the ground, he saw that the trees weren't completely bare. While it was true that they had no leaves, strands of thin silvery thread stretched between the branches and from tree to tree. The strands glistened, tinged red by Lunitari's light, and swayed gently in the night breeze. It was a beautiful sight, and even if Raedon hadn't come here in search of Nearra, he would've dipped down to get a closer look.

The threads were like nothing he'd ever seen before, and he wondered if they were some manner of strange and wonderful plant growth. But as lovely as the strands were, they were going to make it difficult for him to find a place to land. The forest surrounding the grove was thick, and even the most powerful dragons were careful where and how they landed, lest they risk injuring a wing. He supposed he could always try clawing through the silvery threads, but he hated to ruin their beauty, and since he didn't know exactly what they were, he was reluctant to touch them.

If he could use his acid spray to burn through a few carefully selected threads, he might be able to clear a space large enough to land without having to damage too many of the strands.

As he circled low over the twisted trees, he was gripped by

RETURN OF THE SORCERESS

a sudden feeling that he was in danger. Dragons are intelligent creatures, yet like animals, they remained in touch with their instincts in a way other thinking beings on Krynn did not. Raedon didn't pause to question whether his instinct was accurate or what had prompted it. He arced his head toward the sky, beat the air with his wings, and began to ascend as fast as he could.

But before he could gain much altitude, he felt something sticky adhere to his tail. He felt the sensation a second time, then a third, and now the sticky things—he knew without looking that they were threads of glistening silver—began to strike his legs, abdomen, and wings.

Raedon flapped his wings furiously, trying to break free, but the strands held fast. He looked down and now saw that the trees were filled with hundreds of ivory-colored spiders, each the size of a large melon. They were spraying sticky strands from their mouths, and while individually none of the spiders would've been a match for a creature of his size and strength, together they had him trapped.

Raedon kept flapping, but he couldn't rise any higher. As soon as the spiders hit him with their webbing, they secured the strand to a tree branch and fired again. When the spiders had enough lines attached to him, they stopped spinning their silver threads. They grabbed hold of the lines with segmented legs and began to pull their prize downward.

Davyn opened his eyes to walls of gray stone. He felt dizzy and disoriented. He had no idea where he was, couldn't remember how he'd gotten here.

He looked around and was relieved to see that he wasn't alone. His friends were here, too—wherever *here* was.

"What is this place?" Catriona asked.

The companions stood upon a stone floor discolored by dark, unidentifiable stains. In the middle of the floor was a round, rusted metal grate. There was something about the grate that struck Davyn as familiar, but couldn't say what.

"It appears we're in a large chamber of some sort," Elidor said.

"No, we're not," Sindri countered. From his seat upon Ayanti's back, he pointed up. "Look."

They did and saw that there was no roof above them, only sky. Sharp-tipped iron spikes jutted from the tops of the walls, and they too seemed familiar, but though Davyn struggled to remember, he couldn't.

"This is the Pit," Ayanti said in a confused, frightened voice. "We're in Bolthor's Pit."

And then, as if the centaur's words had summoned them, dozens of faces peered over the metal spikes, rough, cruel faces with hungry grins and bloodlust in their eyes.

"I'm not sure how we got here," Elidor said, looking up at the raucous crowd. "But it's obvious *why* we're here—to fight."

Davyn wished he could remember how they had come to return to the Pit. The last thing he remembered was being in Cairngorn Keep, chasing after Nearra.

They could sort out the whys and wherefores of their situation later. Right now, they needed to find an exit.

"Ayanti, what's the best way to get out of here?" he asked.

"There isn't a way out," she said. "Not unless someone lowers a ramp for us."

"We have an elf who can climb a wall as easily as the rest of can walk," Catriona said.

Elidor grinned. "I have a rope in my pack. Once I reach one of the spikes, I can tie the rope off and throw it down, and then the rest of you can use it to climb out."

167

Davyn thought for a moment, then nodded. "Sounds like a plan. Let's get started. We need to hurry before—"

Davyn was cut off by the sound of wood sliding across metal. He looked up and saw that a quartet of burly men were lowering a ramp into the Pit.

The crowd roared its approval.

From the onlookers' reaction, Davyn guessed the ramp wasn't intended as way out, but rather to allow someone—or some-*thing*—else to get in.

Evidently, Ayanti shared his thought, for she called out to the men lowering the ramp. "Don't you recognize me? It's me . . . Ayanti! There's been some sort of horrible mistake! We shouldn't be in here!"

Laughter broke out among the spectators.

"Sorry, Ayanti," Elidor said, "but I don't think they care who you are."

"Look out!" Catriona shouted.

The friends jumped back as the end of the ramp teetered, then came crashing down to the floor of the Pit.

A large shape came into view at the top of the ramp and began to descend into the Pit with awkward, lumbering steps.

Davyn stared at the beast, unable to believe what he was seeing. The monster was a hideous conglomeration, a nightmarish patchwork of heads, limbs, scales, fur, and exposd bone. The main head was that of a white-furred ice bear, and flanking it were the heads of two dire wolves. All three heads growled as the horrible beast came down the ramp, baring saliva-coated fangs and glaring at the companions with hungry eyes. Behind the creature, a black-scaled tail whipped the air, and from its back sprouted a pair of tattered, decayed dragon wings, so decomposed that they were clearly incapable of launching the beast into flight. The bulk of the thing's body was a mixture of white and gray fur, black lizard-scales, and dead flesh. Worst of all were the monster's legs: they were nothing but ivory bone—the front pair avian, the rear feline.

Through the horror that gripped his mind, Davyn felt a tickle of memory. The bear and the wolves . . . the lizard-board and the bone-griffin . . . the dracolich . . . Somehow, by the darkest of magics, these creatures had been merged into a single terrifying entity.

The hybrid monster reached the bottom of the ramp and stepped into the Pit, all six of its eyes focused on the pathetic little beings that were destined to be its prey.

As bad as the sight of the monster was, the stench of the thing was far worse. It gave of a thick, greasy stink like congealed sewage, and Davyn felt hot bile splash against the back of his throat. It took all his self-control to keep from vomiting.

"Now that," Sindri said in delighted appreciation, "is truly an impressive stink!"

Elidor, whose sense were keener than a human's, groaned and covered his nose and mouth with a hand.

The hybrid lurched toward them on its skeletal legs. The five companions slowly retreated to the opposite side of the Pit as it came. When Davyn's back bumped against a stone wall, he realized there was nowhere left to retreat.

Davyn drew his hunting knife. "Then we'll just have to attack first, won't we?"

The patchwork beast opened its trio of mouths and released a combination of ursine and lupine roars, and then it started toward them.

"Now!" Davyn shouted, and he rushed toward the beast, hunting knife held high, prepared to strike . . .

. . . and then he was no longer running, no longer holding the knife in his hand. He stood in front of a painting that depicted

RETURN OF THE SORCERESS

Catriona, Elidor, Sindri, and Ayanti running forward to meet the charge of a hideous hybrid monster.

He blinked in confusion. "What's going on here?"

He then heard a soft chuckle, amused, but not without a certain amount of sympathy.

"Are you all right?"

Davyn turned to look at the gaunt-faced man dressed in black robes and was startled to realize that it was Maddoc, his adoptive father.

His first impulse was to wrap his hands around the wizard's throat and choke the life out of him, but he resisted. "Not that I think you really care, but I'm fine," he lied. "You don't look so well."

"Shaera was killed not long ago. Her death took its toll on me."

Davyn was surprised at how weak and breathy Maddoc's voice had become. Davyn was no wizard, but he understood that the link between a mage and his familiar was created through a merging of their lifeforces. When one died, the other nearly did so as well. But seeing the effect of Shaera's death upon Maddoc was a shock.

Davyn turned away from Maddoc and glanced around the room. He saw that his companions stood before their own paintings, one to a picture, though since Sindri still sat on Ayanti's back, the two of them shared a painting. They all stood motionless, scarcely breathing as they stared at their paintings, all of which depicted the same scene as Davyn's.

"Don't try to yell at them or shake them," Maddoc said. "Simply closing the door activates the enchantment, but it takes somewhat more skill to break the spell once it begins, skill that I obviously possess." He gestured to Davyn's painting, which was now blank. "Do you know why I broke the Gallery's spell for you?"

TIM WAGGONER

"Because you needed someone to gloat to?" he said bitterly.

Maddoc smiled. "Perhaps," he admitted. "One of the problems with being a dark wizard is that there usually isn't anyone to share your triumphs with, certainly no one that's your equal. But I had another more important reason. You are my son and there is unfinished business between us. I would like to speak with you. So I'm giving you a choice. You may leave the Gallery with me, or if you'd rather, I'll return you to your illusion." Maddoc gestured to Davyn's painting.

Davyn was tempted to tell Maddoc to go to blazes, but if he were once again in the grip of the Gallery's enchantment, he would be helpless. If he went with Maddoc, however, there was a chance that he might be able to do something to help his friends and Nearra.

"Very well," Davyn said, doing his best to keep the emotions he felt out of his voice. "Let's talk."

Maddoc acknowledged his adopted son's choice with a nod before turning and walking into the hallway. As Davyn followed, he glanced on last time at his friends. Though their faces were expressionless, he knew that within their minds they were preparing to battle the patchwork nightmare. He silently wished them luck.

CHAPTER

21   A Fireside Chat

Maddoc sat in his favorite chair before a roaring fire, and Davyn sat in front of him waiting for the wizard to speak.

Maddoc leaned back in his chair, steepled his fingers over his stomach, and closed his eyes. A moment passed, then two, and Davyn began to think the wizard had dozed off. The goblins had taken his weapons, but all he had to do was grab hold of Maddoc's neck and squeeze as hard as he could. Davyn was young and strong, and now Maddoc was frail and weak. There was an excellent chance that Davyn could kill the wizard before he could cast a spell to protect himself.

Davyn started to get off his stool, but then stopped. As practical—and satisfying—as killing Maddoc would be, Davyn couldn't bring himself to do it. The person he had been a year ago might've been capable of such an act, but he'd changed a great deal since then, and not in small part due to Nearra. Even though he would be killing Maddoc to protect her, as well as avenge his true father, Davyn could imagine the sorrow and disappointment in her eyes when she learned he had killed for her. Nearra had not only helped him become a better person and she made him want to stay that way.

173

Maddoc opened his eyes then and a sly smile played about his lips. The wizard had been testing him, of course. With Maddoc, everything was a test of one sort or another.

"You might not believe this," Maddoc said, "but in a way I'm proud of you. You're on your way to becoming quite a man."

"No thanks to you," Davyn said. "Is that why you released me from the Gallery's spell? To tell me that?"

"No. The thought merely occurred to me, and I decided to share it with you, that's all. No matter what has taken place between us in the past or may yet take place in the future, you are still my son, and I am still your father."

"You're not my father!" Davyn shouted. "You lied to me, hurt my friends, and you forced me to kill the man who was my true father!"

Maddoc was silent for a time before he responded in a soft voice. "Do you know why I chose to wear the black robes?"

Davyn was surprised at the sudden turn in the conversation. Maddoc had never spoken of such things to him before.

"No. I didn't think choice was involved."

Maddoc kept his gaze fixed on the flames as he continued to speak. "That's true enough as far as it goes. Just as all men and women have their talents and inclinations, so too do wizards. But there's more to it than that. When one begins training at the Tower of Wayreth, one must choose the robes that he or she shall wear, thereby publicly proclaiming a devotion to one order of magic: white for Good, red for Neutral, and black for Evil. At least, that's the way uneducated peasants would describe the orders."

"But not you." Davyn couldn't keep the derision out of his voice.

Maddoc ignored it and went on. "White stands for restraint. White Robes are extremely careful what spells they cast, and they strive to use magic only when they deem it to be truly necessary.

Red Robes believe in balance. They are not as cautious as White Robes, but neither do they completely embrace all aspects of magic, as do Black Robes. They also keep an eye on the White and Black Robes to make sure the former do not impeded magical progress overmuch and that the Black Robes' devotion to total magical freedom doesn't lead to chaos."

"I don't see how—"

"I chose to wear the black robes because I don't believe the gods would've given people the ability to wield magic if they didn't want us to learn all we can about it and use it to the fullest. Magic has no limits, so neither should those who wield it. Some Black Robes seek to increase their power, but my own passion is the acquisition of forgotten magical knowledge. So much information was lost after the Cataclysm, and it's possible that we may never get it all back. But when I learned about Asvoria and discovered the location of her keep, I knew that I would be able to restore at least a small portion of that ancient knowledge. And when I came to believe that I could resurrect Asvoria herself . . . " Maddoc lifted his gaze from the fire and looked at the tapestry that had once held the sorceress' spirit. "I knew then that I could learn all that she knew, and I could take her knowledge to the Tower of Wayreth so that all wizards, regardless of what color robes they wore, could have access to it."

Maddoc then looked at Davyn. "That is my dream, my son. Does it seem like the dream of an evil man to you?"

"No, it's not an evil dream. But evil can result from the pursuit of such a dream."

Maddoc gave Davyn a smile that said *What a charmingly naïve statement*. "The acquisition of knowledge is an ultimate good. Imagine the secrets that must be hidden in Asvoria's mind! Imagine what could be accomplished with such knowledge, such power!"

Davyn thought of the War of the Lance, when Takhisis had attempted to take over the world. When the next battle between the forces of Light and Darkness occurred, would it be Maddoc who commanded the dark army?

"But what of the cost?" Davyn said. "For Asvoria's personality to fully live, Nearra's must die."

"I wouldn't say *die*. More like go dormant. But whatever happens to the girl, isn't the loss of one life worth the knowledge that we will gain? If Nearra could fully understand what was at stake, do you think she would hesitate to sacrifice herself for the greater good? I know you have feelings for her—"

"Not really," Davyn lied. "I mean, she's all right, but nothing special."

"Then why did you come here?" Maddoc asked. "If you no longer care for the girl, why try to rescue her?"

Davyn turned to look at Maddoc. "Because I did care for her once. And to be honest, I wanted to get back at you. You told me you were my father, but in truth, the Beast was my real father, and you were responsible for his transformation."

Maddoc paused before answering, and Davyn knew he was carefully considering his reply.

"Yes, I lied to you. But only to protect you. You were so young, and I feared you wouldn't understand. Your birth parents were my most loyal and trusted servants. I had developed a spell that would allow a person to take on the form of a powerful creature. Such an ability would be quite an advantage to a warrior. Imagine being able to turn into the Beast at will, being able to control its strength and savagery. I approached your father and told him about the spell I'd created. Since Senwyr was a ranger, I thought his affinity for animals would make him the most suitable candidate for the great gift I had to offer if he wanted it. And he did."

Davyn didn't bother to conceal the shock he felt. Could it be true? Could his father actually have *volunteered* to become the Beast?

"Your mother was against Senwyr participating in my experiment and tried to persuade us not to attempt the spell. But I was younger, and like many wizards, full of overconfidence. Your father and I went ahead with the spell, and it was a success—but only a partial one. Your father transformed into the creature that I eventually came call the Beast, but he could not control his new animalistic mind. He tried to attack me, and your mother—well, she tried to stop him and paid for it with her life. But her sacrifice bought me enough time to overcome my surprise and cast a spell to immobilize the Beast.

"I tried many times to change your father back, but I could not. And your father never transformed back into human form of his own accord. Whether because he could not or, and I think this more likely, the part of him that was the Beast wouldn't allow it. Over time, I managed to forge a relationship of sorts with the Beast, and it became one of my servants.

"But because it was my recklessness that made you an orphan, I decided to raise you as my own son, to try to make up in some small way for what I had done. I hope I wasn't too bad of a father to you."

"No. You were a good father," Davyn said. And in many ways, Maddoc had been. He'd taken care of Davyn, taught him, seen to his every need. Davyn was grateful for all that.

"I released you from the Gallery's spell because you are my son, and because of the debt I felt I owed your birth parents. I am prepared to give you one last chance, Davyn. Renounce your friends, renounce Nearra, and help me complete Asvoria's resurrection. If you do these things, I shall forget all about the events of the last year. It shall be as if they never happened. What do you say?"

Davyn was silent, thinking.

Maddoc pleaded. "After everything I've done for you, Davyn. This will be good for us. Good for Krynn."

After several moments, Davyn nodded and said, "I renounce my former companions—all of them—and I will help you obtain Asvoria's secrets."

Maddoc grinned and clapped his bony, trembling hands together. "Excellent!" Then the joy drained out of his face and his tone became deadly serious. "I need your help."

Another test, and one Davyn didn't like the sound of. "What must I do?"

Maddoc reached into a pocket of his robe and brought out a crystalline dagger.

"This is the Dagger of Ulthus. At the proper time during the rite to complete the Emergence, you must plunge it into Nearra's heart. It is a mystic blade and won't harm her physically. But it shall wound her spirit in such a way as to allow Asvoria's personality to assume control of her body. Will you do this thing for me . . . *son*?"

Davyn looked at the dagger. The firelight made the crystal seem to glow with its own internal flame.

Davyn reached out and took hold of the mystic dagger.

"I will." He slipped the blade beneath his belt.

"Oh, and Davyn? I need your assistance with one other task." Maddoc smiled. There was a hint of madness in his eyes.

22 MONSTERS AND SPIDERS

From the corner of his eye, Elidor saw Davyn vanish. One moment Davyn was running to attack the hybrid creature with the rest of them, and then the next—poof! He was gone. But Elidor didn't have time to worry about his friend's sudden disappearance.

Ordinarily, Elidor would've thrown his daggers at the creature's eyes, but since the monster had six, and he had only two knives, he wasn't sure what to do.

"Go for the legs!" Catriona shouted. "The thing can't hurt us if it can't walk!"

As the awful conglomeration drew near, Elidor feinted to the left. One of the dire wolf heads snapped at him, but the elf dodged and avoided its jaws. He darted behind the monster's front left leg and saw the bony joints were connected by leather straps and bits of wire. He slashed out with both of his knives and sliced the leather into ribbons.

The patchwork beast came crashing down heads-first, and Elidor leaped out of the way just in time to avoid being crushed. He rolled as he landed and came up on his feet. He spun around and saw Catriona jump onto the beast's back, right between the decayed dracolich wings. Unfortunately, the hide beneath Catriona was decomposed dragonskin, and her feet broke through and lodged between the creature's ribs.

"By the Oath and Measure!" Catriona swore. She struggled to free herself, but she was stuck fast. That didn't stop her, though. She began hacking away at the monster's necks with her dragon claws and blood sprayed the air.

The hybrid struggled to stand on its good front leg, and then it pushed once, twice, three times until it managed to rear back onto its hind legs. It was attempting to fling itself onto its back in order to crush the annoying pest that kept slicing away at it with her tiny metal claws.

The crowd roared its approval.

"Smash her like a bug!" a spectator shouted.

Then Elidor saw Ayanti gallop forward, Sindri still on her back, the kender's arms wrapped tight around her waist. Ayanti circled behind the beast, careful to avoid its lashing tail. She lowered her head, and when the tail swung out of the way, the centaur charged. At the last instant before collision, she launched herself into the air—Sindri letting out a exultant whoop!—and rammed her left shoulder into the base of the monster's spine.

The monster shuddered at the impact, then pitched forward and slammed onto the stone floor of the Pit. Catriona raised her dragon claws high and slammed them down into the back of the beast's ursine head. She then did the same to each of the wolf heads. When she was finished, the monster's bone legs twitched once, twice, and then fell limp. The creature was dead.

The crowd was momentarily stunned into silence by the outcome of the match, but then they gave voice to their disapproval, booing and shouting curses.

Elidor ignored them and rushed forward to see if Catriona had been injured when the monster fell.

"Are you all right?" he asked.

The red-haired warrior grimaced as she yanked one leg free, and then the other. Both were smeared with foul-smelling ooze.

"I may have to get a new pair of boots, but otherwise, I'm fine."

Ayanti trotted over carrying Sindri, the kender grinning as if he'd just had the time of his life.

"We did it," the centaur said in a tone of wonderment, as if she couldn't quite believe it. "We won!" She frowned. "Hey, where's Davyn?"

Before Elidor could tell her of their friend's strange disappearance, the skin of the patchwork monster's abdomen split open as a swordblade was thrust through from *inside* the beast.

The companions watched in horrified amazement as the blade sliced open the dead creature's gut and then withdrew. Several pairs of hands reached out and gripped the flaps of skin, and then pulled the opening wider until was large enough for a quartet of figures to step out into the open air.

One of them spoke, a kender dressed in wizard's robes of blackest night. "You know the old saying . . . "

"You might have won a single battle," continued a shaggy female centaur with wild, unkempt hair.

"But one battle . . ." added a warrior with short red hair and a black patch over her left eye.

"Isn't the war," finished an elf garbed in the finery of a Silvanesti noble.

And then the newcomers—each of whom was wearing one of the companions' faces—broke out in dark laughter, and the crowd above cheered with renewed enthusiasm.

The match, it seemed, was about to enter a second round.

Raedon's back muscles burned and his wings felt heavy as lead. No matter how hard he'd tried, he hadn't been able to break the spiders' silvery strands. To make matters worse, the spiders had started pulling him down toward them inch by inch. As tired as he was, it would only be moments before he faltered and the spiders yanked him down into the thick of their webs.

Raedon, like all dragons, could cast spells, but he was young and his magical skills were not all they could be. He needed to be able to focus his complete attention on the spellcasting for it to be successful. His current predicament wasn't exactly conducive to concentration.

Well, then, if he couldn't defeat the spiders with his magic, he'd just have to resort to a somewhat less sophisticated method.

He continued flapping to keep himself aloft and curved his long supple neck around. He took aim at several strands that were grouped together, opened his mouth, and shot out a stream of acid. The foul-smelling liquid splashed onto the threads and sizzled and hissed. Raedon grinned in triumph. While the webbing might be too strong to break easily, it wasn't resistant to a good dose of dragon acid.

But Raedon's triumph was short lived. For while it was true that the acid was eating away at the silver strands, it was doing so with agonizing slowness. Not to worry, Raedon told himself. All he needed to do was work up another blast of acid.

Unfortunately, it looked as if the ivory spiders weren't going to give him the opportunity. As if realizing their dinner was on the verge of getting away, spiders began hopping onto the strands attached to Raedon and scuttled along the silvery lines toward the dragon. Raedon didn't panic, though. Instead of shooting acid at the threads he'd hit before, he adjusted his aim, opened his mouth wider, and sprayed a large blob of acid at the oncoming spiders.

TIM WAGGONER

The spiders squealed as the acid struck them, their bodies hissing and popping as they fell to the ground.

Now *that* was more like it! It seemed the spinners of the silver silk weren't as tough as the material their bodies produced. All Raedon had to do was keep shooting acid until either the spiders let him go or they were all dead.

He prepared to unleash another acid blast, but before he could let it go, hundreds of spiders jumped onto the strands of webbing that adhered to him and began climbing upward with frightening speed. Every line attached to him—and there were at least a dozen—was completely covered with scuttling spiders. They obviously planned to overwhelm him before he could kill them all. But so many spiders were climbing the threads that there weren't enough left in the trees to keep hold of the slack they'd gathered.

The lines slipped out of spidery grips and Raedon surged forward. He knew that the strands would soon snap taught, but if he poured on the speed, when they did, some of the spiders might be shaken off. Raedon ignored the pain in his wing muscles and flapped as hard as he could. He shot forward like a crossbow bolt. If he could build up enough momentum, he might just . . . be able . . . to . . .

He felt a sudden jolt as a dozen silver lines drew taught. He wobbled and for an instant he thought he was going to lose his aerial balance and go spinning toward the ground, ivory spiders swarming all over his body.

But then the threads began to snap, one after the other, with plinking sounds that reminded Raedon of lute strings breaking. His wings felt as if they were on fire, but he didn't let up. Finally the last strand gave way and Raedon soared skyward, free at last. Raedon had a mild disposition, even for a copper dragon, but as he exulted in his escape, he let out a mighty roar.

But then he felt something tickling the tip of his tail. He glanced back and saw that the broken silver threads were still attached to his body, and they trailed along behind him like the tails of a dozen kites. Unfortunately, most of the spiders had managed to cling to the lines when they'd broken and had resumed their wire-walking act. The tickling sensation that he'd felt was the first of the spiders reaching his body. It didn't hesitate. It scuttled along his tail, onto the base of his spine, and kept going. Raedon had a good idea what its final destination was—his eyes.

He didn't know if the creatures were venomous, but if they were, their fangs must not have been capable of penetrating his copper scales, or else they'd be biting him now. But even if they weren't venomous, once they reached his soft eyes and the fleshy interior of his mouth and began biting, he would be lost.

As the first of the ivory spiders came crawling up his neck, Raedon angled his head and spit a small stream of acid at it. The spider squealed and lost its eight-legged foothold on Raedon's scales. Raedon was still flying quite fast, and the sizzling, smoking spider was caught by the wind and tumbled away toward the ground.

Raedon had no time to enjoy his modest victory. There were still far too many spiders scuttling toward his face. Raedon continued playing marksman—or marks*dragon*—picking off one spider after another with streams of acid. Sometimes he missed and acid splattered onto his scales, but without any harm to him. Like all dragons, Raedon was immune to his own breath weapon.

Flying with his head turned backward wasn't easy or comfortable, but he had no other choice if he wanted to avoid being eaten. He continue to spit acid, sometimes hitting spiders, sometimes missing. He knew he couldn't keep this up forever. His body could only produce so much acid at a time. But he thought he'd managed to get almost all the spiders. There were only one or two left.

As he concentrated on working up another stream of acid, he wondered where the ivory-hued spiders had come from. They weren't natural creatures, he was certain of that. The threads they spun were magically strong, and they moved more swiftly and operated with more intelligence than ordinary spiders. They were probably the leftover result of some wizard's experimentation, he decided. Human mages were most untidy and often left magical creatures and objects strewn about the land. Ordinarily, Raedon didn't mind all that much, for the mages' negligence often resulted in him acquiring more magic items for his hoard. But these devil-spiders were one bit of mystical refuse he could've done without.

He spit once, twice, three times, and the last of the spiders fell toward the ground, their death shrieks cut short as the acid devoured them.

Raedon turned his head forward once more and let out a sigh of relief. He still trailed half dozen silver threads, but he would worry about removing them later. He was convinced that the spider grove wasn't where Nearra had called to him from. He wasn't sure how he'd gotten detoured to the wrong place, and he didn't care. Now he knew where to go.

He angled in the direction of the large stone keep and kept flying as fast as he could, despite his tired and sore wings. If he could just keep this speed up for a little longer, he would—

A sudden sharp pain lanced through the base of Raedon's wing, and he roared in agony. It felt as if his wing was on fire, and for a moment, that's exactly what he thought had happened—that some spellcaster—human, dragon, or otherwise—had directed a firespell at him. But when he looked back, he saw no flames, only a solitary ivory spider fastened to his wing and plunging its fangs into the tender skin at the base over and over, injecting as much venom as it could.

He tried to perform a mid-air roll in order to dislodge the spider, but his left wing was starting to go numb and refused to cooperate. Raedon then shot a thin stream of acid—all he could produce at the moment—toward the spider. He missed, but the acid splashed close enough to his wing that several drops splattered onto the spider. The creature yanked its fangs out of Raedon's flesh and squealed as the drops began to eat into its body. The spider lost its hold on Raedon's wings, and the wind grabbed it and tossed it away.

Raedon was finally free of his annoying passengers, but it was too late. His wing was beginning to stiffen. If he didn't land right away, he'd soon drop out of the sky and crash to the ground.

Raedon angled downward, jaw clenched tight as he tried to maintain control of his descent. But his wing quickly became worse, until it felt as if it had turned to stone. In the end, he lost control and began spinning, slowly at first, then with increasing speed, round and round, faster and faster, as the ground rushed up to meet him.

23   Dark Reflections

Elidor couldn't believe what he was seeing. "It's like—"

"Looking into a mirror?" his counterpart finished.

"Yes." But not quite. The elf that stood in front of Elidor looked like him physically, but he wore a robe of a Silvanesti noble, the cloth so white that it almost seemed to glow, with a sky-blue sash wrapped around his waist. His blonde hair was longer than Elidor's, and was bound into a ponytail that hung down his back. The elf wore a golden scabbard at his side, the metal embossed with elf runes. He held a long rapier in his hand, the hilt made of gold as well.

Elidor's counterpart held the blade in a comfortable, easy grip, the same way Elidor would hold a throwing dagger or a lock pick, as if it were an extension of his body.

"Who are you?" Elidor demanded. "Did you have something to do with Davyn's disappearance?"

"I don't know anything about someone named Davyn," the other elf said. "As for who we are, I thought it was obvious. I'm you, and they"—he gestured with his rapier at the others who had accompanied him out of the carcass of the hybrid creature—"are them." 187

Elidor examined his doppelganger's friends. Each resembled one of Elidor's companions so closely that they might have been twins, except for some distinct and disturbing differences.

"There's some manner of dark magic at work here," Sindri said.

The black-robed kender sneered. "A brilliant observation," he said, his voice dripping with sarcasm. "You really are as stupid as you look."

"Thanks, I . . ." Sindri frowned. "Hey!"

"And you look completely ridiculous," Catriona's eye-patch wearing counterpart said to the warrior. "You're nothing but a little girl running around Solamnia playing dress-up. You're not a Solamnic Knight, and you never will be."

Aside from the eye-patch, the hard-bitten woman differed from Catriona in several ways. She wore her hair short, the cut ragged, as if she'd hacked off her hair with a dull dagger. She also bore numerous scars on her face, neck, arms, and hands. She wore a battered iron breastplate and metal vambraces with sharp spikes jutting outward. Instead of dragon claws, she was armed with a short sword, the blade nicked and scratched from use.

Catriona scowled at her other self. "And from your attitude, I'd guess you to be a warrior without honor."

The counterpart laughed. "Where we come from, there is no such thing as honor. Only kill or be killed, survive or die."

"This can't be real," Ayanti said, shaking her head in denial. "It has to be like Sindri said, magic of some sort. An illusion."

Ayanti's doppelganger—coat and hair shaggy, wild, matted with dirt and blood—lashed out with a hand whose nails were so long and sharp that they were almost claws. The nails raked Ayanti's cheek and the centaur cried out in pain.

"Did that feel like an illusion?" the wild centaur said in a guttural voice that was little more than a growl.

The other doppelgangers laughed, and above them all, the crowd of onlookers surrounding the Pit cheered.

"You hinted that you are from somewhere else," Catriona said, knuckles white from gripping her dragon claws so tightly. "Where?"

"From Solamnia, of course," the other Elidor said in a tone of contempt, as if he thought it beneath him to directly address a human. "But not *this* Solamnia."

"I don't understand," Catriona said.

"Of course you don't," the black-robed Sindri said, dark amusement in his voice. "That's because you lack even the most rudimentary scholastic training."

The real Sindri leaned close to Catriona. "That means he thinks you're stupid," he whispered.

"I *know* what it means," the warrior snapped.

Sindri's doppelganger continued. "We are from a world much like your own, save that on our world, Takhisis won the War of the Lance."

"And now the Dark Queen rules," Catriona's double said.

Sindri's eyes widened in wonder. "The four of you are really from another world? How did you get here? Can you show me the way? Can I visit your world? It must be so different from here!"

Everyone ignored Sindri, including his dark twin.

"Takhisis sent us here on a mission," the other Elidor said. "To prevent our sickeningly good counterparts—namely, you four—from interfering with Maddoc's quest to possess the power of Asvoria."

Sindri shook his head. "I don't believe you. I can't imagine anything—including Takhisis' victory—that would make me choose to wear the black robes of an evil mage. I don't believe that if any of my friends had been raised in such a hellish world that they would've grown up to become *you*. This is definitely some kind of spell, and as soon as I figure it out—"

"You'll do what?" the evil Elidor said. "Say a few magic words, wiggle your fingers in the air, and make us disappear?"

"Something like that," Sindri admitted. "Though I'm still working out the precise details."

"You'd better work fast then," the black-robed Sindri said. "It's awfully difficult to cast spells once you're dead!" The evil kender wizard gestured and a dagger composed of pure shadow appeared in his hand. He threw the shadow dagger at Sindri, but Sindri raised his hand and a multicolored circle of energy appeared in the middle of his palm. The shadow-blade sank into the rainbow swirl and vanished without harming him. The energy circle winked out and Sindri lowered his hand, grinning with pleasure.

"I did it! I stopped the shadow-dagger!"

But before Elidor or the others could react, their evil counterparts came rushing at them, and the spectators above roared their delight.

The Silvanesti Elidor swung his rapier, the thin, sharp blade making almost no sound as it sliced through the air toward the real Elidor's neck. Elidor managed to deflect the strike, but though the sword blade was as thin as paper, it hit the dagger with such force that pain blossomed in Elidor's hand, almost causing him to drop his weapon.

Elidor heard the clanging of steel as the two Catrionas crossed weapons, the whinny-shriek of the wild centaur as it attacked Ayanti, and the chanting of a dark spell as the black-robed Sindri prepared to fling a spell at the original. But then he had no more time to worry about his friends, for the Silvanesti Elidor pressed his assault.

The Silvanesti thrust his blade toward Elidor's heart, and the thief managed to turn sideways just in time to avoid being skewered. He chopped downward with one of his daggers, hoping to knock the sword out of his other self's hand, or if he was really lucky, perhaps even break his enemy's blade. But whatever metal the elven sword had been made from was too strong for Elidor to do more than leave the slightest of scratches on its surface.

The Silvanesti swung the rapier around in a wide arc in another attempt to part Elidor's head from his neck. But Elidor brought his left arm up and met the attack with one of his daggers. Again, the impact made his hand throb. However, that was far preferable to decapitation.

The Silvanesti moved with such grace, speed, and precision that it was all Elidor could do to retreat from his other's self onslaught and fight defensively, blocking and turning aside blows without being able to strike any of his own.

The Silvanesti took a swipe at Elidor's legs, but the thief jumped nimbly into the air and avoided injury. At the apex of his leap, Elidor heard Catriona cry out in pain.

He turned in her direction and saw that she was on her knees, dragon claws abandoned on the stone floor, right arm cradled against her chest. Blood poured from a ragged wound on her forearm, and the rogue Catriona stood back and grinned, the spikes on her vambrace smeared with crimson.

The rogue Catriona pressed the tip of her sword against the real Catriona's throat and a single pearl of red welled forth. Though there was fear in Catriona's eyes, she didn't lower her gaze, didn't beg for her life. She would meet her death with the same courage and dignity with which she'd attempted to live her life.

Elidor started to go to her aid, when he heard a soft swoosh of air. Fiery pain erupted in his right ear, and he felt warm blood gush down the side of his face and neck. He turned back to his attacker and the Silvanesti laughed.

"Now that I've taken the point of one of your ears, does that make you a Half-elf?"

Elidor reached up to touch his wound and found that two thirds of his ear had been cut off.

The Silvanesti Elidor's upper lip curled in disgust. "You're pathetic. What would your mother say if she could see you now? Though you are a half-breed, you were born into House Royal. If you had fully embraced the ways of the Silvanesti—as I did—you might've been accepted as one of them. But now look at you. You're a disgrace, an insult to every Silvanesti who's ever drawn breath."

Though Elidor tried to ignore his doppelganger's words, they cut deeper than any weapon forged of steel ever could. Guilt and self-loathing filled him, and he was tempted to drop his daggers and let his other self finish him off. He was a half-breed and he didn't deserve to live.

"Don't listen to him, Elidor! He's trying to trick—" Sindri's voice was suddenly cut off. Elidor turned to look at his friend and saw the kender had been caught in the grip of a giant disembodied hand formed from shadow. The black-robed Sindri looked on in cruel amusement as the little mage struggled to free himself from the enchantment to no avail. The evil kender's magic was simply too strong.

Black-robed Sindri grinned and made an exaggerated squeezing motion with his hand. In response, the giant shadow hand tightened its grip on Sindri, cutting off the kender's air.

Ayanti! Elidor thought. Perhaps she could—But then he saw her, lying on the stone floor of the Pit several yards away. The wild centaur stood over her, a forehoof planted in the middle of Ayanti's throat. All the feral creature would have to do was press down hard and Ayanti would be finished.

Catriona, Sindri, Ayanti . . . as impossible as it seemed, they had all been defeated. Only Elidor remained standing.

The crowd began chanting. "Kill him, kill him, kill him!"

The Silvanesti Elidor slowly smiled. "What do you think? Shall we give our audience what they want?" He moved the tip of his rapier in slow circles, as if to taunt Elidor further.

It's over. You might as well give up.

Elidor almost heeded the urgings of his despair. But then he thought of Davyn, who had somehow disappeared before they attacked the many-headed monster. He thought of Nearra, who might even now have had her identity overtaken by the spirit of Asvoria. He thought of his mother, Alloria of House Royal.

Most of all, he thought of his father, Matunaaga, chief of the Tribe of the One-Eyed Crow. After leaving the Sivanesti, Elidor had spent some time with his father's people, learning their ways and customs. Above all else, the Kagonesti valued personal honor—and they never gave up, no matter how hopeless the odds.

Elidor looked into the eyes of his other self and allowed his shoulders to slump.

"Very well," he said in a small defeated voice. "I surrender."

His doppelganger laughed. "Of course you do. Was there ever any doubt?" He started forward, sword tip still circling. "Now stand still, and I'll do my best to make sure this doesn't hurt." He grinned. "Much."

But before the Silvanesti Elidor could fulfill his promise, Elidor threw his knives with blurring speed. One blade flew toward the black-robed kender, while the other streaked toward the wild centaur. Both daggers pierced their targets' throats at precisely the same instant.

As the evil Sindri fell, the shadow hand gripping the true Sindri faded from existence, and the kender fell to the ground gasping for breath, but still alive. The feral centaur stumbled backward. As her dark counterpart collapsed, Ayanti got to her feet, only slightly the worse for wear.

"Blast!" the rogue Catriona swore when she saw what had happened to her companions. The real Catriona took advantage of her other self's momentary distraction to make a sweeping kick and knock the doppelganger off her feet. The rogue Catriona fell hard, slamming her head against the stone floor. She didn't get back up.

Elidor turned to his other self. The Silvanesti gaped in astonishment, unable to believe that circumstances had turned so completely against him so quickly. But he regained his composure and smiled once more.

"Well played, *Brother*. But you just threw away your weapons, while I, as you can plainly see, am still very much in possession of mine. You might have been able to save your friends, but you won't be able to save yourself!"

"Elidor!" Sindri shouted. "I think I've figured out this spell! All we have to do is close our eyes and keep them closed!"

Elidor didn't take his gaze off his other self—and especially his other self's rapier.

"Are you insane?" Elidor said. "If I close my eyes, he'll run me through!"

"Trust me!" the kender pleaded. "It's the only way!"

Elidor considered. Sindri was a kender, and he could be childlike and impulsive at times, but he was also his friend. Elidor knew Sindri would never ask him to risk his life without good reason.

He took a deep breath. "All right," he said at last. "But if I die, I'm never going to speak to you again."

Elidor closed his eyes and waited to feel the Silvanesti's rapier pierce his heart.

TIM WAGGONER

24   THE CHAMBER OF HOURS

Maddoc leaned on Davyn for support as they walked down the corridor. The lantern Davyn held did little to dispel the hallway's gloom.

"I don't think I've ever been on this level of the keep before," Davyn said.

"You haven't," Maddoc confirmed. "I usually leave the entrance to this level sealed."

"For my own safety?" Davyn asked. "When I was a child, that's what you always told me whenever I asked about a locked door or a sealed-off level."

"And with good reason," Maddoc said. "A sorceress' stronghold contains all manner of dangers for a curious little boy." He patted Davyn's arm. "But you're a man now, my son, or close enough to make little difference. And tonight I have need of a very special room that lies on this level.

"I did not anticipate that you and your companions would come to Cairngorn Keep of your own accord. I'd hoped to have more time to recover my strength after Shaera's death before I next attempted to gain control of Asvoria. Still, one shouldn't complain when Fortune smiles upon one, yes? But if I am to 195 perform the Rite of Emergence tonight then I'm going to need to build up my mystical strength fast."

"But how?" Davyn asked. An awful thought occurred to him. "Do you plan to . . . to borrow the strength of another?"

"Worried that I released you from the Gallery's enchantment merely to be a magical snack?" Maddoc chuckled. "Though I'll admit to knowing how to work spells designed to transfer the life energy of one being to another, I'd never do such a thing to you, my son. Besides, the kind of energy I need isn't the sort that can be found in a normal mortal. I need the kind of power that can only be retrieved from another mage."

Sindri? Davyn thought. Was Maddoc planning to steal the life force of the little wizard? Was Maddoc even aware of Sindri's growing powers?

As if reading Davyn's mind, Maddoc said, "And I don't mean the kender who styles himself as a magic-user. A telekinetic ring and a penchant for stealing small objects hardly adds up to mystical might."

"Then who?" Davyn asked. "The only other mage in the keep is Asvoria, and if you drain her power, she'll die, and her magical knowledge will be lost to you forever."

"True, but you're forgetting something, my boy. There's one other wizard inhabiting the keep at this moment."

Davyn frowned in confusion. "Who?"

Maddoc smiled enigmatically. "Me."

They continued walking for several more minutes. Maddoc moved so slowly, at times it felt to Davyn as if they were standing still. But eventually they came to a large oak door.

"This is it," the wizard pronounced. "The Chamber of Hours." He turned to look at Davyn, his expression deadly serious. "Once we enter, I require only that you keep the lantern burning and assist me physically should my body weaken. But I warn you:

where the Gallery is a place of illusion, this is a place of Time—of yesterdays and tomorrows, of pasts that never were and futures that may or may not come to pass. It is disorienting, even to one schooled in the mystic arts. Try your best not to become entangled in anything you see or hear inside. But make no mistake. Unlike the Gallery, the visions in the Chamber can take on physical reality at times, which makes them extremely dangerous. Do you understand me?"

Davyn didn't, but he nodded anyway.

"Good. Then let us proceed."

There was no knob or handle on the door. Maddoc pressed his hand flat against the wood and whispered a few words of magic. The door swung open without a sound.

Since he held the lantern, Davyn started forward, but Maddoc stopped him.

"Best to let me enter first. Just in case."

Davyn wasn't about to argue the point. Maddoc shuffled past him and Davyn hesitated a moment before following.

Unlike other rooms in the keep, the walls and floor of this chamber were made of polished white marble, and the shiny surface reflected and intensified the lantern light. Davyn squinted and averted his eyes from the glare. He blinked several times to adjust his vision and then examined the room. The Chamber of Hours was aptly named, for the walls were lined with time-keeping devices of all sorts: sundials, hour glasses, water clocks, counterweight clocks, there was even a large black globe covered with pinpoints of silver.

Davyn pointed at the globe. "What's that?"

Maddoc opened his mouth to answer, but instead of words, what came out was a low-pitched groaning sound unlike anything Davyn had ever heard before.

"I don't understand. Is something wrong?"

197

Maddoc frowned so slowly that Davyn had to watch closely to detect the movement of his brow. The wizard then reached a hand toward Davyn, the motion also taking a ridiculously long time, as if the wizard was moving through thick molasses. Finally, after what seemed like several minutes, Maddoc's fingers came in contact with Davyn's arm, and suddenly the wizard was moving and speaking normally again.

"Forgive me, Davyn. I should've been more careful to remain in close contact with you. Time flows quite differently in this room, and navigating in here can be tricky."

"You mean that strange noise you were making—"

"Was the sound of my voice, but slowed down many times to your ears. I heard your question and started to tell you that the globe is a magical device for measuring and predicting the movements of the stars, but I barely got out the first syllable before we were caught in different time streams. But as long as we remain in close proximity to one another, our personal time senses should remain synchronized."

"Uh, good." Davyn said. He pointed to a large symbol carved into the marble floor. "What's that? It looks like a sideways figure . . . like the symbol of Mishakal, except it's not blue."

Maddoc laughed. "There are no symbols of the goddess in this keep! This, my son, is an ancient representation of the concept of infinity," the wizard explained. "And it is the center of the Chamber's power, the power to manipulate Time itself."

Davyn looked at the symbol. "You have all these wonders are your disposal—the paintings in the Gallery, this chamber—why do you need to resurrect Asvoria at all? It seems that by taking over her keep, you've inherited so many of her secrets already."

"Having access to some of Asvoria's playthings is not the same as fully understanding them," Maddoc said, "let alone being able to create such wonders myself. I understand only a fraction of the magic this room is capable of. I only hope that fraction will be enough to help to succeed in what I am about to attempt. If not . . ."

"You won't have the mystic strength to complete the Rite of Emergence?" Davyn asked.

"Yes, but that will be beside the point, for if I fail, there's an excellent chance that neither of us will leave this chamber alive."

Davyn grimaced. "Thanks for trying to bolster my spirits," he said sarcastically.

Maddoc chuckled, then said, "Prepare." The wizard began reciting an incantation in an ancient language. Davyn had heard Maddoc cast many spells over the years, but this was different. Sometimes his chanting proceeded at normal speed, sometimes it was slow and drawn out, and other times the words flew out of the wizard's mouth in a high-pitched chatter, making him sound like a black-robed chipmunk. Davyn, mindful of what Maddoc had requested, held the lantern steady and kept his other hand on Maddoc's shoulder, prepared to lend the mage physical support should he require it.

In response to the wizard's incantation, the infinity sign began to glow with a soft yellow light. And then, though Davyn had been sure the symbol was carved into the marble floor, the infinity sign began to rise into the air. When it was at eye level, it tilted toward them ninety degrees, and then stopped. It now looked as if the infinity sign had been drawn into the air with lines of glowing fire.

Maddoc continued chanting and now added complex hand gestures to the spell. The symbol's glowing outline slowly started to fill in with yellow energy. As this happened, Davyn became aware of the sounds of the clocks in the room—the tic-toc, tic-toc; the soft rushing-gurgles of the water clocks; the gentle shhhhhhh of sand flowing through narrow bottlenecks of hour glasses; and even the noiseless movement of shadows across the faces of sundials. He heard them all, and as the sounds continued to increase in volume, the infinity symbol's energy built up until it was blazing like two miniature suns hovering one next to the other.

Maddoc stopped chanting and his hands fell limply to his sides. His knees began to buckle, but Davyn caught him before he could collapse, and with Davyn's help, the wizard remained standing.

"We did it," Maddoc wheezed. "Though it was a near thing toward the end."

We did it. Maddoc had never referred to his son as if he were a partner—an *equal*—before. It surprised, confused, and pleased Davyn all at once.

"Now what?" Davyn asked, speaking in a hushed, respectful voice, for he realized that he stood within the presence of Time itself.

"We begin seeking the proper instant in all the countless moments of eternity."

Maddoc waved his hand weakly, and twin images appeared within the glowing depths of the infinity sign. They were scenes of Maddoc, not as he was now, but before the death of Shaera, strong and healthy. The wizard stood in the courtyard of Cairngorn Keep, holding out a baby bird for a little brown-headed boy to examine.

With a start, Davyn realized that the little boy was he. "This is an image of the past, isn't it? I remember this day. I found a dead baby bird and brought it to you so you could fix if with your magic, and you did. You brought it back to life."

"That's what I allowed you to believe," Maddoc said. "I could not heal the bird's injuries, but I could reanimate the corpse. The body was fresh, and you were young enough not to notice the difference. I disposed of the undead creature later, when you'd gone off to play elsewhere."

TIM WAGGONER

Davyn was appalled to learn the truth behind one of his most treasured childhood memories. "But why would you deceive me like that?"

Maddoc smiled. "Because I could not stand to see you so sad. Nor could I bring myself to disappoint you when you came seeking my help." The wizard waved his hand and the twin images blurred and faded. "But the past is of no use to us right now. We seek the future."

Maddoc gestured once more, and this time the infinity symbol displayed twin scenes of Maddoc with hair that was an equal blend of black and gray. He stood tall, straight, and steady. Clearly, in this future time he had recovered from the debilitating aftereffects of his familiar's death.

"Excellent," Maddoc said. "This should do nicely."

Davyn peered closely at the image, trying to determine the location of the future Maddoc, and perhaps by so doing detect some clues as to precisely how far into the future they were gazing. The background was fuzzy but Davyn thought the older Maddoc was surrounded by crystalline structures of some sort. But as the ranger stared, he realized that those weren't mere crystals. They were gigantic diamonds, the smallest of which was easily twice the size of an adult . The longer Davyn watched, the more clear the setting became, until he could make out several still forms lying near Maddoc's feet. He recognized them—Catriona, Elidor, Sindri—but whether they were unconscious or dead, he couldn't tell.

As the images continued to resolve, two other figures were revealed standing in front of Maddoc and confronting him. One was Davyn himself, sporting a close-cropped beard and holding a bow, arrow nocked and trained on Maddoc.

The other was Nearra. She wore a long white gown embroidered with intricate golden stitchery. Around her neck hung a medallion, and in her hand she held a silver sword. Davyn remembered seeing both objects depicted in the tapestry of Asvoria.

"What's happening?" Davyn asked.

"Pay the scene no mind," Maddoc said, a bit too casually, Davyn thought.

"This is but one future, a potentiality that may or may not occur. But it shall nevertheless serve our purposes well enough."

"And what purpose is that?" Davyn asked.

"I need strength for tonight," Maddoc said. "Since I don't have enough of my own, I'm forced to borrow some. And who better to take it from than myself?" Saying this, Maddoc reached out and plunged his hand into one of the images of his future self.

The Maddoc-to-be stiffened and opened his mouth in a soundless scream. He shuddered, as if gripped by a sudden blast of arctic wind. As Davyn watched, the last remnants of black faded from the hair of his father's future self, and his skin grew wrinkled and seemed to draw tight against the bone, as if every ounce of life was being drained out of him.

The Maddoc-to-be slumped to the ground, and then with a final blinding burst of light, the infinity symbol vanished. When Davyn was able to open his eyes once more, he saw that the symbol was again engraved in the marble floor and its outline no longer glowed.

He turned to Maddoc, unable to believe what he had just witnessed.

"You killed yourself. The you of tomorrow, I mean. You drained all his energy until he died."

Though the current Maddoc's appearance had not returned to normal, his gaze was clearer, his voice stronger, his hands no longer shook, and he shrugged off Davyn's grip. He no longer needed his aid to stand.

"As I said, that was but a potential future," the wizard explained. "It may never come to pass, in which case, the Maddoc I shall someday become will never have to fear being preyed upon by his younger self."

Davyn frowned. "But if that future never happens, then how can you—the Maddoc standing next to me right now—have restored yourself with the life energy of a man who will never exist?"

Maddoc smiled. "It's far too complex to explain in detail. In fact, it even makes *my* head hurt trying to work out all the permutations and implications. Suffice it to say that I am now once more strong enough to conduct the Rite of Emergence." The wizard paused. "And even if this future *does* come to pass and I do perish at the hands of my younger self, it will be worth it to finally acquire Asvoria's secrets."

"Worth your life?" Davyn asked.

Maddoc gazed intensely into Davyn's eyes. "Power—true power—is worth any price." Then the wizard clapped him on the back.

"Let us go. We need to finish a few more tasks before we can begin the Rite of Emergence."

Maddoc started toward the chamber door, and Davyn followed, fully understanding him for the first time in his life.

25   FINAL PREPARATIONS

Davyn stood atop the main tower of Cairn-gorn Keep. It was like a small courtyard. The surface was paved with smooth stone and was about thirty feet in diameter. In the center of the tower roof, four burning braziers, one for each point of the compass, surrounded a table that had been draped with black velvet. Slits had been made in the cloth so that leather straps could fit through. Looking at those straps and knowing they were intended to hold Nearra down during the ceremony made Davyn feel ill.

Maddoc stood a few feet away, examining the sky with an instrument that looked like a sailor's astrolabe, but with more gears and eyepieces.

"The moons are in more favorable positions than I expected," he said. "Not perfect, of course, but I think I can predict a successful outcome for tonight's experiment."

The excitement in Maddoc's voice both angered and sickened Davyn, but he held his tongue. He'd spent the time since their little father-and-son chat helping Maddoc prepare for the rite of Emergence. A small wooden table held numerous mystical tools and spell ingredients. Davyn had no idea what most of them were 205 for, but he'd arranged them exactly to Maddoc's specifications. Close to the head of the velvet-cloaked table rested a stand that held a large spellbook. This was Maddoc's personal spellbook, the one where he recorded the enchantments that he developed. The book was open to the page that contained the instructions for the Rite of Emergence. When Maddoc finished taking his readings of the heavens, he placed the instrument back on the equipment table, then shuffled over to the book to review the rite, which he'd already done a half dozen times, at least.

Close to the edge of the tower's roof, just beyond the braziers' light, crouched the collection of bones, wire, and leather that made up the skeletal griffin. The creature was completely still, but Davyn knew that it would spring to undead life at a single word from Maddoc.

Drefan, Fyren, and Gifre sat cross-legged on the roof close to the entrance to the stairs leading down into the tower. The goblins were playing grue bones and laughing and cursing as they won or lost.

Tucked beneath Davyn's belt was the Dagger of Ulthus, the crystalline knife that Maddoc had given him, the one he was supposed to stab Nearra with at the proper moment during the rite. Though Maddoc had assured him that the mystic blade wouldn't harm Nearra physically, he couldn't stop thinking about how the dagger was supposed to wound her spiritually. That seemed just as bad to him, if not worse.

As he watched Maddoc consult his spell book, Davyn debated what he should do. He could try to grab the book and throw it into one of the braziers. But while there was a good chance Maddoc would be distracted enough by his preparations for Davyn to take him by surprise, he doubted the goblins or the griffin would be caught unawares. He wouldn't be able to get hold of the book before they stopped him. When the ceremony was well underway,

Davyn could stab Maddoc with the Dagger of Ulthus. He didn't know if the blade would deliver a physical wound or a spiritual one, but either way, Maddoc would be finished.

Maddoc looked up from his spell book and turned to the goblins.

"Go tell Oddvar to bring the girl. It's time."

The goblins grumbled at having their game interrupted, but they collected their grue bones and headed down the stairs. Davyn's fingers stroked the hilt of the crystalline blade as he continued to struggle with his confusion and doubts.

There was a knock at the door, making Oddvar jump. He cursed himself for a fool and was glad that no one had been around to see him. He glanced at Nearra's sleeping form.

"It's us," Drefan said. "Maddoc told us to tell you that it's time to bring the girl."

Though the goblin's voice was muffled by the closed door, it was still too loud. Oddvar knew that Maddoc's sleep spell would hold Nearra in slumber until someone shook her or the wizard lifted it, but Drefan's volume bothered him just the same.

Oddvar walked to the door, opened it, and put a stubby finger to his lips.

"Quiet!" he hissed. "Maddoc wants her to stay asleep throughout the ceremony."

Drefan peered past Oddvar's shoulder. "Looks like she's still asleep to me."

Oddvar sighed. "Just do your best to be silent, all right?"

The three goblins nodded, but Oddvar knew they'd forget within moments.

"Have the three of you remained together since last I saw you?"

The shapechanger hasn't replaced any of us, if that's what you're asking," Drefan said.

Oddvar examined the three goblins. None had blue eyes.

"Very well. Let us proceed."

Drefan nodded toward Maddoc's bed. "Do you want us to carry her?"

Oddvar could've managed the job himself, even though Theiwar were not as strong as other dwarf clans. Still, carrying the girl was a servant's task, and while Oddvar was Maddoc's servant, the goblins were his.

"You three do it. But see that you don't jostle her."

Drefan nodded in that vague way of his. The three goblins approached the bed carefully and working in unison lifted Nearra without so much as causing her to stir. They slowly walked her over to Oddvar, and he nodded his approval. Perhaps these three idiots were going to get something right for a change.

"Let's go. And keep a sharp lookout for the shapeshifter. It's bound to try and rescue Asvoria before this is all over."

And then, with Oddvar leading, they began a slow procession down the halls of Cairngorn Keep. If anyone had been present, they might've thought they were witnessing a funeral march, so still and quiet was Nearra.

Someone *was* present, clinging to the ceiling in the form of a tiny mite. As Oddvar and the goblins passed beneath it, the mite released its grip on the ceiling and drifted down through the air like a mote of dust to land on Nearra's shoulder. The mite then scuttled quickly up her neck, over her face, and burrowed into her blonde hair. There, it would wait until the time came to act.

Elidor opened his eyes and found himself staring at a painting. It was an image of the Pit, bandits and mercenaries cheering around the edges, and down inside, the split-open carcass of the hybrid monstrosity. Not far from the beast's corpse lay three other bodies—a black-robed kender, a shaggy centaur, and a red-haired warrior with an eye patch. Standing in the midst of all this death was an elf wearing a white robe with a blue sash around the waist. His rapier dangled useless at his side, and his head was bowed in defeat.

As Elidor watched, the image faded until the painting was nothing but a blank canvas. He turned to see Catriona, Sindri, and Ayanti standing before similar paintings, each one just as blank as his. But he knew that moments ago they'd all depicted the same scene.

"Is everyone all right?" Elidor asked.

Catriona nodded. "Other than feeling a little fuzzy-headed, I'm fine."

"Same here," Ayanti echoed. "Though I doubt I'll ever forget this experience." She shuddered. "What a nightmare!"

"That's exactly what it was," Sindri said from his seat on the centaur's back. "A nightmare that we all shared. This place is a trap created by Asvoria. When we first entered the room the paintings were blank. But when the door closed, pictures appeared on them."

There was something familiar about what Sindri said. Elidor had a vague memory of running down a stone hallway. They'd been chasing someone. They'd come to a room with a door that was partially open. Davyn rushed in, they'd followed and—

"I remember now," the elf said. "So the Pit, that hideous creature, our evil selves were just some sort of dream?"

Sindri nodded. "Whoever is in the presence of a painting experiences a scenario based on his or her greatest fear. The illusion continues as long as you look at the paintings."

"So when you told us to close our eyes in the dream," Catriona began.

"We did so in the real world," Ayanti went on, "and broke the spell!"

"That's right," the kender said.

"You said this place creates nightmares based on people's greatest fears," Catriona said. "I understand why we would all imagine illusions of the Pit and the monster. They're both based on recent enough experiences to be fresh in our minds. But why did we imagine those evil versions of ourselves?"

Elidor shrugged. "It's always difficult to face the darker aspects of one's own self, and even more difficult to conquer them."

"And our counterparts said they came from a world where Takhisis ruled," Sindri said. "Who could imagine a worse nightmare than that?"

Sindri then swayed suddenly, and Elidor grabbed his friend by the elbow to keep him from falling off Ayanti's back.

"What's wrong?" the elf asked, concerned.

"Nothing." Sindri gave Elidor a weak smile. "I'm just weary from using my magic to determine the true nature of this chamber's power. But I'm not as tired as the last time I used my power. I'm not sure, but I think it's getting easier. I should be fine before long."

Catriona looked around. "Hey, where's Davyn?"

"He disappeared from the nightmare," Elidor said. "Just as we were about to attack the monster."

"I noticed at the time," Catriona said, "but we were so busy trying to stay alive that I didn't say anything. Just because he disappeared from the dream-Pit doesn't mean he should've also vanished from this chamber, does it?"

"It's hard to know for sure," Sindri said, "but I'd guess that Davyn somehow broke the chamber's enchantment—or had it broken for him—and then left the room."

Catriona shook her head. "If Davyn got free of the spell, he wouldn't have left us here. He'd have tried to break the enchantment for the rest of us."

"Unless he couldn't," Ayanti said.

"Or someone wouldn't let him," Elidor added, "someone like Maddoc, for instance."

"So now we have two friends to rescue instead of just one," Catriona said.

"We have to find him," Elidor said. "He knows the keep better than any of us. If we're to have any hope of rescuing—" But the elf was cut off by a sudden pounding at the door.

The companions looked at one another.

"Should we open it?" Ayanti whispered.

"We can't stay in here," Catriona said. "The room's enchantment might activate again and ensnare us again."

The pounding kept up, growing louder with each blow.

"We don't have to worry about the room," Sindri said. "The spell won't start up until the door is opened once more. But now that we know the room's secret, we're immune to its effect."

More pounding, louder yet.

"Maybe it's Davyn," Ayanti said hopefully.

"Maybe," Elidor said. But the blows didn't sound to his elf ears as if Davyn were making them. The rhythm was wrong, and it was too intense, as if someone wanted to knock the door down.

"The door won't open from the outside as long as anyone is inside," Sindri said. "Not unless they know the proper command phrase."

"Then we know it's not Maddoc," Catriona said. "He'd surely know such a phrase."

"We can open the door from this side any time we want," Sindri said.

The pounding came nonstop now, in rapid rhythm as if someone were playing the door like a drum. Pound-pound-pound-pound-pound-pound!

"This room is a magical trap, right?" Elidor said. "Then maybe we should put it to good use."

Shiriki watched as her cousin slammed his first against the door over and over.

"It's locked, Kuruk. You might as well face it. We're not going to get in."

Kuruk ignored her and continued pounding.

Shiriki was beginning to worry. Actually, she'd been worrying since Kuruk had collapsed in the cavern. He'd been acting strange. At first she'd attributed his behavior to the wounds he'd suffered. He was far more quiet than usual, and he didn't look at her when she spoke to him. And when he did speak, his voice was flat and emotionless.

And there were other things. He didn't seem to blink anymore, and he moved differently, not with the easy grace of an elf, but with a stiff awkwardness, as if he'd forgotten how to use his body, or was still learning. And then there was the cold. It radiated from him in waves so intense that Shiriki couldn't stand to be too close to him.

He had led them from the cavern, through a tunnel, and up a hidden set of stairs until they had found their way into the main tower of Cairngorn Keep. Now he had brought them here, to this door, though he hadn't said why or what was so important about it. Given all that, she was beginning to have disturbing thoughts. Perhaps this wasn't her cousin after all. Perhaps something had gotten into him inside the cavern. Something bad.

She decided to try reaching him one last time. "What's so important about this door, Kuruk?"

"It's in there. I can *feel* it!"

The emotion in his voice—longing mixed with impatient fury—startled her. "*What* is?"

"The Daystar! I must retrieve it!"

She had no idea what he was talking about and she didn't care. She grabbed him by the shoulder, intending to spin him around to face her. But she gasped as her flesh came in contact with his body. It was like touching a block of ice.

She was about to yank her hand away when the door suddenly opened and Kuruk rushed inside. She stumbled forward, though she would've remained outside if someone hadn't grabbed her arm and pulled her in. She glimpsed a blur of faces—Elidor and his companions—and then she saw the paintings on the walls. One of them in particular caught her attention, and she felt as if it were drawing her toward it, grabbing hold of her, and pulling her in.

Kuruk and Shiriki stood immobile, side-by-side, each facing a different painting. Kuruk's now showed a scene of a cavern much like the one they had passed through on their way into the keep, while Shiriki's displayed a vast battlefield strewn with thousands of dead warriors. Elidor wondered what nightmares the two Kagonesti were now experiencing, but he decided he really didn't want to know.

"It worked!" Ayanti said.

Elidor nodded, but he felt little satisfaction upon seeing Shiriki trapped this way. He knew she was evil, but he couldn't help thinking about the way her lips had felt pressed against his.

Catriona tugged at his elbow. "We should leave."

"Yes, of course."

They turned to go, leaving Kuruk and Shiriki to whatever dark dreams their own minds had conjured. But as they were filing into the hallway, Sindri's eyes went wide. And did the whites have a touch of rainbow colors to them for an instant? Elidor thought they might've.

"Oh no!" Sindri said.

"What's wrong?" Elidor asked.

"They've started. I can sense it!"

"Started what?" Catriona demanded.

"The Rite of Emergence," Sindri said in a small, frightened voice.

26   The Rite Begins

Raedon landed and grimaced as the impact sent a jolt of pain through his swollen, but unfortunately no longer numb, wing. He bent down, coiled his leg muscles and leaped into the air once more. When he was at the highest point of his jump, he spread his wings, held them straight out from his body, and glided.

Even though copper dragons could leap long distances, Raedon knew he needed to reach the stone keep as quickly as possible and he couldn't do so simply by jumping. But he couldn't fly with injured wing, so he was hopping and gliding. It wasn't easy with his wing the way it was, but it was the best he could do. Yet he feared it wouldn't be enough.

As he began to descend, he caught a glimpse of a dark tower in the distance. Orange light flickered at the top. Raedon wasn't certain what the flames were for, but the sight of them made his dragon blood run cold. He couldn't escape the feeling that whatever the fire's purpose, it was a signal that Nearra was almost out of time. He prayed to Paladine, lord of all Good dragons, that he would arrive before it was too late.

He hit the ground, and once again launched himself into the air.

Shiriki stood upon a cold barren plain. The ground was littered with the bodies of slain warriors. The dead stretched in every direction as far as she could see. There were so many that she wondered if the entire surface of Krynn was covered with corpses. The sky was black and starless, though somehow there was still enough light to see by. The air was still and stagnant, heavy with the thick stench of death.

Most of Ansalon's races were represented in the grisly display that surrounded her: elves, dwarves, humans, goblins, ogres, and—most surprising of all—draconians. Shiriki hadn't seen any of the humanoid dragons since the War of the Lance. She'd come to believe that they had all died in battle.

Most of them did.

The voice seemed to echo throughout the world. Shiriki covered her ears as the sound cut through her like cold steel.

So many draconians are here because this is the place where all who fail me are destined to come. These are the Plains of Desolation.

Shiriki experienced a terror beyond anything she'd ever known. Though she had never heard this voice, she knew who it belonged to—her Dark Queen, the goddess Takhisis.

Shiriki fell to her knees and touched her head to the ground.

"Forgive me, my mistress!" she wailed. She had no idea what she had done to merit Takhisis' displeasure, and she didn't care. All Shiriki wanted was to placate the Dark Queen before she visited deadly wrath upon her.

There is no forgiveness for one such as you. You fought in my name during the last great war, but when it became clear that our side was going to lose, both you and your cousin deserted. You told yourselves that you were merely retreating in hope of living to fight another day. But the simple truth is that neither of you wished to die.

Shiriki wanted to deny it, wanted to make excuses, but she knew it wouldn't do any good. Takhisis could see the truth in her soul.

"Yes," she whispered.

At least you show some measure of dignity. But don't imagine for a moment that it will save you. For deserting my army, I sentence you to eternal life here, in a world inhabited by only the dead. You shall not die of hunger or thirst, nor shall you die of age or even by your own hand. Only I can release you from your eternal torment, and though you beg for mercy until the end of Time itself, I shall never let you die.

Shiriki began to sob, but the sound of her crying was drowned out by Takhisis' dark laughter. But then she felt a cold hand upon her shoulder. She lifted her head.

Shiriki found herself looking into her cousin's unblinking eyes. She was back in the room, the one with the paintings, except they were all blank now.

She looked back to Kuruk, wishing he would remove his hand. It felt as if her shoulder were freezing solid.

"What happened?" she asked.

"We were caught in the Gallery's enchantment," he said in his cold, flat voice. "But the Gallery recognized me and let us both go."

Shiriki frowned. "What are you talking about? Recognized you how?"

"We serve the same mistress," he said.

For some reason, Shiriki didn't think that he was referring to Takhisis. But before she could ask any more questions, he said, "We must go. If we are to retrieve the Daystar and—"

He stopped speaking and cocked his head, as if listening to a voice only he could hear. He smiled then, but it wasn't Kuruk's smile. It was a bloodless smile, a viper's smile. "And be present during my mistress' rebirth," he finished.

Shiriki stepped back from Kuruk, or rather, from the thing that wore his form, for she was now convinced that her cousin was truly dead.

"Go on without me," she said. "I've had enough of—"

His hand shot out fast as a striking serpent and gripped her wrist in an iron band of cold. Shiriki struggled to pull free but his grip was unbreakable. With her free hand, she drew a dagger from her belt and plunged it into the base of his throat. The blade slid into the flesh easily, but no blood welled forth.

"Kuruk" didn't react to the wound. He continued to hold onto her wrist with one hand as he removed the dagger from his throat and handed it back to her with the other.

"You'd best hold onto this. You'll have need of it before this night is over."

And then he headed for the door, pulling Shiriki along after him.

Davyn stood next to the table where Nearra lay sleeping, held down by leather straps over her neck, chest, and legs. He trembled, and not because the air was cool this spring night. He held the Dagger of Ulthus in a nervous, sweaty grip as he listened to Maddoc begin the chant that initiated the Rite of Emergence.

"Herthen, simaris, xanthu, olom, ressik, maganti . . ."

The words meant nothing to Davyn, but they struck his ears like liquid fire. Maddoc's face remained impassive as he chanted the words to the spell, but his eyes gleamed in the light from the burning braziers. This was the moment he had worked so many long years for.

Oddvar stood next to the equipment table watching and ready to hand his master whatever instrument he might need. The goblins stood back, weapons drawn in case of trouble. Earlier,

Maddoc had commanded the skeletal griffin to take to the air, and the undead creature now flew above them in slow circles, guarding the tower-top. Maddoc was taking no chances.

"*Parthaquon, vermnassis, yuggonda, lydex, oosensha . . .*"

Davyn gripped the crystalline dagger tighter. He wasn't sure precisely when it would be time for his part in the ritual. He only knew that Maddoc would point at him when he was supposed to act and that it would be soon.

Davyn looked down at Nearra to see if the spell was having any effect on her, but from all appearances, she was sleeping comfortably and completely unaware of what was happening. Davyn was glad for that small mercy. At least she didn't have to lie there awake and afraid while the rite took place.

Maddoc continued chanting, but he glanced up from his spell-book and looked at Davyn, as if to say, *Get ready.*

Davyn nodded and lifted the dagger. This is it, he thought. Paladine guide my hand.

Maddoc's voice rose in volume and then he stabbed a finger in Davyn's direction. Davyn raised the dagger high over his head—

"Stop!"

Everyone turned toward the entrance to the stairs. Catriona, Elidor, Sindri, and Ayanti had somehow escaped the Gallery of Despair and, like all good heroes, had arrived at just the right moment.

Maddoc's face showed surprise and anger, but his chanting didn't slacken. He pointed to Davyn once more, the gesture's meaning unmistakable. *Do it now!*

Davyn flipped the dagger so that he held it point up, drew his hand back, and hurled the crystal blade toward Maddoc with all this strength. "This is for my birth parents," he said. The dagger streaked through the air and plunged into Maddoc's chest.

The chanting stopped and everything was quiet for several long moments. The only sound was the pop and crackle of the brazier fires and the soft flapping of the skeletal griffin's leather wings.

Then Maddoc did something that Davyn didn't expect. He laughed. The wizard reached up and plucked the dagger from his chest. The blade was clean—no blood.

"There is no Dagger of Ulthus," Maddoc said. "It was nothing but an illusion I conjured." As he spoke these words, the crystalline dagger diffused like fog and faded from existence. "I told you I was going to give you a last chance to prove yourself loyal to me."

"It was another test," Davyn said bitterly.

"Of course it was. And you failed. If you'd stabbed Nearra, nothing would've happened to her, but I would've known you were truly my son." A note of sadness crept into the wizard's voice. "But you aren't, are you? You're nothing by an ungrateful brat who's going to die alongside his pathetic friends."

"You can't complete the rite now," Davyn said, ignoring how much Maddoc's words hurt. "The spell was interrupted, and you can't start it again until you memorize the beginning again."

"That would be true," Maddoc allowed, "*if* I had actually begun the Rite of Emergence. What you heard me chanting was nothing more than a minor spell for afflicting an enemy with foot fungus. I'll begin the actual rite now, while my servants slay you all. Farewell, Davyn. Go to your grave knowing that you lost and Nearra's body will soon belong to Asvoria and thereafter Asvoria will belong to me."

Maddoc turned to Oddvar. "Kill them," he ordered.

"Attack!" Oddvar shouted. The Theiwar drew a poison-coated dagger and ran toward Davyn while the three goblin mercenaries went after the others.

Maddoc flipped to another section of his spellbook and began chanting.

"*Reggus, candanta, tremulkulon, morr . . .*"

Davyn kept one eye on the approaching dwarf as he grabbed Nearra's shoulders and shook her.

"Wake up!" he shouted in her ear. "You have to wake up *now!*"

But before he could tell whether or not he'd succeeded, Oddvar was upon him, and Davyn—weaponless—turned to meet the dark dwarf's attack.

27

EMERGENCE

Nearra opened her eyes and saw stars. She started to smile in appreciation of the lovely night when the harsh sounds of battle—sounds she'd become all too accustomed to in the last year—registered on her consciousness. Alarmed, she came fully awake and tried to sit up, but she couldn't move. She was bound to a table by leather straps. She wasn't completely immobilized, though. She could move her head and turned to see what was happening.

Only a few feet away, Davyn was doing his best to keep out of range as Oddvar slashed at him with a poison-coated dagger. Davyn's hands were empty. It appeared he had no weapons. Farther away, Catriona, Elidor, and Ayanti were fighting Drefan, Fyren, and Gifre. Sindri sat upon the centaur's back, holding onto her waist as she fought.

Along with the battle-sounds of clashing steel and harsh breathing, Nearra heard chanting in an alien tongue. She turned her head the other way and saw Maddoc positioned before an open book resting atop a wooden stand. As he chanted, Nearra could feel the power in the words reaching toward her, flowing over her, engulfing her, suffusing not just her body but her very essence. With a stab of horror, she realized what was happening. Maddoc was conducting the spell that would finally give Asvoria control of her body. Nearra didn't want to lose her body, didn't want to become nothing but a spirit unable to affect or interact with the physical world.

But more than that, she didn't want Maddoc to gain control of Asvoria and use the sorceress' knowledge of ancient magic to increase his own power. She had to do something, anything to disrupt the ceremony.

She pushed against her restraints, but they didn't give so much as an inch. She wasn't going to be able to escape that way.

"Maddoc!" she shouted. "You can't do this! Asvoria's too powerful—you'll never be able to control her!"

But Maddoc ignored her. He continued chanting and reached out toward a table full of strange objects. He picked up a small tuning fork and tapped it against his hand three times fast, three times slow, then put it back down. He lifted a piece of knotted silk rope and slowly untied the knot as he continued to chant.

Nearra looked away from the black-robed mage. He was too involved in the ritual for her to stop him by yelling. She looked to her friends for aid, but they were all too busy fighting to help her. All save Sindri.

"Sindri! Help me!"

The kender turned his head in her direction acknowledging her. He continued holding onto Ayanti's waist with one hand while he lifted the other and stretched it toward Nearra. She expected him to attempt to use his telekinesis to undo the straps, but she was surprised to see multicolored tendrils of mist emanate from his fingers. What in Paladine's name were those things?

But before the tendrils had reached halfway to her, Kuruk and Shiriki burst through the doorway to the stairs. What were they doing here?

TIM WAGGONER

Kuruk released his cousin and moved with a stiff, awkward gait toward Sindri.

"Look out!" Nearra cried, but before the kender could do anything, Kuruk grabbed hold of Sindri and yanked him from Ayanti's back. The tendrils of mystic energy winked out as the elf slammed Sindri to the tower roof and began rummaging around in the kender's cape. Shiriki just stood and watched with an expression of disgust and fear.

Nearra saw Kuruk stand and hold up a sun-shaped medallion in triumph. Nearra felt her lips tingle, and then her mouth began to speak, but what came out weren't her words.

"Ophion, do you see it?" the sorceress whispered.

Nearra heard a tiny voice respond close to her ear.

"Yes, Mistress."

"Get it and bring it to me."

"At once, Mistress."

Nearra felt something small, like an insect, crawl along her cheek. It stopped, and then jumped into the air, growing and changing shape as it flew. When it landed, the creature had assumed the form of a large gray wolf with piercing blue eyes.

Ophion bounded toward Kuruk and leaped. Ophion closed his lupine jaws around the medallion and tore it from the elf's hands. The impact of Ophion slamming into Kuruk knocked the elf down, but Ophion landed with animal grace. The shapeshifter whirled about and came running back toward Nearra.

Maddoc's chanting stopped and the wizard shouted, "Kill the wolf!"

At first Nearra had no idea who Maddoc was speaking to, but then the skeletal griffin came crashing down upon Ophion. It dug its bone talons into Ophion's flesh, and though no blood welled forth, Ophion whined in pain. The bone-griffin lifted its beak and then brought it down on Ophion's back, nearly tearing the shapeshifter in two.

But Ophion didn't use its powers to fight back against the griffin. Instead, his neck began to lengthen, gray fur receding, replaced by smooth snakeskin. Ophion extended his wolf head toward Nearra, the sun-shaped medallion still clenched tight in his jaws.

"No!" Maddoc shouted.

Nearra heard the wizard running toward her, but before he could reach the table upon which she was bound, Ophion dropped the medallion onto her chest, and then his head curled back on his serpentine neck.

She felt a warm tingling as magic power surged through her, and the leather straps that held her down evaporated like so much dew in the burning light of day. Her hand snatched the sun medallion from her chest. She sat up and gazed upon the medallion as Asvoria ran her fingers over its surface.

The medallion began to glow and suddenly released a burst of white light so intense that even with her eyes closed, Nearra could see it.

The sorceress slipped the Daystar over Nearra's head and climbed off the table. Nearra tried to reassert control over her body, but no matter how hard she concentrated, it was useless. It seemed Asvoria had at last fully emerged.

Maddoc gaped at Nearra—or rather, Asvoria—in horror.

"The paralysis spell!" he said. "You used the Daystar to nullify it!"

"Of course," Asvoria said with Nearra's voice. "Too bad the girl didn't know how to activate the medallion, or else she could've used it to counter the enchantment that placed me in her body." The sorceress grinned. "Too bad for her, that is. Quite fortunate for me."

Inside their shared body, Nearra's spirit raged in fury, throwing itself against the ethereal walls of the psychic cage that now imprisoned her. But there was nothing she could do. Asvoria had won.

As if a truce had been silently called, all fighting ceased the moment Nearra, no, *Asvoria* climbed off the table. Even the bone-griffin and the shapechanger stopped clawing at one another. All eyes turned toward Asvoria and Maddoc as the two wizards confronted each other.

Davyn felt as if he'd been punched in the gut. They'd failed. Nearra was gone, her spirit destroyed.

Not necessarily, he told himself. If Asvoria could exist as a passenger in Nearra's body for so long, perhaps the situation had been reversed. Perhaps Nearra was now the passenger, unable to do more than watch as Asvoria did as she pleased.

And if that was true, then there was still hope—*if* they could get hold of the Daystar.

Maddoc raised his hands, fingers contorted in mystic patterns. "I can't let you go, Asvoria. I've worked too long and sacrificed too much to obtain the knowledge that you possess."

Asvoria laughed, and though it was Nearra's voice, the dark cruelty in the laughter sounded nothing like her. "You could never hope to stand against me even if you were at full strength. What makes you think you can do so now, weakened as you are?"

Maddoc looked uncertain. A line of sweat trickled down the side of his face, but he didn't back down. "I've made the study of you my life's work. I know more about your strengths and weaknesses than you ever could."

Asvoria smiled. "An amusing bluff, I'll grant you, but that's all it is." She pointed at Maddoc and a burst of crimson light shot forth from her finger to strike the wizard in the chest. Maddoc grimaced in pain, stiffened, and then collapsed.

Asvoria turned to regard the rest of them. "Anyone else?"

The three goblins shrieked and fled down the stairs. Oddvar started after them, but just before he reached the doorway, he turned and hurled his poison-coated dagger at Asvoria. The sorceress' eyes flashed with violet light, and the dagger halted in mid-flight. The metal glowed white-hot, and the air was filled with a sour stink as the poison was burned off the blade and the weapon clattered to the stone surface of tower roof.

Oddvar shrugged. "You can't blame me for trying."

Asvoria smiled. "Actually, I can." Violet energy flared in her eyes once more and Oddvar was suddenly lifted off his feet and hurled toward the edge of the roof, as if he were caught in a gust of wind. Limbs flailing, the dark dwarf was thrown up and over the crenelations.

Oddvar screamed as he fell, but he didn't scream for long.

Like the others, Kuruk and Shiriki stood silently as they watched the dwarf meet his fate. But now Kuruk began walking stiffly toward Asvoria.

The sorceress leveled her finger at the elf, but before she could release a They destroyed my original body, but I was able to transfer my spirit to this form."

Shiriki cried out, "I knew you weren't my cousin!"

Asvoria peered intently at Kuruk, as if using her magic to verify the truth of his words. Finally, she smiled and lowered her hand. "It seems that body swapping is quite the fashion tonight. Come to my side. It was your task to guard the Daystar, and while you failed to keep it from these children, I can always make use of a dracolich."

Kuruk stepped over to his mistress and took his place at her side. Asvoria then looked at Ophion.

"Are you injured?"

The shapeshifter was still half wolf, half serpent, its coils wrapped around the bone-griffin. But with Maddoc unconscious or perhaps even dead, the creature had stopped fighting and stood immobile. Ophion released the griffin, its form blurred, shifted, and rearranged until it once more resembled the black-haired girl that Davyn had first seen with Nearra back in the dracolich's cavern.

Ophion walked over to join Asvoria and Kuruk. "My injuries are minor." It smiled. "It helps if one can toughen the skin as well as shift it away from attacks. I shall heal soon enough."

"About your current shape," Asvoria began.

"Does it displease you? I thought you might be amused if I assumed the form of the girl's sister again. I can become something else if you wish."

Asvoria cocked her head as if listening to an internal voice. "No, that shape will do fine. It annoys my soul-sister."

Davyn's heart leaped at the sorceress' words. So Nearra did still exist! He was more determined than ever to get his hands on the Daystar, but he had no idea how. He glanced at his companions. Catriona watched Asvoria with a mixture of hatred and sorrow and Elidor was doing much the same. Ayanti looked as if she couldn't believe what was happening, and Sindri was sitting up, but he looked as if he might pass out any moment. He was still physically drained from countering the magic of the Gallery of Despair, and being slammed to the ground by Kuruk hadn't helped him any. Davyn doubted Sindri would recover soon enough to be of any help.

Asvoria turned to Shiriki. "And what of you, elf? You served Bolthor, who was at best a minor evil. Will you now serve a much greater and, if I do say so myself, more glorious evil?"

Shiriki glanced at Elidor, and Davyn was surprised at the

tenderness in her gaze. But then she turned away from him and walked over to join Asvoria.

"I serve the Dark Queen. I can think of no better way to do that then by serving you, my lady."

Asvoria nodded, clearly pleased. "Good." The sorceress then turned to Davyn and his companions. "And what of the rest of you? Will any of you pledge your allegiance to me and enter into my service?"

None of them spoke.

"How about you, Davyn? You once served Maddoc. You are no stranger to the ways of evil. And by serving me, you'll be close to Nearra." She smiled. "Or at least what's left of her."

Davyn clenched his fists, but he didn't reply.

"None of you? Ah, well, I can't say I'm surprised. After all, I've had the better part of a year to observe you. Still, I thought it only polite to make the offer." She raised her hands. "When I've finished taking care of you then I can reclaim Cairngorn Keep and pick up where I left off. Ansalon has changed a great deal over the last several centuries, but one thing hasn't changed. The land could still use a strong, firm hand to guide it."

"A hand like yours?" Catriona said.

Asvoria grinned. "Naturally. Now, unless any of you have some memorable last words you wish to share . . . " Asvoria's hands began to crackle with mystic energy.

Davyn spoke up. "There is one thing that I'd like to say."

The sorceress sighed and the energy surrounding her hands died away. "Very well, but hurry up and get it over with."

Davyn shouted, "Raedon, get that medallion!"

CHAPTER
28 ENDGAME

The copper dragon held onto the tower's edge by his front claws. Davyn had no idea how Raedon had come to be here or why he had climbed up the side of the tower instead of flying, and he didn't care. All that mattered was getting the Daystar and saving Nearra.

For an instant, the dragon didn't react, but then he fixed Asvoria with his gaze and scowled, as if sensing what had happened. He opened his mouth and chuffed a blast of slow gas toward the sorceress and her servants.

Davyn felt a surge of hope. The slow gas would immobilize Asvoria and the others, and then they could take the Daystar, and with any luck, Sindri could figure out how it worked and—

But Asvoria gestured and crimson energy flared bright around her hands. Suddenly wind began to blow, so strong it could almost be called a gale. The wind quickly dissipated the cloud of slow gas and then just as quickly died down.

Asvoria frowned at Raedon. "I thought I'd managed to divert you to a grove where the descendants of some of my old pets still live."

Raedon pulled himself up higher, revealing a wing that was swollen and discolored.

"Ah! I see you did get to meet my little friends. Though it appears that their venom might have lost some of its potency through the generations. One bite should've been enough to kill you. Well, I suppose I'll just have to attend to that chore myself." Once again the sorceress' hands flared red.

Davyn knew they had only seconds to act. He turned to Elidor. "Now, while she's distracted. Get the medallion!"

Elidor sprinted toward Asvoria, moving with unbelievable speed. As he ran, the thief drew one of his throwing knives and hurled it toward Asvoria's head.

Davyn held his breath and prayed that Elidor's aim was true.

It was. The knife struck the medallion's chain and severed it just as Elidor reached Asvoria. The elf caught the Daystar as it fell, whirled about, and sprinted back toward his companions. His knife, however, kept flying and lodged in Kuruk's shoulder. But the dracolich took no notice of the wound. He was too busy glaring at Raedon.

Asvoria, suddenly aware of what had happened, shrieked in fury and turned away from Raedon. She unleashed a blast of mystic energy at Elidor, but the elf, warned by one sense or another, hit the ground and rolled. The blast missed him and blew out a chunk of one of the tower's crenelations instead.

"Get it back!" Asvoria screamed. Kuruk lumbered after Elidor and Oddvar and Shiriki followed. Asvoria turned to Ophion. "Deal with the dragon."

Ophion's body expanded, stretched, and took on mass as it transformed into a gigantic scorpion. It scuttled toward Raedon, pincers snapping and barbed tail dripping poison.

Raedon, who had only managed to haul half of his body over the tower's side, said, "Not another blasted bug!"

And then Davyn could spare no more attention for the dragon, for Elidor shouted, "Catch!" and hurled the Daystar toward him just as Kuruk was about to reach the thief.

The medallion tumbled through the air, and Davyn caught it. He half expected to feel some sort of tingling or burning as he touched the magical object, but all he felt was cool, smooth metal.

"Catriona, Ayanti! Try to hold them off!" he shouted.

The warrior and the centaur nodded grimly and Davyn went to Sindri's side. The kender looked as if he was half asleep. Davyn grabbed his shoulder and shook him.

"Sindri, wake up! We need you!"

The kender blinked and looked at Davyn. "Sorry, Davyn. I guess I needed to rest, but I feel better now."

"Good." Davyn shoved the Daystar into Sindri's hands. "This thing is supposed to be able to counter magic spells. Do you think you can use it to banish Asvoria's spirit from Nearra's body?"

Sindri gazed down at the sun-shaped medallion and ran his fingers over its surface. "I'm not certain . . . "

Davyn looked over his shoulder. Raedon, who'd climbed all the way onto the top of the tower, had wrapped his tail around the scorpion's to hold its stinger at bay. But the monster had clasped the dragon's neck in its pincers and was squeezing as hard as it could. Elidor was hacking away at Kuruk with a dagger, but the undead elf ignored the blows. He reached out and touched Elidor's chest. Elidor cried out and slumped to the ground, shivering as if caught in a terrible wintery blast. Catriona fended off the Shiriki's sword with her dragon claws. Ayanti used her hooves to lash out at Oddvar.

Finally, Sindri said, "I think I can do it, Davyn."

Davyn helped Sindri to his feet and the kender held the medallion in his left hand while raising his right. His eyes took on a rainbow-colored cast and tendrils of mist curled from the fingers of his left hand to wrap around the Daystar.

Asvoria turned in the kender's direction as if she sensed the release of his magic.

"By Takhisis' dark soul!" she swore. The sorceress gestured and suddenly the bone-griffin clattered to life. It lunged toward Sindri and Davyn grabbed his friend and dove out of the way of the monster's slashing talons. Sindri and Davyn slammed down on the tower's stone roof, the medallion flew out of the kender's hand, and the mystic tendrils vanished.

The Daystar slid toward Kuruk. The elf was crouching over the shivering Elidor as if about to deliver a death stroke. But when he saw the medallion, Kuruk leaped for it and snatched it up.

Asvoria laughed in triumph as Kuruk hurried over and offered the Daystar to her.

"For you, my mistress," he said.

The sorceress' eyes shone with greed as she grabbed the medallion out of Kuruk's hand. She then favored her servant with a triumphant smile. "You have done well, Frostclaw. As a reward, I release you from my service." She gestured and Kuruk's body stiffened.

Tendrils of a black shadowy substance drifted from the elf's mouth and nostrils. The darkness rose rapidly into the air above the tower, where it coalesced into the silhouette of a dragon. The great beast hovered above the keep for a moment and then it flapped its dark wings. The motion caused the shadows that formed the dragon-spirit to disperse, streaking away in all directions until they were gone.

Kuruk's body remained upright for another few seconds before it went limp and collapsed lifeless to the tower roof, like a puppet whose strings had been severed.

"No!" Shiriki shouted. She ran toward Asvoria, tears streaming down her face, sword gripped tight in her hand.

"Spare me," Asvoria said. She pointed a finger at the attacking elf, and a gout of flame burst forth.

Just as the fire-bolt was about to engulf Shiriki, Elidor leaped forward and knocked her aside. The two elves tumbled to the roof, unhurt, as the flames struck only empty stone several feet away.

Shiriki sat up and looked at Elidor in amazement. "You saved me. Why?"

Elidor shrugged, still trembling from the frigid touch of the dracolich. "It seemed like the right thing to do at the time."

Shiriki smiled wryly. "My hero."

"You people don't seem to understand who you're dealing with," Asvoria said, her face twisted into a mask of fury. "I am Asvoria, one of the most powerful wizards this world has ever seen. And I do not take kindly to interference of any sort. When I try to kill someone, I expect that person to die. End of discussion."

The sorceress pointed at the two elves and released another blast of flame.

Elidor took hold of Shiriki's hand, obviously intending to pull her to safety, but she shoved him away from her as hard as she could. Elidor flew backwards just as flames engulfed Shiriki. For an instant, she gazed into Elidor's eyes with an expression of gratitude and perhaps even love.

Being of magical origin, the flames burned out quickly, leaving behind only a blackened, smoldering husk.

Elidor and the others stared in shock at what was left of Shiriki.

"Enough of this foolishness," Asvoria said. "Ophion, to me!"

The scorpion released Raedon without hesitation and turned toward its mistress. As it went to her, it shifted form once more, becoming a giant eagle. Ophion flapped its wings, took Asvoria by the shoulders, and carried her aloft. The bone-griffin launched into the air and flapped its leather wings as if obeying an unspoken command to follow.

Asvoria was escaping and she had the Daystar.

Davyn felt despair well up inside him. It's over. We've failed . . . and I've lost Nearra forever.

He almost gave up then, and he would have, if it hadn't been for one thing: he loved Nearra, and he would sooner die than fail her.

Davyn ran to Raedon.

"Can you fly?"

" I can glide," the dragon said. "But I don't know how long I can remain airborne."

They couldn't pursue Asvoria then. Davyn thought fast. There had to be another way.

"Catriona, get on Raedon's back! Raedon, go after the griffin and do your best to get underneath it!"

The dragon looked as if he was going to ask why, but he kept his mouth shut and nodded.

Catriona didn't hesitate. She dropped her dragon clawsand leaped onto Raedon's back. The copper dragon ran to the edge of the roof and jumped into the air. Catriona held tight to Raedon's scaly neck as he began to glide after the eagle and the griffin. Even wounded, Raedon began to close the distance between them.

Davyn wished he had his bow, but the goblins had taken his weapons from him earlier. He ran to Elidor. The elf was still staring at Shiriki's remains, tears glistening in his eyes.

"Quick, give me your bow!"

Elidor looked up at Davyn and frowned, not comprehending at first. But then he reached for his bow and handed it to his friend. Davyn plucked an arrow from his friend's quiver, then ran to the edge of the tower. The young ranger nocked the arrow, and took careful aim.

Forgive me, Nearra, he thought, and released the arrow.

The feathered shaft shot through the air and thunked into Asvoria's hand—the hand that held the Daystar. The sorceress

TIM WAGGONER

screamed and she released her grip on the Daystar. The mystic medallion plummeted toward the ground.

"Ophion!" Asvoria shouted, cradling her wounded hand against her stomach. "The Daystar!"

Ophion banked and descended toward the falling medallion, but it was slowed by the weight of its mistress. Before they could get halfway to the Daystar, Raedon flew beneath and Catriona snatched the Daystar out of the air.

Asvoria screamed in rage and Ophion continued flying toward Raedon, but the copper dragon opened his mouth and shot a stream of acid at the giant eagle. Ophion managed to dodge most of the acid, though a few drops landed on his wings and singed the feathers.

As Raedon banked and prepared to return to the tower, the bone-griffin streaked toward the copper dragon. The undead creature lashed out with its claws, striking Raedon's injured wing. Blood and pus burst from the wound and the dragon shrieked in pain. Raedon lurched and dropped half a dozen feet, nearly dislodging Catriona, but the warrior held on. Just as it looked as if Raedon would plunge to the ground, taking Catriona with him, he managed to stop his descent and came gliding unsteadily back toward the tower.

"Look out!" Davyn shouted.

Elidor, Ayanti, and Sindri moved to the edge of the roof, and Davyn, against his better judgment, pulled Maddoc's unconscious form out of harm's way.

As Raedon approached the roof, the copper dragon held out his legs in preparation to land, but before he could touch down, his wounded wing gave out, and he fell. Catriona leaped off Raedon's back in time to avoid being crushed as the dragon slammed onto his side, his injured wing taking the brunt of the impact with a sickening snap of breaking bone.

The dragon slid to a halt and lay still, moaning in pain.

Catriona held up the Daystar. "We got it!" she shouted.

Davyn looked up into the night sky. "It's too late," he said in a hollow, defeated voice. "She's out of range."

Davyn stepped to the tower's edge and watched as the sorceress flew eastward on the back of a gigantic eagle, the bone-griffin following behind. The ranger clutched the top of a stone crenelation with a white-knuckled grip and struggled to control the rage and sorrow seething within his heart.

He continued to watch until Asvoria was swallowed by the night and he could see her no more.

TIM WAGGONER

238

CHAPTER

29 DAVYN'S DECISION

Davyn sat in Maddoc's study, staring at the tapestry that depicted Asvoria. The fireplace held only ashes, and a single candle resting on the side table near the carved wooden chair provided the sole illumination for the room. The lack of light kept the tapestry shrouded in shadow, appropriately enough, Davyn thought.

He heard the door open, but he didn't turn around to see who it was. He didn't care.

"How are you doing?" Ayanti asked.

He looked away from the tapestry and into the concerned face of his childhood friend. But she hadn't come alone: Elidor, Catriona, and Sindri stood with her, and they all looked just as concerned as the centaur.

He turned away from his friends and looked back up at the tapestry. "What does it matter?" he said. "We've failed. Nearra's gone and Asvoria's free to work her evil upon the land."

"We stopped Maddoc," Sindri pointed out. "That's something."

Davyn shrugged. "And how is my 'dear father' doing?"

"Resting in his room," Catriona said. "He's weak as a kitten but I think he'll live."

239

"You didn't tie him up?" Davyn whirled around. "Are you crazy? He'll kill us all!"

Catriona put her hand on her friend's shoulder. "Maddoc claims he's lost his powers. And I believe it. He actually tried using his magic when we were taking him to his room and he couldn't. He could barely walk. He said the battle had taken everything out of him."

"We'll see about that," Davyn muttered. "What about Oddvar?"

"We searched the grounds for his body," Elidor said, "but we found no sign of it."

Davyn turned to look at his friend. "Are you telling me he somehow survived a fall from the top of the tower?"

"I'm telling you only that we couldn't locate his body," Elidor replied. "Perhaps some predator made off with it. Though I must admit, I saw no evidence that such a thing occurred."

"Oddvar is one of the most devious beings I've ever met," Catriona said. "He's far too sneaky to die from something so simple as a fall."

"So he's still out there somewhere," Davyn said. "What about the goblins?"

"Gone," Elidor answered. "They fled during the battle with Asvoria, and it appears they continued running until they'd abandoned the keep altogether."

"Maddoc's other servants fled as well," Catriona added. "I don't know why. Perhaps they were glad to be free of their master at last or perhaps they were afraid of what we might do to them. At any rate, they're all gone."

"And Raedon?" Davyn asked.

"He managed to crawl down the side of the tower and into the courtyard," Ayanti said. "I made a bed for him out of straw there and he's resting. He's badly injured. His wing was completely shattered when he landed on the tower's roof. Worse, an infection seems to have been released into his bloodstream. He's going to need quite a bit of care if he's to have any hope of recovering."

"I tried to use my magic to help him," Sindri said, "but whatever the true nature of my powers are, it seems that healing is beyond them."

Davyn raised an eyebrow. "I'm surprised you're not tired after using your magic."

"I feel fine," Sindri said. "Every time I cast a spell, it gets easier. Now I feel tired only for a few moments afterward. I hope that soon I won't feel any aftereffects at all."

"That's good," Davyn said, though in truth he had no idea whether it was or wasn't. There was so much they didn't know about Sindri's mysterious new powers.

"So what do we do next, Davyn?" asked Catriona.

"What do you mean?" He stood and turned to face his friends. "Don't you get it? We *lost!* There is no *next!* It's over!"

"I understand how you feel, Davyn," Elidor said.

"No, you don't!" But then Davyn saw the sorrow in his friend's eyes and he realized that Elidor did understand. Davyn had lost Nearra to Asvoria and Elidor had lost Shiriki to the sorceress' flames.

He put a hand on Elidor's shoulder. "Sorry. I forgot."

Elidor smiled. "Don't worry about it. It's been a long night for all of us. The question now is what can we do to get Nearra back?"

Davyn removed his hand from Elidor's shoulder and gestured toward the tapestry.

"Even if we could find a way to track Asvoria, how could we hope to defeat her? She's too powerful."

"I don't know," Elidor admitted. "But we have the entire keep at our disposal, all of Maddoc's spell books and magical items.

There must be *something* here that we can use. Maybe Maddoc would even help us?"

"I doubt it," Davyn said. He thought for a moment. "Then again, Maddoc never has been one to take defeat lightly. He'll want revenge against Asvoria, if nothing else." Davyn could feel the first faint stirrings of new hope being born within him.

"Whatever you all decide, you can count me out," Ayanti said. "I'm no warrior. I'm a caretaker of animals. And right now there's a very large, very sick animal in the courtyard who needs my help. Now I'm going to go check on Raedon."

Ayanti gave Davyn a smile before turning and clopping out of the study.

Davyn's friends looked at him expectantly.

He knew they were waiting for him to make the final decision. Like it or not, he was their leader. But after everything that had happened tonight, could he find the strength to lead them once again?

He took a deep breath, held it for a moment, and then released it.

"All right. The first thing we need to do is find out all that we can about Asvoria. Maddoc spent years collecting information about her, and it's likely that he keeps it here in his study. So let's start looking."

Catriona, Elidor, and Sindri grinned at Davyn.

"Right away, boss!" Catriona said. She lit several more candles and the three of them began to search through the books and papers that filled Maddoc's study.

Davyn was mildly surprised to discover that he didn't mind being called boss this time. He looked up at the tapestry of Asvoria.

"Don't worry, Nearra," he whispered. "We'll come for you. And this time, we won't fail, no matter what."

The adventure continues in

DRAGON SWORD

by Ree Soesbee

Released from Maddoc's spell, Asvoria sets out to reclaim her most treacherous weapon: a magical sword. Davyn and his friends have one hope left. If they can locate the sword first, they may have a chance to stop Asvoria and free Nearra.

Only one man can lead them to the sword. And as fate would have it, it's Maddoc, the wizard who started this all. But can Davyn and his friends trust their worst enemy?

Available January 2005

ENTER A WORLD OF ADVENTURE

Do you want to learn more about the world of Krynn?
Look for these and other DRAGONLANCE® books in the fantasy section
of your local bookstore or library.

TITLES BY MARGARET WEIS AND TRACY HICKMAN

Legends Trilogy

*TIME OF THE TWINS, WAR OF THE TWINS,
AND TEST OF THE TWINS*
A wizard weaves a plan to conquer darkness—
and bring it under his control.

THE SECOND GENERATION

The sword passes to a new generation of heroes—
the children of the Heroes of the Lance.

DRAGONS OF SUMMER FLAME

A young mage seeks to enter the Abyss in search of his lost uncle,
the infamous Raistlin.

The War of Souls Trilogy

*DRAGONS OF A FALLEN STAR, DRAGONS OF A LOST STAR,
DRAGONS OF A VANISHED MOON*
A new war begins, one more terrible than any in Krynn have ever known.

WANT TO KNOW HOW IT ALL BEGAN?

WANT TO KNOW MORE ABOUT THE DRAGONLANCE® WORLD?

FIND OUT IN THIS NEW BOXED SET OF THE FIRST DRAGONLANCE TITLES!

A RUMOR OF DRAGONS
Volume 1

NIGHT OF THE DRAGONS
Volume 2

THE NIGHTMARE LANDS
Volume 3

TO THE GATES OF PALANTHAS
Volume 4

HOPE'S FLAME
Volume 5

A DAWN OF DRAGONS
Volume 6

Gift Set available September 2004
By Margaret Weis & Tracy Hickman
For ages 10 and up

THE NEW ADVENTURES

JOIN A GROUP OF FRIENDS AS THEY UNLOCK MYSTERIES OF THE DRAGONLANCE® WORLD!

TEMPLE OF THE DRAGONSLAYER
Tim Waggoner

Nearra has lost all memory of who she is. With newfound friends, she ventures to an ancient temple where she may uncover her past. Visions of magic haunt her thoughts. And someone is watching.

July 2004

THE DYING KINGDOM
Stephen D. Sullivan

In a near-forgotten kingdom, an ancient evil lurks. As Nearra's dark visions grow stronger, her friends must fight for their lives.

July 2004

THE DRAGON WELL
Dan Willis

Battling a group of bandits, the heroes unleash the mystic power of a dragon well. And none of them will ever be the same.

September 2004

RETURN OF THE SORCERESS
Tim Waggoner

When Nearra and her friends confront the wizard who stole her memory, their faith in each other is put to the ultimate test.

November 2004

For ages 10 and up